I0772987

Intent Magic

Other books by William C. Tracy

The Shifting Lands:

Physical Magic

Intent Magic

The Biomass Conflux

Of Mycelium and Men

Down Among the Mushrooms

To a Fungus Unknown

The Spores of Wrath

The Dissolutionverse:

The Five Hive Plateau

Tuning the Symphony

Merchants and Maji

The Society of Two Houses

Journey to the Top of the Nether

The Dissolution Cycle:

The Seeds of Dissolution

Facets of the Nether

Fall of the Imperium

Other Books:

Fruits of the Gods

Anthologies:

Distant Gardens

Farther Reefs

Lofty Mountains

Fiery Deeps

The World of Juno

Lesbians in Space: The Sapphics Strike Back

I Want That Twink Obliterated!

Intent Magic

BOOK 2 OF THE SHIFTING LANDS

William C. Tracy

Copyright © 2025 by William C. Tracy

All rights reserved. No part of this publication may be reproduced, distributed or transmitted in any form or by any means, without prior written permission. No part of this publication may be used in any manner for the purpose of training artificial intelligence technologies to generate text, including without limitation, technologies capable of generating works in the same style or gen-re as the publication.

Space Wizard Science Fantasy
Raleigh, NC
www.spacewizardsciencefantasy.com

Publisher's Note: This is a work of fiction. Names, characters, places, and incidents are a product of the author's imagination. Locales and public names are sometimes used for atmospheric purposes. Any resemblance to actual people, living or dead, or to businesses, companies, events, institutions, or locales is completely coincidental.

Cover art by Serene Chia
Lettering by Audrey Logsdon
Editing by Heather Tracy
Book Layout © 2015 BookDesignTemplates.com

Intent Magic/William C. Tracy.— 1st ed.
ISBN 978-1-960247-48-3

Author's website: www.spacewizardsciencefantasy.com

At least half of a sparring match—potentially the most important half—
is mental, not physical.

CONTENTS

CHAPTER ONE

The Match

The upper stands of the main Chimor arena roared around Silluka. The smell of sweat and roasted maize filled the air. She had never seen so many people in her life, and not even all of them were Huaca.

More importantly, they weren't Huaca she had grown up with. A week ago, she hadn't known this many people existed. She was still coming to terms with seeing them bustling around her from morning until well past when she fell asleep. Chimor never truly slept.

"Will the murder happen soon?" Lugopo thwacked their translation circlet with one of their many arms. It buzzed before saying, "Apologies, mean the *match,* of course."

The little Allwiya was perched on Silluka's shoulder as usual, but they'd found tiny flags somewhere, and held four of them, each in a tentacle as they signed, with two other appendages clutching Silluka's shoulder. Two of the flags were purple with a little jakua head on them. The others were orange, with the outline of a Huaca performing *The Wing Grows,* the first movement of the morning ritual. Their last two tentacles held a collection of metal and wood shards that buzzed and rotated as Lugopo twisted it this way and that.

"Are you charting chayu power again, Lugopo?" Ichu leaned in from Silluka's left. Her brother had been interested in the Allwiya's pet project since the little device had said his chayus were losing power. As much as he worried, Silluka still watched in awe at his smooth and graceful movement when he practiced. That didn't come naturally to her, having not grown up using the chayus every day. She'd always been told the stump she had instead of a right hand would keep her from performing effective chayus. The elders of her village had been as wrong about that as about how many Huaca there were.

"Already showing one Tortoise of power simply from collection of all these people! Such destructive capability!" Lugopo signed with three of the flag-waving tentacles, and their circlet picked up the translation, speaking with a high-pitched, mechanical voice.

"You're so busy looking at that, you are, you will miss the fight," Cosquella said from Silluka's other side. "Our first match between one of the Huaca and one of the Misini. Me, I want to see their capabilities." The tall woman leaned into Silluka's shoulder as she spoke, the rough skin of her arm brushing Silluka's stump. There was a slight breeze through the stadium, and one of the few advantages of being in seats near the top meant they felt it. Cosquella's solid black hair didn't move at all in the wind.

"Stands and smells! You lot are rambling on so much, you'll miss everything." Elder Quilqi pointed with one spindly finger toward the center of the arena. "Look, the challengers are coming out. These matches determine the prestige of the best practitioners—and their gods—in the city. The loser walks away with less honor, and sometimes, less blood. Pay attention, in case you're out there one day."

Silluka didn't miss the implication the elder had put into those words. Her whole village had packed up when the turtlemen's island collided with their new Huaca near the coast. The land there had been rising steadily since her parents had been children, pushed up by the oncoming island. In the destruction, they'd had nowhere left to go, thinking they were the only Huaca in existence, until they came...here. The city itself was breathtaking, towers made of solid stone, each holding more people than she'd ever seen in one place.

A week later, and Elder Quilqi—who seemed to know much more about this world than she let on at first—had dragged them all to this match. She'd implied it was the first in a long while that wasn't between those of the same species. Though the matchups were completely voluntary—

the participants who won gained respect in the city—there was more to it, connected to the gods themselves. Silluka just had to wrangle the reasoning out of the old woman. She was hard to pin down.

The Huaca came out first: a tall, broad woman, nearly as big as Ichu. Silluka had heard nothing about the contestants. In the past week she'd been running around Chimor, on errands from Elder Papaki to bargain for supplies for their new village. The refugee center of Chimor was an area bigger than her whole village, but *inside* the walls.

"She's going to fight a Misini?" Silluka asked. She'd seen the jakua-looking people around but hadn't talked to one yet. They seemed to be aloof, like their animal counterparts. "Do they call on the gods like we do?"

"'We' meaning only creatures with weird bones all over?" Lugopo put two tentacles on non-existent hips.

"Sorry, Lugopo," Silluka corrected. "I mean, do they have chayus?"

"Look!" Cosquella leaned forward, over the heads of the people sitting below them. She pointed to the opposite side of the dirt arena, bigger across than the main square in Silluka's old village. The two figures were indistinct from this distance, but she could tell the Huaca, on her left, had no armor. That meant she must not be as powerful as either the storm warrior who crashed to ground outside her village, nor as Akamu's stone warriors, with their glowing amber outfits.

On the right, just emerging, was a figure wearing even less clothing than Silluka had seen on other members of her species. From this distance, she could see the elongated feet, like a sleek-furred jakua walking on its hind toes, and small ears rising above the contender's head. The Misini was wearing only a belt stuffed with bottles and knives, and a simple scarf, artfully wound around her face, shoulders, and hips. Silluka was about to ask Elder Quilqi if all Misini wore such clothing, but a voice boomed through the arena, and she swiveled to look at an open box across from them, between the two entrances. A paunchy man stood there, the dark glow of the ampuka visible even from this distance.

"Gentle inhabitants of Chimor!" the man bellowed, and beside her, Ichu frowned.

"He's using *Coyote's Howl*," her brother said, "but I've never seen such control of it, to speak rather than just yelling a signal. And he's continuing to use it."

"There's much you have to learn," Elder Quilqi said, but the man was continuing.

"Today marks the first match in many a year, not between Huaca and Huaca, or Misini and Misini, but between a mix of species!"

There were some cheers and clapping from the crowd at that.

"So is that bad or good?" Silluka asked the elder, but the old woman shook her head.

"Hard to say. It's different. The reason matches aren't usually between species is that they channel the gods differently. It is difficult to compare their power, though the Huaca are usually considered one of the strongest."

Then she was drowned out by the announcer.

"It's time for something new, isn't it?" There were a few more cheers from the crowd. Silluka saw the man shake his head. "I can't hear you! Maybe we should simply call it off? Do you want to see how the Art of the slinky Misini matches up against the chayus of the powerful Huaca, or not?"

This time the shouts from the stands made Silluka hunch down in her seat. She'd never been around so many people, and the noise was like a hurricane blowing in from the ocean.

"Is that all? I guess I'll tell these two contenders to pack up. Or do you want to see whose gods are the mightiest?"

This time the roar washed over Silluka like a tidal wave, and she put her hands to her ears. When it was past, Lugopo shook their power-counter.

"Nearly two Tortoises in ambient. Such potential, and untapped!"

"That's more like it!" The announcer shouted back. "Now let's give our contenders the same respect. On my right, our reigning Huaca champion, a Pressure Adept near the peak of her talent, a sure shoe-in for one of our illustrious warrior ranks when she's ready. Give it up for Chyuna, of the Huaca!"

The Huaca in the crowd cheered, and beside her, Cosquella and Ichu roared with them.

"To my left, a mystic in the Art of Changing Sight, a skilled entertainer of her gods, winner of last year's all-Misini matches, cheer for Anuit, of the Misini!"

This time, not many of the Huaca cheered, but they only made up about half of the arena. The other half was the feline Misini, Allwiya, another people with spiky backs, and even a few turtlemen. Together, they hissed, rattled banged on seats, and more. The noise was almost as loud as the cheering.

"What's the Art of the Misini?" Silluka asked Elder Quilqi. "And what's a Pressure Adept?" She still had so much to learn. Akamu had only started to teach them how to connect to the core before he left them in the desert. He'd promised he would see them again in Chimor, but Silluka didn't know when. She snuck a glance at Ichu. She knew he missed the stone warrior. They had made a good pair while they traveled on the sleds.

"You'll see very soon," the elder said. "Now pay attention, girl. We're not just here for fun." She pointed down as the match began.

Chyuna ran across the dirt of the arena, straight for the Misini opposite her. As she did, she gestured with one hand and the ampuka bloomed around her. Her hands curled into claws.

"*Jakua's Claws*," Ichu said. "She must have stored the chayu before now, but it's a questionable attack against someone who already looks like a jakua herself." Ichu had been in so many sparring matches back in the village, Silluka was used to him giving a play-by-play of what was happening.

"Three Tortoises of energy, just from one gesture!" Lugopo signed. "Such deadly force!" They thwacked their translation circlet, but it remained silent, and they made a complex shrug with three arms.

"*Jakua's Claws* shouldn't create that much power." Ichu looked at the elder. "I've never seen it produce more than a sixth of a Tortoise. Lugopo took the name from measuring the entire chayu of *Tortoise Shoulders His Load*, and that's a much longer and more powerful sequence."

"Not when you depend only on what a Physical Adept could produce," Elder Quilqi answered.

However, Anuit simply stood silent, arms crossed, pointed ears twitching. She waited for Chyuna's charge, and the moment before the woman's clawed fingers reached her, Anuit melted into the ground.

Lugopo's arms twiddled their gadget. "Another two Tortoises. What is happening?"

Chyuna ground to a halt, spinning, and made another gesture, dirt gathering from the floor around her to coat her in dull armor.

"I think that's *Caterpillar Weaves His Cocoon*," Ichu said, "but I've never seen it affect other objects."

Silluka glanced to Elder Quilqi, but the old woman's eyes were narrowed, focused on the match. There was a lot she wasn't saying. How much depended on this contest?

Then part of the dirt pulled away from Chyuna, forming into Anuit, right beside her. Chyuna yelped and stabbed with a knife, taken in a flash from her belt.

But it seemed like Anuit's image jumped, flicking from one place to another, and the knife hit nothing.

Chyuna began a chayu, the ampuka glowing around her, and Anuit took the moment to attack, stabbing at Chyuna's dirt armor with her daggers. They slid off, as Chyuna continued, in Dexterity Stance, her arms moving rapidly through burrowing motions.

"She must not have stored that chayu," Cosquella said, sitting up straight to see better. "Why is she inviting those attacks?"

"She's protected by *Caterpillar Weaves His Cocoon*," Ichu answered, "and she's crafting something with Quirra. *Quirra Hides His Nuts?* But no, the moves aren't right."

"*Quirra Digs a Hole*," Elder Quilqi supplied.

"Another two Tortoises! I will need to craft a bigger scale, more powerful than ever before!" Lugopo crooned.

As Chyuna finished her chayu, the ground parted around her, and she dove underground. Anuit stopped her useless attacks and sniffed the air, then stepped into nothingness.

"And now there are no combatants to watch," Silluka said. The others in the stands seemed to have the same reaction, grumbling and complaining.

As the sounds raised to a constant rumble, Silluka saw the announcer step forward, ready to direct the crowd, but just then Anuit fell from the sky, one dagger aimed toward the ground where there was nothing.

Except a mound rose up and spit Chyuna forth, one hand raised above her head. The dagger met her fist and shattered, as the crowd broke out into applause.

Anuit balanced on the broken dagger like a needle balanced on Chyuna's thread spool, then the Misini flowed down to the ground.

Into eight different versions.

They surrounded Chyuna, each with slightly different faces and clothes, none quite the same as Anuit's original appearance, each making different threatening motions with their eight daggers pointed toward Chyuna's throat.

In response, the Huaca knelt down, spreading her arms out like wings. It wasn't *The Wing Grows,* but it was similar. A gust of air blew out from her in all directions, and all eight clones of Anuit staggered back.

"A good ploy," Ichu pondered. "She was trying to find the real Misini among the illusions, but all of them responded."

"Anuit is well trained in the Art of Changing Sight," Elder Quilqi put in. "I haven't seen one with so much potential in many years."

"You want us to fight in matches like this? Why is it so important to you?" Silluka hissed back, as Chyuna went after first one, then another version of Anuit, trying to see which one was real as they all skipped away from her.

"Scattering sands, you'll be their equal in no time, girl," the elder said. "A Pressure Adept is only one little level above a Mental Adept, after all."

Before Silluka could ask more questions, One of the Anuits drew back an arm, throwing her dagger. It arced through the air, and Chyuna, through some other sense, or some chayu she'd stored, sidestepped out of the way. But the dagger curved in its flight, and another Anuit threw her dagger, then a third, fourth and fifth.

The daggers made a storm around Chyuna as she frantically sidestepped, the last three Anuits adding their daggers to the frenzy.

"I thought this was supposed to be for honor, it was," Cosquella asked. "Is it supposed to be deadly?"

"Of course not." The elder waved a hand at Silluka's girlfriend. "You'll see. Chyuna will..."

Chyuna stepped out of the way of three daggers aimed at her heart. And right into another, which plunged through her eye.

She fell lifeless to the ground as the crowd erupted in boos and angry shouts.

CHAPTER TWO

Strength

Ichu glanced around before he opened the doors of dark polished wood, inset in the stone building. Elder Quilqi had taken them here on the first day they'd arrived in Chimor, and he hadn't been back since. Now he wanted some answers, and the elder had been stingy with them so far.

The city was still in an uproar about the match yesterday—the first one to end in death in over twelve years. It wasn't a good sign from the first fight to pit different species together. Misini had been more visible in the city since then, some carousing in the streets with strange, minty drinks that seemed to act on them like fermented maize did on Huaca. Ichu was put in mind of the village's Jakua when their handlers let them roll in a spicy-smelling plant they liked.

What was the elder's game, saying they would have to fight? His sister had done seemingly impossible things, but many people in this city were advanced far past even Silluka's feats. Did Elder Quilqi really think she could train them so fast? Not with her reluctance to answer his questions.

He had just arrived, yet Chimor was changing. There were so many powerful people here, he had to learn how to become the best body caster he could. He also had to find out more about the Huaca, the Misini, the turtlemen, and any other species. There were more here than he had thought existed in all the world. He'd only known of his village of Huaca and the few Allwiya who lived in the garbage dumps. He'd been completely wrong about them, until the elder opened his eyes.

Once inside the building, he let his eyes adjust to the gloom. It was darker here, since the street outside was still in shadow, even late into the morning. The buildings in this district of Chimor were taller than the tallest trees around the Huaca back on the coast. That village didn't even exist any longer, buried as the turtlemen's island collided with theirs.

In the middle of the square room, guarding the stairs up to higher levels, was a desk with the same woman behind it as the first time they had come here, working by a single candle. Her armor was similar to the storm warrior who had crashed to ground when they fled the village. It gave off its own sapphire glow in the dim light, letting her work with ease. She didn't look up from her sheets of vellum, where she was scratching glyphs that reminded Ichu of parts of chayus. His sister was the one who could read, though maybe he would have to learn, now they were in this city. Yet another task for him.

"I seek an audience with Nina?" he addressed the desk in general. He was used to people seeing him when he arrived. In the village, he had been the champion of many sparring matches. Now, he didn't even know if he could stand up to his little sister.

"I'm sorry, *Administrator* Nina is tied up with work today. Please come back at a later time." The receptionist emphasized the title, all without looking up.

"I...I arrived before with Elder Quilqi," Ichu tried again. He didn't want to depend on the strange elder for everything, but her name seemed to have power here. "The person you call 'ancient one'?"

The receptionist finally did look up at that, though there was none of the deference shown when Elder Quilqi was here. She didn't wear a helmet, as the storm warrior on the coast had, though Akamu had shown him how warriors could summon and dismiss them with simple gestures. The rest of her armor sparkled like waves on a sunny day, and it fitted to her form close like no metal could do, even down to the tiny ridges of sapphire overlaying her fingers. Creating the armor was a process tied to storing chayus—a principle Ichu was far from understanding. From what Elder Quilqi had hinted, there were many levels beyond what the citizens and elders of the Huaca considered the pinnacle of perfection—that of learning as many chayus as possible and summoning the ampuka with each one. Such power was only the lowest level of Adepthood—a Physical Adept.

"And for the ancient one, Administrator Nina may have time in her busy schedule. For you, I can answer any questions you have at this time." She didn't look like she wanted to answer any questions.

Ichu's mind spun. He had barely a plan coming here in the first place, save some vague idea to ask Nina for help with learning what was the next step past Physical Adept. The elder was so focused on Silluka's progress, she had barely addressed Ichu the last week they'd been here. He needed to learn. He *had* to learn.

"I want to be a warrior. How do I do that?" The words just popped out.

The receptionist gave him a considering glance, and Ichu rocked back on his heels. The look itself had *power*. Then she blinked and the pressure against him disappeared.

"You're barely a Physical Adept. And you're how old? You must be half again my age." She laughed, not unkindly, but with enough humor that a spear of embarrassment passed through him.

"I can learn," he shot back. "The ancient one you're so reverent of picked *me*, along with my sister and two others, as her champions. Do you doubt her?"

That sobered the woman up. She stood up from her desk and came around to Ichu's side. She was a slight woman, shorter than his sister and with barely more muscle. It was no wonder she was the receptionist for the stone and storm warriors here rather than helping outside of Chimor. Ichu straightened as she approached him, his shoulders above her head.

"The ancient one shows up every decade or so, as Administrator Nina tells it, usually with some fanciful tale of which god is going rogue this time, or what island is coming our way. But Chimor has stood here for thousands of years. It's the oldest settlement on this island, in the center of this island. I'd imagine it's even older than the ancient one and has withstood all her tales so far."

Ichu stared up at the stone ceiling above him. The entire building was wrought of one piece, stone crafted by the power of the core by Huaca practitioners. Many buildings in the city were the same. He'd assumed it was maybe a hundred years old, but *thousands*? Could anything stand so long against the storms, earthquakes, and volcanoes that plagued their lands? Neither his village nor his parents' had lasted more than fifty years.

They'd passed into what Akamu had called the "stable desert" on the way here, where the storms and earthquakes faded away to nothing. He'd assumed that meant only they were more rare. He'd only been here a week. Did they *never* have such weather here? He could only imagine what his Huaca could have built if they didn't need to migrate inland every fifty years or so.

"Then you certainly have resources. Can you teach me?" he pressed the woman. "I'm sorry, I haven't even asked your name." He put on a winning smile—the one that had brought men and women to his bedchamber back in the Huaca.

The receptionist lifted one slim eyebrow. "I'm Ganaki, of the storm warriors." She turned a hand palm up in question.

"Ichu," he said. "Champion and best bodycaster of the Huaca. My Huaca, that is."

"Bodycaster? I suppose that's another name for a Physical Adept? And you're proud of being at only the first step of Adepthood?"

"We didn't even know of other stages before coming here," Ichu said. "In my village, we perfected each chayu, each stance, until we knew it with our full body, until we could connect to the ampuka with it just by starting the movements."

"Then how could you adjust a chayu for the intent of your goal? Or store sections of a chayu to release when you sense your enemy's weakness? It seems a very limited style." She gestured to herself. "I've only mastered the Elemental Adepthood of air so far, which is why they keep me here until I can join one of the warrior bands. One must master at least two elements before being accepted, and most master three of the four before choosing their primary mastery."

The words washed over Ichu, and he scrambled to grasp the meaning. "This is exactly what I've come here to learn. How do I go from a bodycaster—a Physical Adept—to the next stage?"

Ganaki crossed her arms, the sparkling stone of her armor catching a stray beam of light from a window and casting a rainbow of colors on the floor. It coated her from neck to toes, segmented sapphire. "You are much older than the usual Physical Adepts, and most of the Mental Adepts, unless they simply have no aptitude for the chayus."

"Then you're at the stage after that? Elemental Adepthood?" The elder had done a poor job of explaining what the adepthoods meant. She seemed to be dismissive of them.

Ganaki shook her head, a small smile on her face. "You do come from a long way away from Chimor, don't you? This is something taught to every child here. Simply performing the chayus and showing a connection to the ampuka—what you call bodycasting—is the level of the Physical Adept. You tap into the ambient ampuka with no ability to control or manipulate it or understanding of how it connects to the core."

Ichu opened his mouth to debate the description, but at Ganaki's glare, he shut it.

"Do you want to learn or not? That's what I thought. Now, the revelation of a true connection to the core starts the journey to the Mental Adept. The surge of power that comes with it shows the practitioner's skill, but traditionally the test before judges only comes at the height of skill for that adepthood. Only after those higher than you judge your skill as passing, can you say you are truly one of those adepts."

Ichu thought back to escaping the collision of the turtlemen's island, the earthquake that separated the front sleds from the undesirables following...and what Silluka had done, how her entire body glowed.

"So, someone might suddenly fly when they become a Mental Adept?"

Ganaki's eyebrows shot up. "Flying? Uncles, no. That might be an effect of understanding the Elemental Adepthood of air, but I only got there myself last year. Did you see someone do this?"

"I...perhaps it was a leap through the air. We were traveling during an earthquake." Had Silluka skipped over the Adepthoods Ganaki was describing? Was that why Elder picked her out—did she have so much potential? But Ganaki was speaking again.

"After the realm of the Mental Adept, then one will start the journey of the Pressure Adept, sensing a new realm of connections between the gods, the core, and all your surroundings." She lifted her hands, gazing around the room, and Ichu got the feeling she saw much more than he did. Maybe that one candle was even more unnecessary than he thought.

"Only then does a practitioner start to understand how the gods of the Huaca affect us, as they descend into the realms of the Elemental Adept." She shrugged. "And that's where I am now."

"But there's more after that?" Elder Quilqi had never been so clear on where Ichu's journey would take him. This one woman had given him more information than the elder's weeks of implications.

"There's always more," Ganaki said. "Another way to use the chayus, to channel the gods, to interact with the world. Administrator Nina is one of the only Huaca in the city to pass out of the realm of the Elemental Adept, and she won't say what happens then." A frown creased her face.

"So to become a warrior like you, I need to become a Mental Adept, then a Pressure Adept, and then an Elemental Adept?" He gave a firm nod. "Then that's my goal. I'll become an Elemental Adept and more."

Ganaki watched him and again that pressure pushed him back. He straightened against it. "I admire your goals," she said, "but you have a long way to go, champion and best bodycaster Ichu. You have a strange shadow over your connection to the core, and I fear it could make your journey much harder."

Ichu swallowed. She could see the effect of the vial he had swallowed? Elder Quilqi had told him it had contaminated his core with the turtlemen's god, that he had a separation from the gods of the Huaca now. It would make progressing as an adept harder, but he didn't know it would be so evident to everyone he met here. He changed the subject, trying to keep Ganaki talking so he could learn as much as he could.

"And the other species, the Allwiya and Misini and others, they go through this process too?"

"Oh, Tiyus, no." Ganaki laughed again. "Each species has their own gods. That's where their power comes from. And each god has a different way of expressing their power. You arrived with an Allwiya, did you not? Do you imagine they perform chayus like we do?"

Ichu frowned. "I suppose not. Then what do they do?"

"Ask them," Ganaki said. "I assume you saw the match yesterday or heard about it. All I know about the Misini is they get their powers of illusion by entertaining their gods. Do you think Uncle Sky or Aunt Harvest want to be entertained?"

"The chayus honor the gods and express their perfection," Ichu objected. "They don't want entertainment from us."

"The Tiyus, Tiyas, and Tiyes don't, that's true. But they aren't the only gods. Chimor may have belonged solely to the Huaca far in the past, but we welcome all species here now, and their gods. That means there are plenty of places to learn about them. Ones that are not here."

Ichu almost missed her pointed hint. He was thinking about the turtlemen who had followed them across the desert. They had disappeared before the sleds encountered the crazed Allwiya in the desert, driven off by Akamu and his stone warriors. But Akamu had said they would be back. There was a whole island of them marching toward Chimor. It was why Akamu was still out on patrol. Would the turtlemen—the new ones, who followed their new beliefs—also be welcome here? It was another reason Ichu had to learn.

"When do you think I'd be able to test for Mental Adept?" he asked.

Ganaki went back to her desk. "Come back when you have a strong connection to the core and don't bleed the ampuka from you like a dying prey animal. Then we'll see."

CHAPTER THREE

Adepthood

"You must be ready to test to Mental Adept as soon as possible," Elder Quilqi told Silluka as they turned between tall stone buildings in Chimor, Silluka's stump wrapped around Cosquella's large arm. She'd barely had time for a spare moment with her girlfriend since they got here.

They had all been shaken after the death in the match the day before, even the elder. The matches were almost never fatal, and it had cast a pall over the mixed-species competition. Supposedly, Anuit was under investigation by the heads of the Misini in the city—something called The Clowder.

Silluka's brother had gone off into the city this morning, saying he wanted to find a group to practice with. Silluka knew he was scared about what the vial had done to him. *She* was scared what it had done to him. His connection to the gods was weaker, and the arena fights were all about the gods, though the elder hadn't said how. She suspected that was why Elder Quilqi was pressuring her to aim for heights even her brother—the best bodycaster in the Huaca— couldn't achieve. What did she see in Silluka that she hadn't seen in any of the other inhabitants of Chimor?

"I failed my test to be a citizen, or I guess a Physical Adept," she said. "*You* failed me at my test. How can I be ready to test as a Mental Adept? Can I even test again?"

Elder Quilqi waved a hand. "What your village called 'undesirables' don't exist. If you fail a test, you can always try again later. You're a Physical Adept if I say so. You crossed that threshold when you started to show the ampuka. But to test for Mental Adept? You *aren't* ready. Yet. That's why you need to practice. Understand your connection to the core and learn how to store it within your *sunqu*. You'll need that to be able to save an entire chayu within for later use. These are only the basic steps of adepthood, and you'll need to leap past them to have any hope of challenging the Eztli Mecatl, or even others in this city. My champions must be strong to withstand what is coming."

The elder was unusually talkative today. Maybe because they were away from the refugee camp, and the elders. Silluka had claimed a small hut with Ichu, Elder Quilqi, and Cosquella. Lugopo lived next door with Muola and the other Allwiya who traveled with them, insisting they needed more space for their creations. Why such a tiny creature needed more space than she did, she wasn't sure.

"And what is coming?" Silluka asked.

"A reckoning for which gods' people survive," the elder said. "The more species that exist on this island, the more powerful the entities they will attract. You don't want to meet most of them, especially not as you are now. Come on."

She sped up before Silluka could ask more, taking them somewhere deeper in the city. Cosquella was looking at her worriedly as they hurried along behind. She shifted the large net she carried, Lugopo riding on top.

"What does she expect you to do, does she?"

Silluka shook her head. "I don't know. You'll help me train, won't you?"

"I wouldn't miss it, me. I never get tired of watching you move." Cosquella winked at her, and Silluka wondered once again how they'd found each other, both outsiders from their people, Silluka with her stump and Cosquella with her rough skin and large size.

The rest of the refugee camp—mostly Huaca and elders from her village—all seemed concerned with such trivial matters, like which hut was nicer and how to negotiate with Chimor officials about better accommodations. Silluka had seen enough of the city already, and who was respected in it. Those with power were in control, and the remains of her village from the coast had none. The people of Chimor were called "perfectionists" behind their backs and treated with as much disdain as the Huaca used to treat the undesirables—what Silluka had been destined for. But there was so much more at stake. Even the elder sounded nervous about these powerful entities she'd mentioned. Were they other gods, eager for followers and control? Adepts so high on the ladder they might as well be gods? She'd have to press the elder for more answers later.

The former undesirables, on the other hand, seemed to be faring far better in Chimor than they had back on the coast. Most had left the refugee center already for jobs in the city, as apprentices and helpers, accountants, drivers and porters, and more. It was what they had done in the village to get by, but there, labor and creation were looked down on in favor of perfection of chayu technique. In a city this size, those Huaca who didn't practice chayus far outnumbered those who did. They worked hard, and in return, those who had no ability for the chayus were protected by those who did. Silluka had to keep practicing so she could protect them too.

"This place you know in the city, you say it is a better place to practice?" Cosquella took up the conversation in the silence. She carried a net of what looked like wood and metal splinters over her shoulder, Lugopo clinging to the outside. The little green and blue Allwiya clambered over the parts, their translation circlet occasionally making remarks like, "This connection can be deadlier!" and "Such power in this area. But can the suit transfer it?" and other vaguely unnerving and threatening statements.

"Blocks and roads, it's not a 'better' place to practice. It's *the* place where people practice in Chimor. Or one of them anyway." The elder put her hand on her lower back and stretched as she walked. "This isn't the village square where hopefuls gather to practice when they feel like it. Chimor has gymnasiums and schools, divided into which Adepts can attend. There are ones for each species here."

"A school where daring Allwiya channel the world-breaking might of the unknown gods?" Lugopo piped up from their trawl over the net. They smacked the translation circlet with one tentacle. "That is, where they might learn of how best to gain new insight?"

"And ones for the Misini, and the Kawchi, and whatever those jellyfish creatures call themselves. They're new since I've last been here. I suspect there's a school starting up for the Eztli Mecatl, too."

Silluka shuddered at the mention of the turtlemen. The creatures had followed them all across the land, and she'd even glimpsed some at the match. There were already a lot of species here.

"Those would be the ones who fled past my father's farm, they would," Cosquella said. "The ones who used the old ways, branded as heretics, they were. They wouldn't even say the name of their god who had abandoned them. I'd hope, I would, any school here follows the old ways."

"I hope so as well, but yes, that is a conundrum," the elder mused, turning down a side street with certainty. Silluka followed behind with Cosquella and Lugopo. She still got lost, more often than not, in the huge city. "The gods don't often change like that, and with the troubles I've heard of Adepts failing to contact Uncle Smith and Entle Love, I wonder if there's more to what's going on than I know."

"Is it possible to contact a god directly?" Silluka asked. Bodycasters gained power associated with one of the uncles, aunts, or entles depending on what chayu was performed, but she'd never heard of anyone actually *talking* with one of them.

"It's not possible for *you* to speak with a god, girl," Elder Quilqi chuckled. "Burn yourself to crisp before you opened your mouth. But someday, maybe."

"What sort of Adept can speak with a god?" Silluka asked.

"All three pass deadly plans to me directly!" Lugopo called from the net.

"And I believe we fought a bunch of your people driven mad by them, they were," Cosquella answered.

"Humpf!" The translation circlet literally spoke the word. Silluka looked back to see Lugopo waving a couple tentacles in the air.

"Each god speaks with their people a different way," the elder clarified. "The Huaca have more gods than any species I know of, and their power is similarly great. Thus, it takes more experience working with the power of the core to be able to communicate on their level. The squids only have three insane gods—all barely coherent themselves—so their gods whisper to them from childhood."

Silluka looked back for Lugopo's reaction, but the tiny blue-green Allwiya shrugged bonelessly. "Fair."

"The Misini I've had a few dealings with over the years. They've been here the longest of the other species in Chimor. I know they call their gods 'The Clade,' and from everything I can determine, they're hedonists, rewarding those Misini that are the most flamboyant or risky in their endeavors."

"But one species can't learn techniques of another god, can they?" Cosquella asked. "That's what I was told by the Eztli Mecatl who traveled through our farm. They taught us reasoning, farming methods, and food preservation, but nothing of their gods, they didn't."

Elder Quilqi gave Cosquella a long, unreadable look as they passed through a narrow alley. Silluka thought of her girlfriend's rough skin, strange hair, and inability to connect to the core. She insisted it was a skin condition passed down by her mother, and Silluka believed the other woman believed that.

"Until now, girl, I've always said that was the case. But with so many islands coming together, there's going to be...er...cross pollination. Most times that leads nowhere, but I'm beginning to rethink my conclusions on that score."

"What do you mean by cross...oof!" Cosquella was suddenly gone from Silluka's side, and she spun to see a Misini who had emerged from an inset side doorway just as they were passing.

"Watch your step, ya?" The Misini's ears were back just like an angry jakua, teeth bared. They were dressed in revealing silks, barely concealing their curvaceous form, though it was protected by fur. Their face was more like a Huaca's with a long jaw, but furry, and they had wide angry eyes with slit pupils.

"Sorry, I didn't see the door, I didn't," Cosquella apologized, getting to her feet. Lugopo had clung to the netting during the impact and was busy checking its contents.

Silluka started. This wasn't just any Misini. She recognized her stance, her bearing.

"You're Anuit," she blurted.

"Which is what to you, Huaca?" Anuit hissed.

"We...saw your match," Silluka said.

"So did most of Chimor. You want an autograph, ya? The Clowder wants enough of Anuit's tail already."

"I...no...I..." Silluka looked to Cosquella for help, but the big woman's shoulders were tensed, her hands up in fists. Anuit noticed at the same time she did.

"You think you can take Anuit on, big woman?" A knife appeared out of mist and dropped into Anuit's open paw— her fingers had pads, Silluka noticed, but were dexterous like a Huaca, with a thumb that flipped the blade this way and that. "Or maybe the one-armed weakling wants a piece?" Anuit stepped toward Silluka, and she stepped back, despite herself. She hadn't been ready for this level of vitriol.

"Fur and fangs! We want none of your charades, Misini," Elder Quilqi cut in. Silluka could feel the pressure of the old woman's gaze, though it wasn't even directed at her. Anuit narrowed her eyes, but even her shoulders dropped under the elder's notice.

"At least one of you is competent to give Anuit a challenge. Not like most of the miserable Huaca in this city." The knife disappeared from her hand. "Your feuding gods having nothing on The Clade. I should go back to Ninun where Anuit is respected, can perform for real."

Before Silluka could say anything else, the Misini spun away and stepped into nothingness, gone in the blink of an eye.

"What a pleasant bony person," Lugopo chirped from their place on the net. They flicked the translation circlet. "Delightful. A boon to travelers. Full of gratitude." They flicked it again. "I am not certain if the sarcasm filter is working correctly."

"It's working, squid," the elder said.

"Are all Misini so combative?" Cosquella asked, dusting herself off.

"Not usually," the elder answered. "Flamboyant, yes, rude, yes, aloof, yes, but not so directly argumentative. She's scared. I don't think she wanted to kill Chyuna in the sparring match. I wonder if a god put her up to this."

"But you just said the gods don't speak to Adepts."

The elder held up a finger as she began walking again. Silluka scurried to catch up. "Misini practitioners are called Artists, not Adepts. What do you call yourself, Lugopo?"

"Our glorious Supplicants to the three mighty ones must pass challenges by each god to grow our might and power!"

"There you have it," Elder Quilqi said. "Adepts, Artists, Supplicants, each species has their own word for it. Ah, here we are."

Silluka thought there was something else she was going to ask, but the elder had stopped in front of a large open building, its roof held up by columns as big around as Cosquella's arm span. Inside were dozens, no, *hundreds* of Huaca, all practicing chayus. Silluka even saw one man with only one arm, and another woman with a wooden leg from the knee down. The ampuka glowed around some, but not all.

"This is the gymnasium for Physical and Mental Adepts in Chimor," Elder Quilqi said. "You'll become very familiar with this place as you train. Go on now, find a free spot and I'm sure Lugopo will set up their inscrutable contraptions to measure and record everything."

"My creations are perfectly scrutable!" Lugopo said from the top of the net. Cosquella rolled her eyes as they strode in.

Lugopo gathered a few looks from practitioners, but Cosquella no more than usual. There were people of all shapes and sizes here, though all seemed to be Huaca.

They found a free corner and Lugopo dragged the suits out of the net. They'd made one for Cosquella in the last week to match Silluka's. Hers had to be reassembled after the fight with the many-legged vehicle of the desert Allwiya. The right arm—a hollow construct that mimicked a hand where she had none—had been crushed to splinters, and joints all over the suit had burst and splintered during the fight.

"Get into the SCUIT." Lugopo signed with three tentacles while pointing with a fourth. "I will trap you in it!" They smacked their translation circlet. "Lock you in it." Smack. "Close. Close you in."

"I think your circlet is hiccupping," Silluka said as she pulled the mesh weave over one foot. It was made of small bits of wood and metal, sometimes woven together, and sometimes connected by tiny joints. The overall product was stiffer than a fur sock, but still pliable. Around her joints were a comparably larger number of tiny joints in the suit so it flexed the way her body did. Lugopo had somehow created the thing, with inspiration from their gods, to lock out Silluka's movements within the perfect range for the movements of chayus. She wasn't sure how exactly it worked, as it seemed to adapt to whatever chayu and stance she used. It merely restricted and perfected her form. With it, she could connect to the ampuka nearly twice as fast and generate an extra half Tortoise of power, or so Lugopo said.

"No hiccupping. The translation circlet is always correct!" Lugopo ignored her glare and pointed at Cosquella. "The big woman shall don one as well. Even more destructive capability!"

Cosquella took another semi-rigid weave of wood and metal. "She's right though, she was. It sounded as if you said 'scoot' instead of 'suit.'"

Silluka pulled the mesh up around her middle and fed her stump into the right sleeve. The end of that limb was different than the others, and heavier. The weave of wood and metal was denser there, though some light shone through the empty space where her hand would have gone. Inside, she felt a layer of woven material cover the end of her stump. As she flexed the partially formed muscles in her arm, the fingers and wrist of the suit moved as if she had a second hand. She was almost more impressed with the detail in the hand than the rest of the suit.

"SCUIT!" Lugopo said. "Silluka named it, so I drew inspiration from Crawling Dark of Squirming to give me a name to strike fear in our enemies!"

"'Scoot' strikes fear in people?" Cosquella asked.

"Situational Correction Unit (In Testing)!" Lugopo looked between Silluka and Cosquella. "I had little to work with." They concentrated, their tentacles fiddling together like twiddling fingers. "What about Scaling Chayus Up In inTensity? Striking Up In Triumph? Setting Upon Enemies Together? No, that would be SUET..."

"I'm sure it will come to you," Silluka told them. "This new arm feels different though. Did you change it?"

Lugopo scrambled up Silluka's leg and clung to her arm. He was only about the size of her hand, so it wasn't a lot of extra weight.

"Yes! Calculated strength of desert Allwiya iron and made improvements in density and impact resistance." They knocked on the arm with a tentacle. "Adjusted mesh rigidity for lacking bones. Turns out yours are good for something!" They flopped a tentacle around limply for emphasis. "No bones good for squeezing enemies to death, but not for punching them to pulp!" They looked between Silluka and Cosquella again, then tapped their circlet. "That is, bones help with punching."

Silluka flexed her forearm muscles and the suit made a fist, then she tapped a nearby column with the knuckles of the mesh hand. She hadn't used the original suit for long, but this felt even more solid.

"Punches and practice! You won't get anywhere if you keep standing around jawing, girl," Elder Quilqi said. "You need to practice your intent and learn to store the energy from the core. If this thing helps you get there faster, fine, but don't use it as a crutch. Remember, do the chayus as they fit to *your* body, not everyone else's."

Silluka held up her faux hand, wiggling the fingers. She was already getting better at controlling it. "So does this change my intent for the chayu?"

She'd never been good as a bodycaster back on the coast. She'd even avoided the test for citizenship—the equivalent to a Physical Adept here—until it was nearly too late. She'd been dragged before Elder Quilqi and the other elders by Hufi and his patrol just before the turtleman had attacked— and Hufi had been killed in the fight.

Everyone else in the village believed that every physical part of the body had to be in the exact right place to call forth the ampuka—the glow of energy. But as the elder and Akamu had shared later on, that was a way of forcing the core to power the chayu and was much more exacting than the technique of using one's intent. Using intent was the basis of the Mental Adept. It meant bringing the mind into the chayu rather than only relying on the body. The mind could map out what the chayu *could* do, rather than what the physical practice implied. Rather than performing a chayu in a set stance, like Basic, Dexterity, or Speed, the intent behind the chayu let practitioners change the end result. Rather than using each chayu for one application, now the end result blossomed into many, depending on the intent behind it. It meant Silluka, with only one hand and an unfinished right arm, could achieve the same result from a chayu as her brother could. But the suit was another layer between her intent and her body.

"You've seen the problem with that contraption firsthand," the elder chided. "When you used the suit to activate chayus while fighting the desert Allwiya, your intent was with two whole hands. When that insect-vehicle crushed the suit's hand, your intent no longer matched the energy you'd channeled from the core to power *Tortoise's Heavy Foot*. The shape wasn't right, and it failed. But it also tangled the energy around your *sunqu*. If I hadn't straightened it out, you'd be relearning chayus with your brother."

"But the suit helps my connection to the core," Silluka objected. "And Lugopo has strengthened the hand so it won't break again."

"Which is why I'm willing to entertain this unusual circumstance, if it moves you through the Mental Adept stage quicker," Elder Quilqi answered.

"And what of me?" Cosquella asked. She'd been a conundrum for both the elder and Akamu. Teaching her how to use the morning ritual to open the connection to the gods and the core led to barely a whisper of the ampuka.

Elder Quilqi shook her head. "You're a strange one, and no mistake." Cosquella frowned. "Oh, don't take it wrong, child. It's not an insult. You're strong as a stump and I'd bet on you versus an Eztli Mecatl any day, but the energy of the core seems to slide off you. Maybe that suit will help, and maybe not. It's worth a try."

"My inventions are the deadliest possible!" Lugopo tapped their circlet. "That is, they're successful and strong."

"We'll see." The elder gestured to Silluka and Cosquella. "Go on then, run through the morning ritual and see what happens."

Silluka hadn't yet performed the morning ritual with Lugopo's creation. It had only been completed shortly before the attack and destroyed soon after. Lugopo and the other Allwiya had spent the time traveling to Chimor to rebuild it.

She settled into the chayu—one even she was innately familiar with. It had been the way to warm up back home in the village, taught to every child. It started with *The Wing Grows*, progressed through several other common moves like *Giving Water*, *Praise the Sun,* and *Root Drinks Water,* but the last move, *Pray*, had always been omitted, the elders of the village saying it would bring down the might of the gods on whoever performed it.

Akamu had later revealed the morning ritual was *meant* to connect the practitioner with the gods and was the first step to learning how to actively channel the power of the core of the planet, where the gods lived.

As Silluka went through the motions of the chayu, she worked to envision herself with two hands. It was easier with the visual of the new hand the suit provided, but she still felt mentally off balance, and as she finished, the glow around her was a weak thing, nothing like what she had accomplished on a rocking sled in the middle of a desert beset by earthquakes.

Cosquella was ever worse. The big woman had never had luck summoning the ampuka, even when she did the right moves, but she also moved jerkily, like her body was trying to resist the chayu itself.

"Terrible," Elder Quilqi commented from where she sat beside a column. Other practitioners moved around them, but only a few gave their strange suits a second glance. A few others had sections of armor. Were they training to be city guards? "Do it again but match your mental state to your body. If you want to use the squid's crutch, you need to accustom yourself to it."

So the afternoon went, Silluka and Cosquella both repeating the morning ritual again and again, trying to summon the power of the core. Her physical moves in the chayu were more exact, and if she were simply trying to bring the ampuka into being with *Tortoise's Heavy Foot* or *Quirra Hides His Nuts,* she would have no problem, but the morning ritual had a different use. It was meant to bring the power of the gods and the core into her *sunqu*—her center—to store and be used later. The ampuka itself was a measure of inefficiency, showing how much power leaked out from the performance.

"I can't," Cosquella finally panted, after many repetitions of the morning ritual. Silluka had managed to connect to the core a few times, trying to wrap her brain around having *two* hands instead of one. It was a strange sensation, and she felt off-balance. Cosquella still hadn't made the connection at all. Her movements in the chayu seemed choppy and abrupt, as if she was lacking fine control of her hands.

"No, you can't," Elder Quilqi agreed. "Maybe that skin condition from your mother also keeps you from performing a chayu with enough exactness to attract the gods of the Huaca."

"That's a strange way of putting it," Silluka said. "What other gods would she be..."

"Medical attention needed!" The shout from across the gymnasium scattered her question, as Silluka's head whipped around to the source of the cry. A Huaca was standing over Ichu—when had he gotten here? He looked as if he might faint at any moment.

CHAPTER FOUR

Tearing Apart

Ichu eyed the crowd of people practicing in the gymnasium, and quickly noticed his sister, the elder, Lugopo, and Cosquella in one corner moving through the morning ritual. His sister had...both hands? Then he realized she was covered in a strange net of material. Lugopo must be testing out their contraption. Cosquella was pulling on a similar one. It was a good idea, in theory. A shame something like that couldn't help him.

He'd practiced the forms since he was a child. His physical coordination was better than almost everyone else he knew, and that wasn't a boast. He was simply *good* at the chayus. He liked the movements. His body was trained over decades. He could slide through the moves of even complex chayus like *Foam Tossed in the Waves* with barely a thought.

And that was the problem. He moved around the gymnasium in the opposite direction from his sister, putting many other Huaca between them. Better for him to practice on his own. He *had* to get better. This new way of thinking about chayus rather than simply performing them was alien to him. Even before the turtlemen's island collided with their village, he'd felt himself slowing down, like the elders who no longer summoned the ampuka except to teach others, or in emergencies.

The promise of an increase in power, anything to catch up to his sister—Silluka! Who'd never practiced if she could avoid it. Now she was the one with more power than him, as if his years of practice meant nothing.

So, he'd taken the full vial Lugopo had rescued from the first turtleman they killed. He'd snuck around like a weakling, using *Quirra Hides in the Brush* to cover his movements and steal the vial of power.

He barely remembered drinking it, save for the rush of speed, and strength. His skin had been like metal, his focus sharp.

And then it had all bled away when the power of the vial left him, and Silluka, with the elder's help, had to save him once again.

Elder Quilqi had told him he'd ingested parts of turtlemen in the vial. It was how the Eztli Mecatl got their power, and why they were more powerful the fewer of them there were. It was as if they concentrated the strength of their fellows in their body. It wasn't at all how the Huaca did things.

The Misini were different as well. And so were the Allwiya, though he'd never really thought of them as having power from their gods. There was so much the elders in his village had been wrong about. They'd taught their Huaca was the *only* Huaca, the holy place blessed by the gods. It was not.

Ichu began to practice. Akamu had told him to do the complete morning ritual, including the last move, to link with the core. But after the vial, the link was even weaker than before. The core felt far away, in a manner the ampuka never had when he was in his prime. The vial had tainted him somehow, with the mysterious single god of the turtlemen.

Raven Spreads Her Wings. Giving Water. Praise the Sun. He moved through the morning ritual, almost without thought. He'd performed this every morning since he was a child.

He almost paused when he got to the last move, *Pray,* but he was supposed to do that move too, now.

Rather than the rush of energy, his *sunqu* felt like it was tearing apart, moving in two directions at once across his body. It had been this way, ever since the vial, and Elder Quilqi warned him he would have to work harder even to stay at his same level.

He grimaced and pushed the pain away. Again. He needed to do it again.

The second time through, he doubled over around his middle. A few others turned his way, concerned. No. He would not stop.

The third time his head started pounding, and hunger twisted his belly. He'd brought a handful of dried berries with him, and ate those, but they didn't help. The sweat of the practicing Huaca around him became a nauseating odor.

The fourth time through, he stumbled as he finished, pitching into another Huaca as he fell. The woman took one look at him and yelled, "Medical attention needed!" at the top of her lungs. He tried to tell her he didn't need anything, that he only needed to get his balance, but the room swam around him, narrowing to a tunnel.

He blinked, and people jumped around him. He blinked again and Silluka was standing in front of him, still in that strange suit, with both hands.

"Did you grow a new hand?" he tried to ask, but his mouth felt strange and stiff.

"We need to get him to a healer," an older voice said. Elder Quilqi. Someone large propped him up under his shoulder. He recognized that craggy skin. Cosquella. He walked with her, out of the gymnasium and down the street, but not far.

"In here," the elder's scratchy voice said, and they passed into another building.

Things happened. He thought he saw a large Allwiya, as big as him, but they had too many arms. The arms reached for him, laid him down, moved across his body, taking away the confusion and pain as they did.

When his vision cleared, he saw the entire group surrounded him, along with a strange, jelly-like creature that floated above the ground. Lugopo was on Silluka's shoulder, as usual, and he could see now the creatures were completely different. Countless thin, wisp-like tendrils wrapped around his arms and legs, and he tried to sit up.

"What—?"

"Calm down, the healer is only doing her job," Elder Quilqi said from over his shoulder. "Nu'oona, how is he?"

What emerged from the strange creature was a crooning cry he only gradually realized was made of words.

"I can take the pain from him, but there is trouble deep within this one. His center is tangled with that of another."

"He drank a brew of power meant for an Eztli Mecatl," the elder replied.

Nu'oona's arms twitched in surprise. Her body had no visible eyes or mouth, like a globe of semi-clear water, yet she still spoke.

"That is unusual. It is normally fatal to channel the god of another species. Some have tried before. None have succeeded."

"Have you heard of the new god of the Eztli Mecatl?" Elder Quilqi asked. Nu'oona's limbs retracted fully from Ichu, leaving red lines on his arms and legs that faded quickly to his normal copper coloring. The lines looked painful, but instead radiated cool calm.

"The few Eztli Mecatl I have spoken to in Chimor say they are refugees and that their god punished them for heresy. You are saying this is one effect of that?"

Ichu tried to imagine this creature floating across the city, maybe buying vegetables or meat from a market, waving to friends, wearing a hat to shield it from the sun. His mind rebelled at the thought.

"The turtlemen here—the Eztli Mecatl—do they use vials to gain power or strength?" he asked.

Nu'oona's waving arms paused in their languid motions before starting back up again. "Vials? Perhaps, but not as a way to gain power. They are a people of science and research, and their vials are a way to share that insight and knowledge."

"This is how their new god is corrupting their ways," Cosquella said. Nu'oona turned, though Ichu wasn't certain how he knew the creature's face was toward her. Three frond-like limbs extended.

"May I examine you? You have an interesting condition, similar to this one." More fronds pointed at Ichu.

"Me? This is just a skin condition, it is." The more Cosquella gave her reasoning, the less believable Ichu thought it sounded. Her craggy face was screwed up, arms crossed in front of her.

"May I?" Nu'oona repeated.

"I...guess."

"And you? Now you are out of danger, may I establish a new rite?"

Ichu realized the question was directed at him. These "rites" must be how she healed. Maybe how she connected with her god. "I...suppose so."

Frilly tendrils caressed his legs as they also connected with the rough skin on Cosquella's arms.

"Interesting. There are similarities here. Both of your cores are misplaced from where traditionally they are located in the Huaca."

"Misplaced? Is that dangerous, is it?" Cosquella exchanged glances with Ichu. Now he was interested in the answer.

"Dangerous?" Nu'oona's blobby center twisted upward as if in thought. "I do not think it is dangerous intrinsically, or you would not be alive. How you use it might be dangerous, as this patient has discovered. I have heard of this rarely, mostly in those unable to connect to their gods. I would be happy to learn more of it in the future, if you are willing to send me updates."

"That...may be helpful," Ichu said. If someone was willing to help his condition, from a medical perspective, maybe it would help him connect with the core again.

"What is the distance from the *sunqu* location to its normal placement for a boney person?" Lugopo asked. They had out a piece of paper and were writing glyphs on it. "Perhaps I can recalibrate my chayu measurements based on *sunqu* distance to Tortoises generated. But how to apply on a mass scale..." They trailed off, lost in thought.

Elder Quilqi had one thin hand on her chin. "It is unusual indeed. The gods don't mix with each other, not like this. Of course, they're usually on separate islands. The other species are newcomers here, relatively speaking. The whole concentration of power around Chimor is out of the ordinary." She'd been quiet, by the door the whole time, though Ichu could feel her presence looming. Even a look from the elder went straight through him. He wondered what sort of adept she was. If Nina was her daughter, and she had passed beyond what many here capable of in the city, was Elder Quilqi similarly advanced? Or had she stalled out at an earlier level? He had to know more.

"The turtlemen just arrived, their island coming closer over the last decade." Ichu sat up, then counted off on his fingers. "You said the Allwiya arrived a few hundred years ago."

"When our bold ancestors conquered the seas and steered their island to this one for new adventure!" Lugopo added.

"Yes, and the Kawchi before the Allwiya and the Misini before them," the elder said.

"Are you a Kawchi?" Ichu asked the floating creature. It drew its arms in and made a coughing noise. Ichu realized it was laughing.

"No, we are the Yakurikra, and before you ask, our island has not joined this place."

"You haven't?" This from Cosquella.

Several tendrils waved. "My people are skilled at moving across water. Our island is some distance away but drawing nearer. It will be here in several more years."

"Then who are the Kawchi?" Silluka asked.

"The hedgehog people, of course," Elder Quilqi answered. "They have a useful, though specific, set of skills." She looked at Ichu. "You were leading to a question?"

Ichu thought for a moment. He did have a question, but he wasn't even sure what it was. The elder eyed him with a slight smile, as if she saw where his thoughts were going.

The pressure of her gaze seemed to press him deeper into the soft table he sat on.

"Is the *sunqu* different in other species?" he finally asked. It wasn't exactly what he wanted to ask, but it was close.

Nu'oona was the one to answer. "It varies by the body type." She pointed one tendril to her central blob. "My *sunqu* is here." She pointed low in Lugopo's blobby head. "Theirs is there. You know where yours is. It is generally near the center of the body's mass."

"And an Eztli Mecatl?" Ichu pressed.

"They are heavier than Huaca, and more powerfully built. I have not had the opportunity to investigate one of the few that are in the city as I have done to Huaca, but I could hazard a guess where it is."

"And mine specifically," Ichu said. "You said it was misplaced. Is mine halfway between a Huaca's and an Eztli Mecatl's?"

Nu'oona turned their blobby middle upward again, several tentacles rising. "I believe that would be a good guess."

"Is the solution as simple as bringing the chayu to a different place on my body to connect to the core?" he asked the elder.

She shook her head. "As I said, I haven't seen this particular oddity before, and I'm not certain how it happened. Those few whose *sunqu* are misplaced never connect with the core at all, but you still can. It's worth a try, though be ready to acknowledge your hypothesis might be wrong." She waved toward Silluka. "There are dangers to cutting yourself off from the core or misplacing the flow to your *sunqu*. I don't want to have to untangle yours, along with...whatever you did to it."

"You have untangled another's *sunqu*?" Nu'oona asked the elder. "That is an impressive feat. I have only achieved it once, in very controlled circumstances."

"I've had some unconventional experiences," Elder Quilqi said vaguely. "They've helped prepare me for strange chayus and how they're used."

Ichu looked to his sister. He'd heard a little bit about this, but it happened while he had been affected by the vial. She'd broken the false hand of the first iteration of the strange suit Lugopo designed for her. She'd handled the desert Allwiya's vehicle mostly without his help, though he was supposed to be the one to protect her. Because she had been using her intent, losing the hand while she was channeling a chayu had changed the effect, tangling how the power was used. He'd never come across anything like that while bodycasting, even when he'd taken a spear to his leg in the middle of a disastrous hunt with untrained youths of the Huaca. It seemed the higher levels of adepthood came with their own cautions.

"What are the risks of being a Mental Adept?" he asked the elder. She dipped her head in acceptance.

"A good question, and one no one else has asked yet. Because using intent to shape the chayu allows you to change it, there are dangers involved. Stray too far from your original intent in the chayu, and the effect will falter. Change it drastically, and your *sunqu* might even suffer."

"And the adepthoods after that?" Silluka asked. "Are there other risks?"

"More than you can count," the elder said, "but you don't have to worry about those yet. Focus on your progress to Mental Adept first."

Ichu got up from the table. Nu'oona's office was small, a station hollowed out in the solid stone of this edifice. There was patchwork on the stone wall where once there must have been an entrance to a different part of this place. It was all one piece, like many of the buildings here, different dwellings bored out at many heights.

Behind him, the office was open to the air, welcoming any who walked in to use Nu'oona's services.

Elder Quilqi looked across everyone gathered, as Ichu turned back. "You all are weak, compared to most people in this city. You're finding the roadblocks in front of you, but remember, all roadblocks can be removed." She gestured to Ichu. "Try using the new placement of your *sunqu* when you practice. Cosquella might try the same, since you two seem to be similar somehow."

Cosquella frowned at that, but nodded.

"Now, I think we've taken enough of Nu'oona's time. Hopefully we won't be needing her services again any time soon." The elder placed a few spokes—the currency of Chimor—in a bowl by the door and they departed, leaving the floating tendril creature to her job.

Ichu placed a hand low on his belly as they walked. He'd been aware of his *sunqu*, even before Akamu had taught him of it. If he focused deep in his body, he could tell it was different somehow. Was that the way the gods told them apart? How did that work? Why did the gods of the Huaca not grant their powers to an Allwiya, or a Misini, when they inhabited the island the Aunts, Uncles, and Entles were under?

He didn't know the answer, but Elder Quilqi had given him some information. Maybe it was time he sought out the other half, by talking to one of the elusive Eztli Mecatl refugees.

CHAPTER FIVE

Jakua's Fight

Over the next several days, Elder Quilqi pushed Silluka through her chayu, again and again. With the suit, without the suit. Gradually, she started to understand how her hand changed her intent. She moved differently with it and without it. She had to cover for the reduced manipulation when she was without Lugopo's suit and often used more Dexterity or Reflex stances in her chayus. With the suit on, she innately used more Strength, Basic, and Blocking stances.

Cosquella and Ichu both practiced with her, and she thought the glow of the ampuka was gaining strength around her brother again. Ichu disappeared a few times, giving the excuse that he was keeping an eye on people's movements through Chimor. Cosquella, on the other hand, saw barely any difference whether or not she wore the suit.

Five days after Ichu's incident with the Yakurikra healer, they were all practicing in the gymnasium again, Lugopo fiddling with their various measurement devices. *Quirra Hides His Nuts*, one of her favorite chayus, was the benchmark they'd chosen to chart Silluka's progress. The elder had told them she would meet them there later but had errand to run first.

"Nearly three Tortoises of energy! Such destruction!" Lugopo announced.

"This chayu isn't for destruction," Silluka told them. "It's meant for stealth."

"Such stealthiness!" Lugopo said. They were right, though. Silluka was getting stronger.

"You get stronger while we founder, you do," Cosquella griped. "I cannot feel if my *sunqu* is in some different place or not. I cannot feel it at all, and this suit does not help!" She began to unfasten the clasps, and Lugopo scuttled over to help. Just like Silluka had been practicing with and without hers, Lugopo was trying to gauge how much Cosquella's suit helped her. It didn't seem to do much to perfect her stances and movements. It was like the gods simply wouldn't let her access the core.

"I wish I could help more," Silluka told her. The past week they had pushed themselves, practicing every day, all day. Silluka had barely seen any of Chimor and hadn't had much chance to talk to her girlfriend. "Why don't we take a break from this? I saw a café yesterday that had roasted choca beans. We can go now, if you want."

Cosquella pulled the rest of the suit off, Lugopo muttering over it as they smoothed it out. "Yes. I'd like that, I would. I think I'm more cut out for punching things, me, instead of chayus. Give a chance for us to—"

"Ah, there you are. Perfect timing."

Silluka turned at Elder Quilqi's voice, clenching her teeth. The old woman held a rolled parchment that looked ancient. She presented it to Silluka, who took it with a frown. The last time Elder Quilqi had her read a new chayu, she ended up almost dying.

"Cosquella and I were just about to take a break. Can this wait?"

"Not if you want to learn this Chayu."

"It looks like a long one," Silluka said. The parchment was bulky and heavy. It promised the rest of the day practicing, and no roasted choca with Cosquella.

"Rolled scrolls! It should be, child. Do you know how much wrangling I had to go through to get one of these from Nina's storage? They're supposed to be kept in the center used for Mental Adept testing, but almost no one pays attention to that. Except Nina's receptionist."

Silluka heard Ichu grunt in amusement, off to her right. She unrolled the top of the parchment, taking note of the title glyphs at the top. Even the title had a slew of arrows and modifiers on it. She gave Cosquella an apologetic look. The tall woman rolled her eyes and waved Silluka on.

Maybe they could go to the café tomorrow. She turned back to the elder.

"*Jakua's...Fight*? This isn't one I've heard of. Maybe Ichu has..."

"He hasn't heard of this one either. It's not one of the little chayus you've been practicing up until now. This is all of the form of *Jakua*, a chayu with ties to Tiyu Tiksimuyu, Uncle Earth."

Ichu, covered in sweat from multiple rounds of the morning ritual, came over, wiping his brow. He hadn't had any more incidents like the one that took them to the healer, but he hadn't made much more progress than Cosquella.

"Is this to prepare for stored chayus? Akamu said he would teach us those later."

"It is, but you are not ready for this, by a long shot." The elder glared at Ichu until he retreated. "Practice finding your *sunqu* first."

Silluka wanted to go to him, but the elder was standing over her, exuding that field of pressure. "You, on the other hand, need to learn how to store an entire chayu, a real chayu, to test for Mental Adept. This is one of the easier ones and will get you started. You're going to have a challenge, though. If you store this chayu with the suit on, you'll only be able to use it with the suit, and vice versa."

"The suit makes that much difference?" Silluka held up the suit's constructed right hand, moving her fingers in and out. It still wasn't as dexterous as her real hand.

"I told you not to use it as a crutch. It's going to be twice as hard for you to learn these chayus as a whole if you want to use them with that contraption."

Silluka unrolled more of the chayu. There were some unfamiliar symbols at the top, after the name.

"What are these?"

The elder looked over her shoulder. "Ah, you wouldn't know of those yet. That is *Jakua's Fight*, the mental chayu at the beginning to let your body store these chayus rather than activate them."

Silluka puzzled over the symbols. They were reminiscent of the beginning of *Flying Quirra*, in what the elder had called a Mental stance.

After that, she saw the first few moves of *Jakua's Claws*, followed later by *Jakua's Legs*. There were more of the *Jakua* chayus later. They switched stances between chayus, but interestingly, only the original stance was specified. Silluka had learned from the elder herself that the stance the chayu was performed in changed the effect. It was the basis of using her intent, a component of learning to be a Mental Adept. She looked at the suit's hand again, then back at the scroll.

"This is only in the first stance for each part of the chayu," Silluka said. "Don't Huaca who learn this know they can change stances in a chayu by now?"

Elder Quilqi gave her a searching look. "They do."

"So when they store this chayu, does it have to be stored separately for each type of stance, or say, could I use *Jakua's Claws* in Reflex stance rather than the Basic stance it's taught in?"

"A good question, and not one many pick up on at first. Yes, when the chayu section is released, the footwork may be modified to adjust the outcome. It's better to store it in the stance you want to use, but it's doable to change."

"Then how is that different from whether I have two hands or one? Shouldn't adjusting the effect of the chayu take that into account as well?"

Elder Quilqi crossed her arms. "Changing where your feet are placed is different than your mental picture of how many limbs you have. Is your mind that fluid? Rivets and splinters! I'm not saying it can't be done, but remember what happened when the suit's hand was destroyed mid-fight? I won't be there to untangle your *sunqu* every time you mess up."

"Then I better not mess up." Silluka squatted down at the base of a pillar and began to study the scroll. Cosquella would understand. She glanced up to see her back muscles rippling under her clothes as she moved through a chayu. She and Ichu worked side by side to practice.

Silluka frowned and went back to studying the scroll. She'd have to work twice as hard to learn *Jakua's Fight* with and without the suit.

* * *

It was several hours later before Silluka even attempted to practice *Jakua's Fight*. She knew most of the parts, but not all of them. Some were obscure, like *Jakua Blinks His Eyes*, which she thought was meant to reset the body during a fight, giving time for all combatants to recoup. Others were well known but hard to implement, like *Jakua Leaps Up a Tree*, used to evade opponents. One was even part of the morning ritual, *Jakua Crouches and Lashes His Tail*. Together, the chayu gave a whole repository of moves, countermoves, strikes, and defenses. It was an entire suite of fighting techniques. Many other chayus were utilitarian. If she mastered all parts of this chayu, she'd have been able to take on Hufi and his entire patrol at one time. The thought gave her pause, knowing how far she'd come since thieving on the streets of the Huaca by the coast.

She realized Cosquella and Ichu had already left for the day. When had that happened? Had they told her goodbye? They must have. Cosquella always did. She must not have heard them. Maybe she could catch up with them for a late evening meal.

Just as Silluka was getting ready to go back to the refuge center, Elder Quilqi appeared from whatever errand she'd disappeared on. Silluka sighed and sat back down. The old woman had a talent of showing up just when she was about to quit and making her practice more. Was she really that worth the attention of someone called "ancient one"?

"Why me?" Silluka asked. She held up her stump. "I'm not a good practitioner. I wasn't even able to become a citizen. Why trust me with all this? Why push me?"

Elder Quilqi sat down on a bench, her old face surprisingly gentle. Most of the gymnasium was clear, the other Huaca having gone home to whatever else they did in Chimor. Merchants or laborers maybe, or soldiers. She'd seen a group of people using *Tortoise Shoulders His Load* to bring crates of food through the front gate. Sun slanted in between tall buildings and made a sliver of sunlight across the tile floor. The elder considered her for several moments.

"You were a spot of interest in a bland village of perfectionists," she finally said. "One who knew of the techniques they practiced, but not hidebound by them. I had been there for several years at that point, observing them for some hidden strength that might have come about by their methods. I've been looking for ways the Huaca might regain some of their might. Too many skilled practitioners have left..." She suddenly tilted her head, breaking off her sentence. "Do you know, I actually looked in on the village your parents lived in on the coast, back when they were children? The elders had not quite calcified then, and I thought there could be some promise of their techniques. Papaki especially had potential, but...it was not to be."

Silluka did some quick math in her head and looked at Elder Quilqi in a new light. Ancient one indeed.

"Do they remember you?"

Elder Quilqi pursed her lips. "Papaki might have an inkling, but I don't think the rest do. In any case, it's not important. What you think of as a weakness"—she pointed at Silluka's stump—"gives you an opportunity to think about life a different way. Many of the most powerful Huaca started that way. It will help when you have to fight for real."

Silluka blinked, all her thoughts driven away by that statement. "Wait, fighting? Fighting who? When?"

"In the arena, for one. It's a good first test. You can't hold a candle to most in Chimor now, but I have a feeling that will change soon. And the only way to move up here is to show your strength."

"Why fight though? Can't I show my strength in different ways?"

Elder Quilqi sighed. "Of course you could. That would be my preference. But remember what I said when we first arrived here. The islands, each with their gods, are joining up. And the gods are not ones to easily share their power. When they come into conflict, that conflict is passed down to their peoples. Anuit's victory will not be the last of the deaths. And frankly, I don't want you to be one of them. You've still seen very little of this island, and none of the world outside it."

"But why would anyone want to fight me?" Silluka still hadn't figured that part out.

"Because you're with me, of course. Godly contests, girl, I thought you got that part." The elder leaned forward, still seated. "I already told you all these species gathering here will attract powerful and unpleasant people. You've seen the state of your people in the refugee camp. They'll stay there as long as possible, and by the time some of them really understand Chimor and how backwater they seem in comparison, we'll be inundated with those who can challenge the gods. The Eztli Mecatl are just the beginning. Now, you can stay with them, spending your life waiting for the next handout and hoping not to be crushed under a powerful adept's thumb, or you can continue on this path, and go...I don't know how far." The elder lifted a hand skyward.

Silluka thought of spending more time with Cosquella in the refugee camp. None of them had much money, or anything else worth much in Chimor. The elder continued to give her opportunities she couldn't pass up.

"And you think I really have a chance to affect this conflict you say is coming?"

"I've seen many champions in my time. I can recognize potential. It's up to you to act on it."

"Then I'd best get back to this," Silluka said, hefting the scroll. She would have time to spend with Cosquella later. For now, practice.

* * *

The next day, Silluka began learning *Jakua's Fight*. Lugopo checked the power output, as usual, and adjusted the connections on both her and Cosquella's suits.

"It would be better for me to train in simple sparring matches than to practice this, it would," Cosquella grumbled. "This suit does nothing for me."

"Made more adjustments this morning," Lugopo signed. "Accounting for change in *sunqu* is hard, but not past my capabilities. With this suit you will rain great destruction!"

"Try it again. With me this time." Silluka tried to buoy her girlfriend's spirits, but Cosquella was frowning, though she stood for the morning ritual. Performing it first would open her connection to the core, which would aid her in *Jakua's Fight* afterwards. She understood now why Akamu's stone warriors were so drained after the desert Allwiya attack on their sleds. They had to perform chayus for the next several days to store all the parts they'd used up. They couldn't even help Ichu when he was injured, leaving it up to her and Elder Quilqi.

Ichu was gone that morning. It was unusual for him, but he'd been frustrated with his lack of progress. Maybe he was taking a break today?

She started the morning ritual with Cosquella. Both of them wore Lugopo's suits, and Silluka visualized the chayu with both physical hands. She'd learned on the journey here to use a mental version of her missing hand to fulfill the form of the chayu, but with this, she didn't need to. She had a physical hand, which lined up with the picture in her head.

They started slow. Cosquella knew the movements, but her fine control had always been shaky. She could punch through a wall, but her hands shook while she was writing or performing another detailed task. That meant getting the moves exactly correct was hard for her. Akamu had said the core's power seemed not to know where to attach to Cosquella. If it never happened, she'd never be able to test for even Physical Adept. Silluka watched Cosquella's uneven moves. Maybe she was better suited for punching and sparring matches.

And that was fine, if it had to happen. There were no undesirables in Chimor, Akamu had told them. Simply Adepts who followed the path, and those who didn't. In a city this size, there were plenty of both.

Together, Silluka and Cosquella performed the morning ritual. The pressure built in her, rising up like sap through a tree. It connected her to the core of the planet and the gods who resided there. Back in the village, a well-performed chayu caused the ampuka to bloom around the practitioner. But she'd learned that was just the energy escaping. Capturing it and sending it to one's *sunqu* was what made a true connection possible. A more experienced practitioner would show little of the ampuka.

They completed the last move, *Pray*, together, elbows coming to their centers, hands unfolded in front. Silluka gasped as the energy became a font through her.

"Capture it quickly! Place it in your *sunqu*!" She grated the words and heard Cosquella grunt in acknowledgement. Out of the corner of her eye, she could see the glow was faint around Cosquella, as if the chayu had been performed badly. Except with the help of the suit, Cosquella had been nearly as exact in her placement as Silluka.

Silluka strained, bearing down on the energy to compress it to her *sunqu*. When she was done, she looked to Cosquella again. There was a warm glow in her middle, raging to get out. She needed to channel it into *Jakua's Fight*.

"Anything?"

The other woman breathed out a sigh. "It's better with you, it is. Maybe better with this suit. But the energy, it doesn't stay within me. Am I broken, am I?"

"Over six Tortoises of power! You grow again, ready to bend the world to your might!" Lugopo was signing with three tentacles and holding up their measuring device with another two.

"Wasn't it five and a quarter last time?" Silluka asked.

"Indeed!"

"And what about Cosquella?" Silluka looked to her girlfriend.

Lugopo fiddled with their measuring device, twisting several components. "Hm. Much lower. Only half a Tortoise. Such disappointment." At Cosquella's dark expression, they tapped their circlet. "Such potential for improvement!"

Cosquella looked ready to rip the suit off but Silluka went to her, placing her real hand on the taller woman's shoulder. She had to reach up. She stood on tiptoes and pressed into a kiss.

"We'll figure this out. I believe in you."

Cosquella growled. Her hands were gripped tightly enough to make the joints in the suit creak.

"I'm useless."

"You're not. We'll find the best way to use your talents here."

"If I can't even be a Physical Adept, then what use am I here? I should find a job in the city like all the other undesirables, I should. Maybe they need a farmer. Or a lumberjack."

Silluka tried not to shake the larger woman, though she wouldn't mind seeing her chop wood. Her shoulders moved like serpents when she flexed. "You took out a turtleman with your bare hands. You carved through to that giant Allwiya's brain! How can you say you're useless?"

"To overpower gigantic Allwiya speaks of massive prowess!" Lugopo signed. "You use your many bones to good effect!"

Cosquella snorted, despite her obvious anger.

"Now, I need to do something with these six Tortoises in me, or I'm going to explode," Silluka told her. This time she was pleased to hear Cosquella's belly laugh. "Do you want to try to perform it with me?"

"Naw. I'll slow you down, I will." Cosquella waved a craggy hand at her—one that would nearly reach around her entire middle. "I'll hold the scroll and give you hints if you go amiss."

Silluka got another quick kiss, then took in a deep breath. The energy in her *sunqu* begged for release. "I'd welcome your support. Let me have one last look." She read through the scroll again from beginning to end, memorizing the sequence. She thought she had a grip on even the unfamiliar chayus. There was a pattern to them, after all. They were all parts of *Jakua's Fight*. Together, they formed a whole. She could just see the web of movements in her mind. The jakua used its whole body as a weapon, and that was what this chayu represented. Except she wouldn't act on the effect of each chayu. She was doing this to store it within her.

She gave the scroll back. "Ready."

"I am ready as well, for unlimited power of my creation!" Lugopo swung up to Cosquella's shoulder, their power sensor held in two tentacles.

She felt the shape of the jakua as she began *Jakua's Fight*. Was it one jakua? All of them? *The* Jakua? Whichever, she could feel her muscles move like the great cat's as she went into Mental stance, envisioning the battle. *Jakua's Claws* were next, a brief chayu where the suit hand and her real hand curled into talons, ready to hook and scratch. She'd seen it many times with the jakua handlers in the Huaca. The next chayu section was a new one, *Jakua Observes*, during which she held a Reflex stance and made only movements with her head and neck. This was another mental chayu, like *Flying Quirra*. *Jakua's Belly* came after, another new chayu that tensed her midsection in a rippling motion. A series of small internal moves expanded her torso. She felt her spine lengthen with the effort, pushing her neck forward. In practice, it would strengthen the softer parts of her body to take an impact.

And then...what was next?

"Jakua Springs Back," Cosquella prompted her. Of course. She crouched down, in a modified Strength stance, then uncoiled, pushing back across the floor. Her feet danced through a series of moves that would avoid projectiles, or distance strikes. It could just as easily be used to climb an unstable support. That was followed by *Jakua's Legs*, as she regained her footing. She could start to see the shape of the fight. So many diverging pathways, depending on what the situation was. Jakua had found a foe or been surprised by one. Jakua snuck around the enemy or made a frontal assault. The shape of the battle glowed in the air around her in the colors of the gods, the rich brown of Uncle Earth, the purple of Entle Magic, the orange of Aunt Harvest.

She fell into the next logical chayu segment even though she didn't remember the order. *Jakua Crouches and Lashes His Tail*—part of the morning ritual—made so much sense here. A shadow formed in the air behind her, whipping back and forth. The practical uses for it began to unfurl in her mind, from propelling her forward with great speed, to stabilizing her balance. It would depend on the stance she used.

The energy she'd stored in her core began flowing into the chayus, strengthening them as each segment added another layer to jakua's battle with their opponent.

A movement caught her eye as Elder Quilqi sat beside Cosquella, watching intently. A pressure crowded against her as Silluka continued through the chayu, then dissipated as the elder sat back. She was only a quarter of the way through and Silluka had been moving continuously for at least a quarter of an hour, maybe more. Lugopo continued to watch their device, writing down numbers here and there on a pad held in yet another tentacle.

All three of her witnesses watched her, Cosquella occasionally prompting her with a word or gesture from the scroll when she looked like she was faltering. Sweat streamed down Silluka's face and back. The gymnasium floor around her was filled with highlights, the remnants of Jakua's fight and outlines of the great beast, which slowly faded from the air. Even the morning ritual was not this long. Performing it multiple times gave breaks between repetitions. There were no breaks here. This was a fight, and to pause was to die. The power in her *sunqu* radiated outward to all her limbs, fading deeper into her. No, not fading, but storing. She felt lighter the longer she moved, as if she was being buoyed up by a force beneath her.

As she progressed, she found other adversaries. During *Jakua Leaps Up a Tree*, the target was no longer on the ground, and she fought differently, more defensively. It was also useful for movement in high places. In *The Bush Conceals Jakua*, the opponent was larger and more powerful, and she had to hide and leap out to best use her skills.

Finally, the room a mass of shadows around her, Silluka completed *Jakua Licks His Wounds*, then, at last, *Jakua Rests*.

As she paced through last few movements—a Reflex stance, checking her surroundings, then a Basic stance, her back arched in a stretch—the shadows pulled toward her, coalescing into her core. The whole fight was etched before her eyes, and she felt she could reach out and pluck part of it into being.

Then she realized Elder Quilqi was on her feet, coming closer. The old woman was staring as if she would bore a hole through Silluka, but she felt nothing. In fact, everything seemed washed out around her.

"—too strong. How is your connection...girl? I need...break...movements and measures!"

Why were the elder's words so faint? Behind her, Lugopo held up their device in triumph. The construct vibrated, then one end fell off, but the Allwiya seemed happy because of it.

Elder Quilqi came closer, shouting into her ear. "You have to finish storing the chayu, girl. Otherwise, it will rip you apart! You're taking far too much from the core for this chayu. It must be that Allwiya-cursed suit."

Silluka concentrated and the last of the haze around her faded, rolling into her body, forming impressions of a jakua pacing through grass, swiping at enemies, dodging, rolling, leaping, and more. Her *sunqu* was empty of the power from the morning ritual, but her entire body buzzed.

The room came back into focus. Had that haze of light...been from her?

Elder Quilqi put her hands on her hips. "Well, at least now you're not lighting up this entire section of Chimor. Fiery core, girl, you don't do anything by halves, do you?"

The suit creaked around Silluka, and she realized it was warm to the touch...no, *hot* to the touch.

"Get it off!" she said, as the wood started smoking and the metal singed her flesh. She began to strip out of it, while Lugopo swung down to unfasten the clasps on her legs.

"Ow. This is pain. Hurting. Searing tentacles. Ah!" the circlet emitted a string of updates as Lugopo signed and picked at the fasteners. Silluka stripped from the top, and before long, let the suit fall to the floor behind her. She massaged her wrists and legs where the metal had left bright red marks on her flesh.

"This is unusual." The elder watched the suit as if it might get up and start dancing. "I would have warned you against performing a full chayu in the suit if I knew this would happen."

"But it worked," Silluka answered. "I can feel the power this gives me. I think I can release parts of the chayu, too, just like Akamu." She raised her hand, but the elder pushed it down with a shake of her head.

"None of that now. I don't doubt the power. That's the problem."

"Over twenty-two Tortoises of energy!" Lugopo chirped. They held up a blackened object. "Look! You have destroyed my carefully constructed measuring device!" They tapped their circlet. "It will take days to replace!" They tapped it again. "This has succeeded past what I imagined!"

Elder Quilqi frowned down at Lugopo. "I can keep the girl's power from flooding the city like a beacon, but I can't do anything for an Allwiya." She glanced around the gymnasium, where a few other practitioners had stopped to watch. Several pointed in their direction. "We'd better hope..."

She cut off as a beam of white splotched with black, like a diseased fruit, projected up from the ground under Lugopo. The little Allwiya frantically gestured with their tentacles, then froze, held in place as if captured by a giant hand.

"You have attracted my attention, little one. Come, serve me and undergo my challenge. Grovel before Whirling Abyss."

Elder Quilqi sighed. "The problem with bright students is that they tend to attract the attention of their gods."

CHAPTER SIX

Mixed Magic

Ichu watched the turtleman stump down a side street that afternoon in Chimor. He'd noticed her the past few days, always following the same path. He'd seen her talking with Huaca, Misini, and the spiky people, the Kawchi. He'd seen her give carefully wrapped packages to several people, and guessed she was a healer of sorts. Perfect to start his education, especially after his failures practicing with his sister and Cosquella.

He headed after her, once she dropped off a package with a mother Huaca and child. She looked like she was heading back home for the evening.

The turtleman—or woman, as it were—threaded a maze of pathways near Chimor's edge. It wasn't the same area as the refugee camp, but it wasn't far. If Cosquella's timing was correct, the turtlemen had only been here for maybe a few years, though long enough to settle into the city.

Ichu hadn't bothered to use a chayu to sneak after his target. Not that his chayu did much these days, especially compared to what Silluka could do. He tried not to be jealous, though it was difficult when he seemed to fail more than he succeeded in learning the path of the Adepts. Still, he was continually amazed by his sister's growth. She'd be able to take on any other bodycaster in the old village by now, and most of the elders.

Thus, he was surprised when he rounded a corner and came face to face with the turtlewoman. Her beady red eyes bored into him, craggy arms crossed. She was just taller than him, topped with a bonnet, and wore nondescript beaten fiber clothing that blended into the stone walls of Chimor, nothing like the plates of steel the fighters had worn when chasing them from the coast. Her back was rounded and solid, not quite a shell, and her beaky mouth frowned, more mobile than a true reptile.

"Why are you following me, are you, Huaca?"

Ichu faltered, caught off guard. "Can you teach me your magic?" he blurted.

That seemed to surprise the turtlewoman, who blinked and uncrossed her arms. "How would a Huaca learn Eztli Mecatl magic?"

"I drank a vial from one of your warriors. It corrupted my *sunqu* somehow. Can you help me?" So much for any attempt at subtlety. His mouth seemed determined to run away from him even as the mere thought of the vial filled him with longing for more of it.

The turtlewoman squinted in disbelief. "A vial? Impossible. This is new magic. Our true god is dead, he is. Our magic no longer works. What do you really want, do you?"

Dead? Ichu blinked. Could gods die? Evidently, they could. That was new information. Akamu only knew their god had changed in some way. He had to find out more.

"Please." Ichu tried to put his need into his voice. "I used to be a champion of my people. Now my chayus are weak. I need help."

"Hm." The turtlewoman grunted, then turned and stomped down the alley. "You are ignorant, you are, but fortunately I have a soft spot for helping others. Come. I will explain."

The turtlewoman's home was a single room excavated into the stone block of a building on the edge of Chimor. Much like where Nu'oona worked, it looked like it had been carved out long after the building was first erected, remains of previous inhabitations filled in with stone and mortar to make this new apartment. Inside were racks of reagents, complex devices worthy of an Allwiya, a small sink and several herbs in pots above it, and a table with yet more equipment, mostly for grinding and preparing ingredients. There was a small bed tucked against one wall, which looked almost smaller than the turtlewoman herself.

"I am Amoxtli, I am. Sit." She gestured at two rickety chairs by the table. "Tell me why you want to learn our magic, you do, and how you think it might be possible."

Ichu introduced himself, then related his village's flight from the new island's collision with the coast, the turtlemen's attack, their use of the vials, Ichu taking one, and what Akamu and Elder Quilqi had said about his damaged *sunqu*. Amoxtli frowned through most of his description.

When he was done, she sat forward, her beaky mouth working. He got the feeling she would have been an old woman, had she been Huaca—an elder—but was harder to tell with other species.

"First," she finally said. "There is a distinction, there is. You use the term 'turtleman.'" She waved off his rising objection. "I will not debate the physical resemblance. You all look to me of shaved, tail-less quirras, you do. The Misini are like stretched, awkward jakuas. 'Turtleman' is as good as any." She held up a thick finger, topped with a wicked, curved claw. "But those who chase you and drink unwilling sacrifice, name *those* turtlemen." She put a hand on her chest. "We of the dead god are Eztli Mecatl, we are. The true ones. The fugitives."

Ichu was filled with questions, but also aware of his tenuous guest status. He nodded. "Eztli Mecatl then. Thank you for explaining, Amoxtli. Will you tell me of the difference between the magic you knew and what the...the turtlemen use?"

Amoxtli waggled her head side to side. "We have always been a people of sacrifice. Together, we are greater than we are singly, we are. We searched for answers in the sea surrounding our island as it sped through the world ocean. One of us might boil, then drown in the boiling seas, but ten of us giving just a pinch of strength, and one can withstand the heat by dispersal. Do you see, yes?"

"I...think so," Ichu said. "I saw firsthand how the turtlemen attackers grew stronger the fewer of them there were."

"Paah. A perversion." Amoxtli held out both hands, raising and lowering them like a balance. "We make an individual strong by lending them ability as tribute when needed. In the absence of a god, the turtlemen take strength from others to fulfill their needs. As their comrades fall, they hoard power."

Ichu squinted. It was a subtle difference. "So the old ways are based on giving, and the new ways, on taking?"

"Smart for a shaved quirra, you are."

Ichu chuckled, then grew serious. Now he would find out if Amoxtli could actually help him. "I've taken a portion of the god of the Eztli...pardon, the *turtlemen* into myself, and made a connection. I can no longer connect to the chayus like I used to. So...after some medical advice and that of an elder acquaintance of mine, I've come to you to see if I might be able to use the abilities of the Eztli Mecatl instead." He'd been mulling it over since Nu'oona's words.

Amoxtli sat back, a dark look on her face. "That is...not how that works. A vial distilled of my people, whether of our dead god or of the turtlemen's perversion, should have no effect on you, it shouldn't. The Misini's feckless gods will not accept entertainment from you. The Kawchi's quorum will not let you summon with one of their members. It is impossible, it is."

Now Ichu sat forward, realizing Amoxtli must have thought he was embellishing his tale. "I promise you, my story is true. I used to be the best...well, Physical Adept, I suppose it's called here. Now my training has faltered, and I can no longer summon the ampuka. An elder of my people tells me the vial corrupted my *sunqu*. Perhaps it happened when I ingested a vial created without a god's power? Is there some way you could determine this for yourself? I don't wish to impose on you..." he trailed off. He had imposed plenty already.

"A bit late, but I'm used to requests from other species, I am. I have found my place as a healer in Chimor over the last few years. Plus, your story intrigues me, it does. What has happened to our magic since our god died?" Amoxtli huffed to her feet and came around the little table to Ichu. She leaned close to his forehead, a raspy noise coming from her beaky mouth. Was she...sniffing him?

She placed both rough hands on his shoulders, pushing him back into the chair. Her hands were warm, radiating through his thin shirt. She moved one hand over his heart, the other over his stomach and pressed again. Ichu's heartrate rose as if he was warming up for chayu, and his stomach growled. She moved her hands to his, on the arms of the chair, her rough fingers running down his.

"Sit tight, you," she said, her mouth turned up in a rueful grin. She moved both hands down to his navel, where his *sunqu* should have been, then her hands dipped lower, just above his groin, fingers pressing in. Ichu felt his chin rise, his shoulders reaching back for the safety of the chair. Heat filled his belly, energizing him, and he struggled not to pant.

Amoxtli chuckled as her hand moved again, this time both on his thighs, then with a grunt, she got to her knees and felt under his knees, and then his feet. Now his legs burned as if he had run for miles.

She stood again with a breath of effort, then crossed her arms. "A little less jumpy than a quirra, but not much, you aren't."

He couldn't sit any longer. As soon as Amoxtli wasn't looming over him, he sprang up, feet propelling him back and forth across the small room.

"What did you find?"

Amoxtli's face soured again. "I do not like to admit this, I don't, but you are right. You felt my sacrifice for you, yes? That proves there is a connection between us."

That was enough to make him stop pacing, at least for a moment. "You were...giving energy to me?"

She nodded. "Our ways are that of sacrifice, as I said. You get a little stronger, I get a little weaker. The direction might be reversed in the future if my need is greater than yours."

He thought he saw the difference between the Eztli Mecatl and the turtlemen a little clearer. "Then it's a partnership. Neither party loses, because the one you give to can give back to you."

"Indeed. The sacrifice of others' bodies to perfect your own is the easiest application of our magic. More subtle gifts come later."

Ichu narrowed his eyes as he started pacing again. "Like the levels of Adepthood for the Huaca. Our first step is Physical Adept, where we perfect performance of chayus. You perfect sharing your body's power with your people."

"As good a summary as any," Amoxtli said. "Now slow your step, you. An old woman like me can't waste too much of my body, and you shouldn't waste it either."

Ichu stopped abruptly. His urge to pace, his racing heart, his elevated breathing. He was using *her* energy, not his own. He blinked, visualizing this gift fivefold, or tenfold, from several Eztli Mecatl. No wonder the turtlemen were powerful, if they could do this, or some perversion of this.

"How do I give it back?" he asked.

Amoxtli opened her hands to the sides, standing before him in her nondescript clothing. "You saw what I did. Give of your *sunqu* to mine. When we make a connection with others, the sum is more than the parts. Our god adds"—her expression soured— "*used* to add his portion as well, and a giver was never so drained they couldn't function. Some went years, lending all of their abilities to our brightest minds and cleverest crafters. They lived average lives at the mercy of our now-dead god, they did." She sighed. "Now the transfer is not bolstered. We refugees must give only of ourselves, limiting our might. We are especially weak before the *turtleman* warriors, who have no qualms about stealing the lives of their people."

"Then I *am* using up your energy! Please help me return it," Ichu insisted. He extended his hands toward her, waiting for instruction.

"Breathe first, little quirra," Amoxtli said. He wouldn't have accepted that from most people, but even an elder

Eztli Mecatl like Amoxtli stood a head taller than him. "The more you expend, the less you have to give. Find your *sunqu*—where it really is, where my hands were."

Ishu closed his eyes, forcing his breathing to a slower pace. As if he'd just finished a complex chayu and needed to prepare for the next one. He remembered the gentle pressure from her old hands, low—very low—on his belly. It was even lower than he thought. Nu'oona had agreed it might have moved between where it was on a Huaca and an Eztli Mecatl. He opened his eyes and took in Amoxtli, still standing there, waiting. She was taller than him, yet her legs were shorter, the rounded bone of her back curving under like a shell. Naturally her *sunqu* was even lower than him. On him, it would be below his torso, between his thighs. Could a *sunqu* exist *outside* of the body?

Suddenly a blaze of energy rushed through his tissues. He *had* been wrong, the whole time. *There* was his *sunqu*, below where his torso ended. And now he could feel the web of connection from him, to her. It was still there, a warm touch where her hands had connected with him, giving freely, bolstering him.

He took two steps to the old Eztli Mecatl, placing his hands on her shoulders, as she did to him. Feed back the power she had given. It was a gift while he used it, and now he returned it freely. He moved his hand lower, one over her heart—a little more central in her chest than in his—and over her stomach. His heart slowed. He cupped each of her rough hands in his. Then hands low on her belly, lower even than his *sunqu*. His breathing evened out. He knelt and placed his hands on her thighs, her knees, and finally her feet. At each touch, a little went out of him, until he was...simply himself again.

He stood up and dipped his head to her. This was a holy connection between them. Literally. An homage to her dead god.

"Thank you for your knowledge, Amoxtli," he said. The words felt right, but there was more. "If you need a gift from me in return, simply call on me."

For the first time, a true smile, lifting her hard mouth, crinkling her eyes, crept on her face.

"You understand the gift, little quirra," she said. "I would not be offended if you visited me again. There is more I believe I can teach you."

"But you have your own business to attend to today. I apologize for taking up your time." He had accosted this woman on the street and demanded she teach him. Just like her magic, she had given him a gift.

He stood straight, struck by a thought. It would take practice, and some experimentation with where he now knew his *sunqu* resided.

"May I visit you tomorrow?" he asked. "I believe I may have a way to give more back to you."

The bony ridges above her eyes rose. "You seem inspired." She gave a sharp nod. "I have some time late morning tomorrow, after my errands are over."

"Then please, a gift for you." He reached out with both hands, this time one over her heart and the other reaching down to her *sunqu*. He gave some of himself—the energy of the mature to the waning of the elderly. He would not need it, and if his idea worked, he could give even more back to Amoxtli.

Her shoulders lifted as he took his hands back, this time a deeper, searching look in her eyes. "A true gift, from a noble Huaca. I thank you."

Ichu took his leave.

* * *

He returned to Amoxtli's home, late the next morning. He didn't tell Silluka where he was going, hoping the explanation after the fact would be good enough. He'd run through the morning ritual several times, attempting to capture the power of his core into his *sunqu*. It was harder than it had been before he took the vial, but getting easier, now he knew the new placement of his center.

Amoxtli grumbled at his arrival, but he thought he saw a lift in her walk as she crossed back to her chair on the other side of the little table. She didn't sit down though, putting her hands on the back. Her thick nails curled down to touch the wood. Was she...excited?

"You seemed as if you had a revelation yesterday before you left, you did," she began.

"I did." Ichu paced again, the energy from the morning ritual filling him, even if it was not as much as he used to feel from a well-executed chayu. Lugopo would probably say it was only a couple Tortoises or so in strength, rather than the five they had measured before. "For whatever reason, I have a connection to both the gods of the Huaca, and the Eztli Mecatl—dead or not. But all our power comes from the core, does it not?"

Amoxtli nodded her old head, obviously waiting for the end result.

"You said with your god dead, he was not able to support your gifts to each other. But I *do* have the support of my gods."

She stood up straight at that, hands coming off the chair. "I think I see what you mean, I do."

Ichu opened his hands, palms up. "May I?"

The old Eztli came closer. "I will accept your gift."

He went through the ritual she showed him the day before, placing his hands on shoulders, heart, stomach, hands, core, thighs, knees, and feet. With it, he willed the stored energy from his *sunqu* as he would while using the benefits of a chayu. The morning ritual did not have a specific purpose, merely to connect to the core and flood a Huaca with energy for more powerful chayus. He fed everything he had stored that morning into Amoxtli, feeling her heartbeat stabilize, her joints creak less, the arthritis in her hands and feet leave her.

He stood up again afterward, feeling no weaker than he had the day before. He hadn't needed to give much of himself. Nearly all was the energy he had stored that morning.

"Oh. Oh, shining seas." Amoxtli clasped his face in her old hands. "You have done what none have since our god died, Huaca." She spun away quickly, looking through a cabinet hung on a wall.

"We spoke of the vials, what you drank to make this change to yourself. That method has been lost to us, it has. Without the power of our god, storing ability like that would drain a person to nothing. It cannot be done."

She spun back, walking spryly, a glistening vial and a cork in her hand. "But no more."

Ichu took a step forward before he could stop himself. The *need* that rose up in him was overwhelming. Just seeing one of those vials again—he hadn't known how much he wanted one. There had been none available. But now...

"That's how the turtlemen gain power."

"They abuse their power." Amoxtli raised the vial, her other hand a warning. "These should be used for the good of all, they should, when an artist needs a burst of inspiration, or a crafter must finish a project under a deadline, or in the aid of others. The turtlemen have reversed this process, and can suck in the essence of those around them to fill one of these, they can. They take, remember."

Ichu forced his hand down. He hadn't realized he'd reached for the vial. Was that why it was such a need? Because the one he'd drunk was built on taking from others? But he had used it as Amoxtli said, in the aid of others. He'd used it to save his sister. So why was he punished by it?

"What do I need to do?" he asked.

"Provide me enough power from the core to fill this. Then I will gift it back to you to power your progress. It will be good simply to make one again, it will."

"Could I make one myself one day?" he asked.

Amoxtli twitched her head. "Debatable. Eztli Mecatl went through several stages of perfection from our god to learn how to make these. I do not know what the turtlemen must do, or how your abilities lie."

"Then do what you must," he told her. "I'll prepare now. I'll need to go outside."

Ichu left the small home. There wasn't enough space for more than the simplest chayu inside, and he wanted something substantial for his first test.

He steadied his breathing, closed his eyes, and set his stance. Then he began the morning ritual again. He'd used up the power he'd stored from that morning, gifting it to Amoxtli. She was welcome to it. Now he performed it again to open himself to the core.

When he finished, the surge of power felt a little stronger than before, and he compressed what he could into his *sunqu*.

Immediately after, he began *Eagle Watches from on High*. It was not a chayu used often, but its effects were easily felt. The shape of a great bird formed around him as his arms and fingers brushed wide, then close, his feet in Dexterity stance. The last time he had performed this chayu, he had been looking for Silluka, just before the first turtleman arrived. Now, he knew so much more, and the power he'd stored in his *sunqu* surged into the chayu, giving it shape. It was of Tiye Kwirpuyay—Entle Magic, and their power filled him, a purple aura surrounding him.

He finished, then looked left and right. Little signs he had not been aware of stood out to him now. Where one of the Misini had crossed in front of Amoxtli's home while he'd been inside. The chips in the stone around the door, telling when and how this entrance had been made. A scratch on the wall, at Amoxtli's head height, made by a stone two years ago.

Ichu went back in the house before the chayu could begin to fade. He wanted to give as much of this to Amoxtli as he could.

"You are ready, then?" She held a vial in one hand, standing straighter than ever, her head high. He tried not to stare at the vial.

"I am ready. How do I move this chayu to you?"

"The heart and *sunqu* connections are the same. What is the nature of the chayu?"

"*Eagle Watches from on High*. It increases sight and allows the mind to make connections it would not otherwise. Used for tracking, or hunting."

"Or research, possibly?" Amoxtli touched her temples, eyes, and ears with her free hand. "These connection points as well. You may feel there are more, you might."

The points she had indicated on herself burned in his vision, as if the sun shone on them. His hands went to her chest and low belly first, creating the link to him, offering his power. Then he touched his fingers to her temples, her eyes, her ears, and after consideration, her mouth and neck. He stepped back as the rush of power left him.

The world was mundane again, but Amoxtli turned her head this way and that, her eyes wide.

"A powerful ability. And a good choice to test." She held the vial to her forehead, eyes closed. Inside it, a mist coalesced until it was viscous liquid, the same purple as Entle Magic's aura.

She blinked, as if keeping tears from falling, then offered the vial, cork in the top.

"It worked. For the first time since our god died, for nearly two decades, it worked." Her gnarled hand trembled ever so slightly.

Ichu took the vial from her gingerly. The need to drink it almost overwhelmed him, but he resisted it. He had to save this. The last time he'd drunk from a vial, he'd almost died. Surely this was different though? He had no way of knowing. This was a new magic. He pushed his need away again and stowed the vial in a pouch on his belt.

"Perhaps now we can both find our power again."

"Yet I should not have any power, with my god dead," Amoxtli said. "I do not understand how this works, I don't. I still cannot feel him."

"Even the power of the gods comes from the core," Ichu suggested. "Regardless, I would like to come back again, if you will have me, to explore this power and to make new vials."

"I would welcome it, Huaca," Amoxtli said.

CHAPTER SEVEN

The Challenge of Sanity

"Lugopo!" Silluka ran to the beam of light surrounding the little Allwiya, but it was as solid as rock. She pressed against it, trying to get to them.

She raised her hand to pound the surface and hissed as the burns on her wrist pulled.

The burns. She'd stored all of *Jakua's Fight*.

"How do I release a chayu?" she called to Elder Quilqi. Akamu had made a simple motion. But which part was which? And which section would she use? *Jakua's Claws? Jakua Crouches and Lashes His Tail?*

She raised a hand, but fingers like iron closed around her wrist, stopping it from moving. Silluka jerked, but the fingers didn't move, didn't even tremble.

"Elder horrors, girl, think before you act!" Elder Quilqi's fingers released her wrist as she relaxed, letting her hand fall to her side. "Don't interfere with a godly assessment of a candidate, and especially not one other than your own. You won't like what happens."

Cosquella appeared on her other side, pointing into the light. "They're talking, they are."

Lugopo seemed able to move again, and all their tentacles were gesturing wildly, their eyes roving the room. If their translation circlet was picking any of it up, Silluka couldn't hear it.

Elder Quilqi squinted, her mouth moving as she silently translated. "Bargaining. Begging. Explanation, and...yes, I thought so. Everyone back!"

Silluka pulled Cosquella away as the speckled white light surrounding Lugopo shattered into pieces, and they dropped to the floor with a thud.

Lugopo continued to sign, seeming not to even notice their drop to the floor. Their translation circlet began spouting off what they were signing.

"Building. Yes. For you, Whirling Abyss. The destruction of enemies! Fabrication of—yes! It can be created. I need only...but no. Those materials do not exist. However, with enough pressure? The core itself! Yes! That can be used...no. With no place to stand. Must endure heat of a thousand suns! I only need..."

"They're becoming crazed, like Wallwa, they are." Cosquella pulled Silluka farther away. "The Allwiya who nearly killed my father, they did. We have to help."

She moved forward, but Elder Quilqi reached out again, stopping the big woman's movement with one finger on her shoulder. Silluka started at the strain evident in Cosquella's face. This was the woman who had carved into a giant Allwiya's brain and killed a turtleman with her bare hands.

"Do not interfere. Lugopo will come out unscathed. Or they won't. We cannot interfere."

Silluka turned to her. "Why not? What is going on?"

Elder Quilqi checked to make sure neither of them was going anywhere, then sighed. She watched Lugopo's writhing form over their shoulders. The circlet was still translating stops and starts of ideas, as if Lugopo had revelation after revelation, but no means to act on them.

"I believe it is the first challenge of the Allwiya gods, much like when you become a Physical or Mental Adept. Manylegs of Reaching, Crawling Dark of Squirming, and Whirling Abyss have always been more hands-on than the Huaca Aunts, Uncles, and Entles."

"Was this what Wallwa went through?" Cosquella asked.

"From your description, likely, though I assume that was a test of Manylegs of Reaching, not Whirling Abyss, whose attention Lugopo has drawn."

"You know a lot about the gods of the Allwiya," Silluka said. "I don't think I even know that much about Uncle Sky, or Aunt Sea."

"I've seen quite a few things over my years, girl," Elder Quilqi snapped.

"Can we help them, then?" Cosquella stared at the trembling Allwiya. They moved one way, then another, as if each new idea struck before they could act upon it.

"We can give them a focus." Silluka went to her suit, discarded on the floor. It was still warm to the touch, but not hot. She waved it in front of Lugopo's wide eyes, and their pupils started to follow the motion.

"Careful, girl," the elder grumbled. "I don't want to have to explain to your brother how Whirling Abyss smashed you without a thought." But she didn't stop Silluka this time, which Silluka took as implicit permission.

"Lugopo, look! This was your creation. This was what caught the attention of your god."

"...with turrets on the side to— Yes, the suit!" Their eyes fixed on it, focused. "Such great power. Connection to the core is optimized, but with more exacting dimensions. Maybe spikes to connect it to all the bones. Would be permanent, but worth the risk."

"I...don't think I like that one." Silluka shivered at the thought of the suit sending spikes into her bones. No, the shivering was not just from the image. There was pressure on her, bending her down, like a huge storm was imminent. She gritted her teeth. "What else?"

"Stronger joints! Yes, with predictive knowledge of chayus. Movements could be input—"

"Great. How would you do it?" Silluka's knees creaked, her back bending. It was like a giant hand—tentacle?— pressed down on her. She'd be crushed to the floor soon, but she hoped to narrow Lugopo's focus down.

"I..." Lugopo's tentacles waved helplessly, and the circlet tone turned to one of distress. "*I don't know.* The ideas are here! They overwhelm me! Ah, to overwhelm. With flame emitters on the heels, movement could be doubled, tripled!"

"What would you need for that, would you?" Cosquella asked. "I could use some flames on my heels, me."

"Yes, but fuel lines would need to be routed along legs? Tank on back? Bones are hindrance, but helpful. Could draw energy from blood? No, death rate too high..."

Silluka finally gasped and lowered the suit. She couldn't hold it any longer. The second she did so, the pressure on her disappeared and she spun to Elder Quilqi. "They're not going to become a crazed Allwiya, are they?"

The elder shrugged. "I couldn't say. It's between them and their god. But Lugopo's a strong one. I have high hopes. Well, hopes, anyway." She gestured them over. "Come now, leave them to their test. You didn't need anyone's help when you tested for me."

"You're not a god," Silluka said.

"As you say," the elder said. "I still think you don't want Whirling Abyss' full attention on you for more than a few seconds, do you?"

Silluka swallowed at the feeling, like a giant carefully pressing an insect to the floor without squashing it. She watched Lugopo, still mumbling to themself, or maybe to Whirling Abyss. She would stay, would watch over the little Allwiya until they passed or failed. How would she know?

How *did* she know? Ever since she'd learned there was more to the world than just bodycasting, more to the world than her village, she'd been trying to understand it.

"How do you know someone is an Adept?" she asked Elder Quilqi.

The elder raised white eyebrows. "Can't you tell, girl?"

"I can't," Cosquella said.

The old woman seemed to think. "Yes, I suppose that would be after Mental Adept, wouldn't it? It's been a long time since I was there."

"What would?" Silluka sat down on one of the benches in the gymnasium, and the others joined her, while they watched Lugopo sign to the air. It was rare to get direct answers from the old woman.

"The ability to know another's strength in regard to yours." She gestured at Lugopo. "They're on to something, with their measurements of Tortoises. That hasn't been done before, that I'm aware of. But they're going to need a new scale soon."

"Silluka made twenty-two Tortoises when she went through *Jakua's Fight*," Cosquella added. "How high would the scale need to go?"

Elder Quilqi laughed. "*Jakua's Fight* is one of the simplest of the full chayus to store within your *sunqu*. Silluka is powerful, but she's still only starting. Imagine storing *Life Tree*. It takes nearly a day to perform completely, which is why generally healers and those warriors going on patrol are the only ones to bother storing it."

"So, what, hundreds of Tortoises?" Silluka asked.

Elder Quilqi only looked at her, then she cocked her head to one side. "You know now your power is drawn from the core of this planet, yes?"

Silluka nodded.

The elder sat forward. "The core, girl. Molten rocks! Do you have any idea how big that is? Do you even understand the size of the world ocean?"

"What do you mean?" Silluka shared a confused look with Cosquella.

"Chimor is on the edge of the stable center of this island—continent really. The distance you traveled from your village on the coast to here? That's not even a third of the size of this island. The islands that used to be free-floating in the ocean. The civilizations of the Misini, and Allwiya, and the others have joined this one. Where did they come from? Did they calf off from other lands? What you call the burning ocean surrounds everything here. That doesn't mean there aren't other lands as big or bigger than this one out there."

"What does that have to do with the core, does it?" Cosquella asked.

Elder Quilqi made a round gesture with her hands, spreading them out. "This is the world, yes?" She made a pinching gesture with her fingers, holding them close together. "This is the size of the island we live on in comparison. The core is the center of the world, a place of liquid rock and fire. Pure energy. Think how big that is, and how big this island is. How big *you* are in comparison. What would you need to do to tap into even an infinitesimal fraction of that power?"

"So, we'll need a bigger scale," Silluka said. She looked to Lugopo again. The white aura, spotted with dark specks like a molding mushroom, surrounded them and the immediate area around them. She remembered the first time she'd seen that, before she ever left the village. Lugopo had a tool they said showed the blessings of the gods. Had they lost it when fleeing from the village? Or used parts of it to make their new Tortoise-measuring device? It didn't really matter. She also remembered the device barely touched Elder Quilqi before her aura exploded into light. Right now, when Lugopo was in the presence of their gods, the aura expanded in a radius around Lugopo wider than Cosquella was tall. Was that an indication of the power the god was investing into Lugopo?

They sat for some minutes watching the test, Silluka mulling over questions in her mind.

"What stage of Adept are you?" she asked Elder Quilqi, a little later.

The old woman grimaced, as if the question itself was distasteful. "High enough to teach you everything you need to know," she said. "For now, you only need to be aware of what is required for your testing to Mental Adepthood. You have a good start, storing *Jakua's Fight*, but you'll need to show the judges at least three complete chayus. I'll get you the scrolls for two more. Perhaps *Tortoise's Growth* and *Quirra's Day*? Those fit your style well."

Silluka frowned at the evasion but let it go. "And then I can test?"

"Didn't you say it was merely a formality, it was?" Cosquella put in.

"Yes and yes. The minimum required full chayus to store is three. You'll have to perform all three for the judges." The elder turned to Cosquella. "This method has been put into place to formally evaluate Huaca. That doesn't mean it's correct. Silluka crossed into the realm of the Mental Adept when she correctly enacted *Flying Quirra*—part of *Quirra's Day*, I might add, though even a few of the Elemental Adepts can make it work so effectively. You are a bit of a mystery, girl. But even though you have used the techniques of a Mental Adept, you are not ranked as one until those higher than you officially say you are."

Silluka tried not to get lost in the rush of information. "But I've already stored *Jakua's Fight*. What happens if I try to store it a second time?"

Elder Quilqi waved a hand. "Nothing of consequence. It may boost the effectiveness an inconsequential amount when you learn to release the parts. But releasing chayus is a good test of ability in the next realm of Adepthood. If storing your intent and the shape of the chayu is Mental Adept, then marking the place you have stored it and learning to release it effectively is that of the Pressure Adept. You still have a lot to learn."

Silluka blinked, processing.

"I have much work to do, I do," Cosquella grumbled. "Perhaps the gods of the Huaca simply do not like me."

"The gods aren't even aware of you, girl," Elder Quilqi said. "The Huaca gods are so powerful even the Elemental Adepts barely register their notice. Unless or until you offer something truly new, you'll likely escape their attention, thankfully." She shifted and stood. "Ah, it looks like Lugopo has survived their test."

The white, splotchy light was receding, leaving Lugopo looking even more boneless than usual. Silluka rushed to them.

"Are you alright?"

Lugopo signed weakly, and the translation circlet's voice was scratchy, as if it had a throat that had been yelling. Or screaming. "I live, blessed by Whirling Abyss. Such new concepts to explore! Every object I create shall be even more dangerous!" They tapped the circlet. "They will kill many!" Another tap. "They will have even more potent abilities!"

"Then you've passed your challenge? Are you like a Mental Adept now?"

Lugopo's tentacles waggled. "These are not the puny Huaca gods." They smacked the circlet. "The extreme power of the three Allwiya unknowable ones means only one may touch my mind at once. Only one portion of the Challenge of Sanity has been administered. I shall be on my guard from tests from Crawling Dark of Squirming and Manylegs of Reaching."

"When?" Silluka asked.

"Soon? Later? In many years? They are called unknowable for a reason."

"So they might happen at any time, they might?" Cosquella frowned down at Lugopo.

"When it is least expected!" Lugopo seemed excited by the prospect. "But now, I believe I need to lie down."

CHAPTER EIGHT

Returns

The vials watched Ichu from across the small room he slept in. He had visited Amoxtli almost every day the last two weeks, though he hadn't shared that with Silluka or the others yet. They'd been congratulating Lugopo on their challenge, then Silluka had been busy committing huge scrolls of chayus to memory. What he did with Amoxtli felt both personal and like it had larger implications. He wanted to explore it more before Elder Quilqi told him it was impossible.

He'd gotten a glance at *Quirra's Day* while she studied it—a complex mess of writing. If he had been taught to read like his sister, would he be studying full chayus? Even he didn't recognize all the chayu she'd named from it. He'd learned every single one the elders taught in the village. He'd seen the room of dusty scrolls in the back corridors of the elders' building, where every chayu in the world—they'd told him—had been studied, recorded, and assessed for use in the village. He'd known there *were* more chayus, but thought they were simplistic, or not of use. The elders, he'd thought, had the ear of the gods.

But all that was a lie. Would he even be able to make use of a full chayu like *Quirra's Day*, now his *sunqu* was changed? The vials sat in judgement. Each one was a slightly different color.

There was purple, blue, orange, brown, yellow, and a couple that swirled with multiple dots of colors, unmixed. Each was the color associated with one of the Huaca Aunts, Uncles, and Entles, all except the pink of Entle Love and the steel gray of Uncle Smith. Both had resisted efforts by he and Amoxtli. Chayus tied to those gods just didn't work as well as the others. Something was happening there, but he didn't know what.

He picked up the purple vial that contained *Eagle Watches from on High*. He had no reason to need it now.

But he *wanted* it.

He put down the purple vial and his hand clenched into a fist. Ever since seeing vials again, they'd called to him. He could resist their call. The more he got used to handling them without drinking from them, the better. He didn't want to be overtaken by that need when he should have been protecting his sister, or the others.

He picked up the blue vial instead. This contained *Foam Tossed in the Waves*, one of Aunt Sea's chayus. He'd tried to pick ones that were hard, or took a long time to perform, to make the process worthwhile. *Foam Tossed in the Waves* gave the practitioner an innate sense of balance and movement, so much they could walk through a storm and not get wet or throw a pine needle to embed in a slab of wood.

He didn't need its effects right now. He didn't. His hand clenched around the vial before he made himself relax. Crushing it would solve nothing.

The orange vial, then. *Quirra Hibernates in the Winter*. It was a powerful chayu attributed to Aunt Harvest. One that kept the body from harm, even in dire circumstances. Was it possible it could help him in storing energy in his *sunqu*? He hadn't tested it when he first performed the chayu, merely passing it on to Amoxtli for storage. But now...what if... He raised his other hand to the cork.

There was a knock at the door of his room. Ichu almost dropped the vial, but placed it carefully in a drawer—added the others—and answered the door.

"Akamu?" He sucked in a breath at seeing the man again, then leaned forward and engulfed him in a hug. "You came back," he murmured into the other man's shoulder. It had been weeks since he'd last seen the stone warrior.

Akamu turned his head for a kiss. "Then I suppose you haven't found some other person to warm your bed?"

Ichu released Akamu, but trailed his hands down Akamu's arms, pulling him inside his room. "Not at all.

Chimor is so large, I haven't had time for any of that." His eyes darted to the drawer with the vials, safely closed. That was a discussion for another time. A lot had changed since Akamu left. "Elder Quilqi has been preparing Silluka and me for our Mental Adept tests." Mostly Silluka, since he was still so weak. That would change, though.

"That's actually why I'm back now, to serve as a judge on Silluka's test."

Ichu tried to keep the hurt from his face. Not to serve as a judge for both their tests?

"But you came back for me too?" There were lines in Akamu's face that hadn't been there in the desert. Ichu traced the signs of worry with his eyes.

Akamu's eyes turned soft. "I did. But the Eztli Mecatl are coming in force, close behind us. My stone warriors have been fighting back, and we've been aided by the fire warriors, but they are a strong foe. Honestly, we needed to come back to Chimor simply to regroup."

"The turtlemen," Ichu said. At Akamu's confused look—he'd missed those high cheekbones, that long hair tied back—he continued, "I've been talking to one of the Eztli Mecatl in the city. She's one of the original ones who fled the island. She sees the invading force as turtlemen. She regards herself and the others here as the true Eztli Mecatl. There's even differences in their magic—" He cut off before he mentioned the vials. They would complicate everything.

"You should be keeping far away from Eztli Mecatl magic after what happened to you," Akamu said, suddenly stern. "Several of my warriors have died since we last met. They are a dangerous species."

"Not all of them," Ichu insisted. "Amoxtli has been helping me." He closed his mouth, but the damage had already been done.

Akamu stared at him and a physical weight pressed on Ichu, like when Elder Quilqi looked through him, though not as strong. Was that the power of the Elemental Adepts? He gasped as the pressure disappeared.

"I am sorry to do that, but I had to check if the corruption from the vial you drank has spread."

Ichu drew up to his full height—just taller than Akamu. "And?"

Now Akamu looked confused. "It is...better? I think? But different. What have you been doing? I do not get the sense I usually do from one in the realm of the Physical or Mental Adept."

"That's what I've been working with Amoxtli on. We've discovered...." He didn't want to say. He hadn't even told Elder Quilqi about this since he wasn't sure what was happening, but he wanted Akamu to understand that he was healing and growing in new ways.

"You've discovered something about...the turtlemen?" Akamu reached for his hand again. "Whatever it is, you can tell me. I can help now I'm here."

"Did you know their god is dead? Not just changed?" Akamu's grasp was firm, but his eyes grew worried.

"Dead? Can a god die?"

Ichu exhaled a sharp sound, not quite a laugh. "That was my first question. I assumed you would know. After all, I thought you were a god when you first found us."

Akamu smirked. "Sorry to disappoint. But this is important news. I'll have to tell the other warrior leaders. How do they even channel from the core without a god?"

"I discussed this with Amoxtli. We wondered if that's why the vial affected me, making a mix of our magic."

"That's not possible," Akamu said quickly. "The gods are jealous of their peoples. Experiments between them have happened in the past but have never ended well." He gazed at Ichu for a moment longer. "You couldn't have petitioned the gods at your Adept level. Even I would have to go through an intermediary. No, this is impossible."

"The gods answered the pleas of our village elders in the village. Is this so different?" He made the sign of Uncle Sky in the air—fingertips touching, hands viewing where clouds would be.

"How do you know that motion? The elemental signs are only taught to Elemental Adepts in training."

Now it was Ichu's turn to be confused. "The elders regularly called on the gods, each by their own sign. Is that not the case here?"

"But your elders are barely Physical Adepts themselves."

Ichu sighed. Even before the vial, he had been told he was not up to the task. After years of being the champion of the Huaca, it was infuriating. The vials. They were the key here. The proof. He couldn't keep them hidden.

"It sounds like there's a lot that doesn't work quite like it does in Chimor," he shot back. "Seems like you don't know everything after all. Maybe our elders had a reason to go to that coast in the first place. Look!" He took his hand back and jerked open the drawer, the vials rattling in it.

Akamu took them in with a glance, his back straight. "Where did you get those? And where did the colors come from? The turtlemen I've fought only have vials tinged in red and maroon."

"I *made* them, Akamu. That's what I'm telling you. Magic isn't as limited as you think. It's a mix of our magic, Amoxtli and me. The Eztli Mecatl work differently than the turtlemen. They're not bad people. Something changed after their god died."

Akamu's mouth was a hard line. "You're correct. Something did change. This should still be impossible." But he opened his hand when Ichu offered him the orange vial with *Quirra Hibernates in the Winter*. He studied it, then blinked and the pressure increased in the room again, though not directed at Ichu this time. Was it a stored chayu? Elder Quilqi did the same thing. Or was it merely the capability to use more power?

"The chayu in this...is pure," Akamu finally said. "I could use this, as could you, with no ill effect to your *sunqu*. In fact, I think one of the Eztli Mecatl could use this too. No one has ever done anything like this." He stared at Ichu. "Could it be...?"

"It's not hard," Ichu said. "Amoxtli and I can generate one or maybe two in a day. I haven't used any vials yet, but I was almost certain they would work, and now you've confirmed it." His hand itched to take up one of them and drink it down. Akamu had given him implicit permission. He wasn't certain if the vials themselves were addictive, or he just wanted the feeling of power like when he was the champion of their village. He *would* resist it.

"You can store any chayu like this?" Akamu asked, and Ichu frowned.

"We've had trouble with a few, usually the ones most firmly in the realm of Entle Love and Uncle Smith, but—"

"Entle Love too?" Akamu said. "That means the problem is even bigger than I thought."

Ichu took the vial back from him. "You know something about this already? How?"

"Because with your information, I know who killed the god of the Eztli Mecatl," Akamu said. "I thought it was merely a contest, though, not fatal. Maybe there was another connection forged when it happened. A way for the magic of the Huaca and the Eztli Mecatl to mix. He was the second born. He's almost as strong as Entle Magic."

"Second born?" Ichu's mind went back to the nursery rhyme they all learned back in the Huaca. "Death and Life begat us all, Death and Life begat the gods. Firstborn is Tiye Kwirpuyay, Entle Magic, by which all is done. Second is—"

"Don't say it," Akamu interrupted. He looked around the room, as if gauging its solidity, then rolled his hands into a ball, spinning the gesture out to both sides. Ichu's ears popped and he swallowed. That had been a stored chayu, even quicker released than drinking a vial. From the change in air, he guessed this was *Tortoise's Hard Shell*, maybe from an Unmovable stance? He'd seen it performed by an elder when he was young, but it had fallen out of use in the Huaca. With such speed, was his new discovery ultimately useless?

"Now." Akamu leaned in, as if even his chayu keeping others from hearing might be suspect. "Secondborn is Tiyu

Llamkay, Uncle Smith. I have evidence he interfered with the Eztli Mecatl's god, and he must have gone so far as to kill them. I have never heard of such a thing, but who can tell the mind of a god? But your vials further prove it. He must have left some...residue of his deed, connecting the Huaca and the Eztli Mecatl. That and the lack of a godly focus for the Eztli Mecatl must be why the vial affected you in the first place, and why you were able to create more."

Ichu blinked back at the man. He'd never even thought of the gods having personalities, or motivations, or schemes. They were just there, and protected the Huaca from the worst storms, earthquakes, and volcanoes. Uncle Smith was...he was the god who made the Huaca's bodies, according to myth. Chayu directly affecting the body's prowess, like *Eagle's Downy Coat* or *Tree's Hardwood* were said to come from Uncle Smith. How did that factor into him murdering another god—one of another species?

And how did the turtlemen still have magic?

"The other vials," Ichu said.

"What about them?"

"If Uncle Smith killed their god, how are the turtlemen still using magic at all? Amoxtli said they prey on the lives of other turtlemen, but is there sufficient power?"

Akamu shook his head. "I'm not certain. They may have a way to tap into the core directly, without the guiding power of the gods. It would burn them out quickly. Maybe taking it from others mitigates the strain while giving them great power."

Ichu thought of his sister, falling into a deathly sleep after flying over that chasm. Had she used the core's power without a god's help? If so, how? Was that ability what Elder Quilqi saw in her?

"Enough power to besiege Chimor?" he asked.

"Just as you say."

"Have you told Elder Quilqi what you found out about...him?"

"I haven't even told Administrator Nina or my warriors. You're the first, in fact, and we need to keep it that way.

Tortoise's Hard Shell can even keep the gods from hearing, for a time, but word will eventually get to them. This is the second time I've had to hold this shell. I don't think I'll be able to a third time without him noticing."

"He would personally notice us?" Ichu asked. His eyes widened. "You mean Uncle—" Akamu was vigorously shaking his head. "You mean the god we were discussing?" Akamu nodded.

"What does that even mean?"

"The ancient one seemed to think the gods were coming into conflict. The Huaca used to be dominant in these lands a few hundred years ago. Then the Misini began to gain in power, challenging our chayus with their art. The Allwiya came next, with their gadgets, revolutionizing the city. Then the Kawchi and the Yakurikra, and now the Eztli Mecatl. The Huaca have the most gods of any species we've met, but they're outnumbered now by the others. They are in decline, and the others are in ascendance."

Ichu tried to take that all in. There was so much more here than he knew. The village he'd grown up in had been simple: practice the morning ritual. Learn all the chayus. Become the best bodycaster he could.

"Is that why it's also hard to store chayus by Entle Love?"

"Perhaps." Akamu rubbed his jaw with one hand. "She was always one of the weakest of them, though she's third born. There are machinations in process we are too insignificant to understand, powers that are far above anyone's ability in Chimor. It's good to stay out of the gods' notice, if possible, ours and other species."

Ichu held up the vial. "Then are the gods aware of these?"

Akamu waggled a hand. "From what I can guess, likely not. Administrator Nina or the ancient one would know more. It's such a small aspect of their power it's equivalent to accounting for one missing hair." He must have seen something in Ichu's expression, because he gestured for the vial again. "But the potential you have for this, that's the amazing part. How close does the ancient one say you are to testing for Mental Adept? She only mentioned Silluka in her message."

"The Yakurikra healer I went to told me my *sunqu* had moved. That's why it's been so hard for me to connect to the core. But I'm adjusting to the new location, and my connection is getting stronger."

"Moved? That's not poss—" Akamu broke off, his mouth pursed. "It seems I should stop saying that. But your *sunqu* is based on your body. For it to move is as foreign as..."

"As using another species' magic?" Ichu suggested.

"A good comparison." Akamu waved the issue away. "The point I was making was that when you are firmly a Mental Adept, you could use this same skill to store a whole chayu, like *Life Tree*. If I had multiple vials like that, my warriors would need not fear any turtlemen."

Ichu rotated the vial. It was about as big as his thumb. "Could an entire chayu, rather than a chayu section, even be stored in one of these? Would the vial break?"

Akamu held out an arm. He didn't have his amber armor on, and he displayed one muscled forearm. "A full chayu is stored through the body, rather than just in the *sunqu*. The segments of the chayu naturally migrate to the areas of the body they're associated with. *Branches Withstand a Gale* is kept here, for instance." He tapped his forearm. "*Tree in the Wind* is in the calves, of course. Perhaps the turtlemen have larger vials for bigger storage? Perhaps not. Divining the methods of another god is problematic. I have watched the Misini's art my whole life, and I am no closer to understanding how they please their gods. That's why what you are doing here is risky."

"But necessary, if our gods are weakening, and committing...indiscretions?" Ichu suggested.

"You may be correct," Akamu said. He reached out for Ichu's shoulder. "But for now, it's been a long time since I've seen you, and *Tortoise's Hard Shell* will give us several more minutes of privacy, if you wish."

Ichu smiled back.

CHAPTER NINE

Steam and Mist

"Another match is announced!" Lugopo signed to Silluka. The little blue and green Allwiya was perched on her shoulder as usual, as she made her way to the gymnasium to practice. For nearly two weeks, Elder Quilqi had been pushing her to learn all three chayus completely, so she no longer needed any prompting from their respective scrolls. *Jakua's Fight*, *Tortoise's Growth* and *Quirra's Day* buzzed through her brain morning and night.

"Another one? Like the one Anuit fought in? What about the Huaca whom she killed?" She and Lugopo were alone today. Elder Quilqi was off on another mysterious errand, and Cosquella said she hadn't gotten a day out of her suit in so long she was starting to fasten it up in her dreams. It still seemed to make little difference in what she did. Silluka could tell her girlfriend was getting disheartened by the practice, despite Silluka's attempts to distract her with hugs, kisses, and sweet rolls from a bakery they walked by every day.

"Another murder from Anuit, yes!" Lugopo said. "Except this time against the Allwiya. Who shall be murdered now?"

"I thought the fights *weren't* supposed to end in death," Silluka said.

Lugopo tapped their circlet. "Wondering which one will win, of course. No murdering. Certainly not."

Silluka shook her head. Lugopo was finally recovering from their test with Whirling Abyss, though they hadn't created any new inventions in the last week. They said it still made their tentacles ache to channel concepts from the gods. She, on the other hand—she glanced to her missing one—had not successfully stored either *Tortoise's Growth* or *Quirra's Day*. Both were more than twice as long as *Jakua's Fight*. She stretched her arms behind her back.

She'd gained some muscle from practicing so often. The chayus kept her from getting too stiff, but she was continually tired at the end of the day.

"When is the match?" she finally asked. The whole city would be there, especially after the last one.

"Tomorrow! Muolo and the other Allwiya who arrived with us have already secured seating to watch the carnage!"

"I hope you got extras. I wonder if Akamu wants to come with us. I'm certain Ichu will want him to." The stone warrior had devoted as much of his schedule as possible to Ichu while he was recuperating from engaging with the turtlemen's march across the stable desert. They often didn't leave Ichu's room until the sun had been up for a while.

"We have bought enough for everyone to glory in the murder!" Lugopo tapped their circlet. "That is, to enjoy the killing. The match. Muolo has been doing good business among the refugees, making and selling new designs. I will help as soon as I am healed."

* * *

Word had spread by the end of that day, and the next morning, there was a palpable aura of excitement across the city. Silluka wondered if even the gods were watching. This was for them, if the elder was right, and she usually was. Despite Chyuna's death in the first match between species, the whole city wanted to see another matchup.

Cosquella wrapped Silluka's stump around her arm as they started toward the area. "How does an Allwiya fight, anyway? Unless they found another one as big as the one in the desert. Maybe I could sign up to fight one like that, I could?"

Silluka did a double-take at her girlfriend. She had a terrific black eye, the bruise creeping across the rough skin of her face.

"What happened? I don't see you for one day and you get in a fight?"

Cosquella looked embarrassed for only a moment. "It's no issue, for me. Just got in a friendly tussle."

"It doesn't look friendly."

The tall woman sighed. "It's only...I couldn't take the practice any longer, I couldn't. Some of the undesirables from the refugee center—the ones who can't perform the chayus—they set up a brawler's club, they did."

"So you decided to go hit people for fun?"

"Basically, yah." Cosquella had a huge grin on her face, her left eye squinted half-shut. "No chayus, no gods, no magic. Just these fists, me. It's what I'm best at."

Silluka shook her head, but she could see why Cosquella liked it. "How did your opponent fare?"

Cosquella grinned even wider. "His friends are carrying him to this fight on their backs. He didn't want to miss it but couldn't get out of bed. We're going to meet up again next week."

Her eyes lingered on Silluka's shoulders, bare today as it was warm. "I like what these chayus are doing to you, I do. Maybe you want to come join us for a brawl sometime?"

Silluka laughed. "I think I'd fare even worse than your opponent."

* * *

They finally got their seats in the arena. This time, the ratio of Allwiya was much higher in the crowd, as were the Misini. Fewer Huaca were here, which let Silluka pick out the other species easier.

They were all in a line, two seats with five Allwiya crowded into them, then Silluka, Cosquella, Elder Quilqi, Ichu, and even Akamu at the end. She hadn't seen any of the stone warriors from the desert yet, but maybe they were somewhere else in the city, or here in this arena, for that matter.

The same large Huaca announcer stood up on the other side of the ring of seats, *Coyote's Howl* amplifying his voice.

"People of Chimor, are you ready for our second match between species?"

Shouts, screams, hisses, and the clank of metal on metal answered him. The Allwiya had brought noisemaker devices of all types to voice their approval. Lugopo had some sort of crank that generated an annoying croaking sound. Silluka wasn't used to this much noise and ducked her head.

"You can do better than that!" the announcer shouted. "When was the last time we saw an Allwiya in this area? Do you want them to go home in sadness without even fighting?"

"We must generate such noise it brings our compatriot forth!" Lugopo's circlet broadcasted. They hadn't finished building a new Tortoise-measuring device, but cranked their noisemaker, and the other Allwiya with them brought out their own devices. The arena erupted in clanking, screeching, and hammering sounds.

"Come on then, help the little ones out!" Cosquella cried, clapping her hands together. Silluka winced, but joined in.

"That's more like it!" The announcer gestured wide with his arms. "Now folks, the first contender needs no introduction, the Artist of the Misini, defeater of Huaca, and knife-enthusiast, Anuit!"

There were a few boos in the cheers this time, especially from the Huaca in the audience. The death of one of their members wasn't being mentioned, but Silluka could see glares thrown toward the Misini in the stands, and she'd seen fewer of them on the streets since the last match.

From the left side on the arena floor, Anuit stalked out, dressed in the same revealing fabrics as last time, twirling a knife.

"And our new contender, their first time in the arena, inventor extraordinaire, blessed supplicant of Crawling Dark of Squirming and Manylegs of Reaching, Tolor the Allwiya!"

Creaks, hums, and thumps filled the arena, especially from the seats with Allwiya hanging onto them. On the right side of the dirt floor, a large door creaked as two Huaca attendants pulled ropes to roll it up to three times their height. The crowd silenced, waiting for Tolor to crawl out.

"Are they late or something?" Cosquella asked. Silluka shook her head.

"Ha! Hear that?" Elder Quilqi cocked her head.

Silluka listened over the stray tweet or whistle from the noisemakers. There was a rhythmic thumping coming from the right door. *Thum. Thum. Thum. Thum.* Silluka's mind threw out memories of the crazed Allwiya's contraptions in the desert.

A giant Allwiya squeezed through the door. The thumping was each of its tentacles striking the ground.

"There's another one of them?" Cosquella was standing in her seat, and Silluka pulled her back down.

"No. Look! It's mechanical!"

As if to emphasize her words, gouts of flame erupted from holes high on the contraption's head. A sheet of shining copper folded over, revealing a bank of swirling colors—leaves and berries expertly arranged into the symbology of the Huaca.

PREPARE FOR DESTRUCTION, it announced.

"Ah, such elegant locution!" Lugopo called.

The copper flap moved back up for a moment as the eight great legs stamped fully into the area, lifting the main body higher than a Huaca was tall. The noisemakers were going wild again. Then the flap dropped, showing a different arrangement of plants and leaves.

TOLOR SHALL REIGN SUPREME

"What does it say?" Ichu leaned over to Akamu beside him. Silluka had forgotten their parents had never taught him to read. Akamu whispered something back. Evidently the stone warrior could.

"Hopefully Tolor doesn't put me out of a job!" the announcer laughed, and the sound swirled around the arena. A wave of chuckles sounded from the Misini and Huaca. "Then, if we're ready, let's see what these two can do! Remember, no killing this time!" His last words were nearly lost in the noise from the crowd.

This time, Anuit was the one to rush forward, tiny against the looming mechanical Allwiya. Silluka guessed Tolor was hidden somewhere inside it, probably pulling wires and levers to make their contraption move. One giant arm reached up to slap her away, but Anuit stepped into mist and disappeared.

The copper plate dropped.

TRACKING

The mechanical beast's round glass eyes glowed green, and Silluka thought she could make out a shape behind the left one, multiple arms moving.

"It's like the brawler's match, this one," Cosquella said. "No chayu to recognize. Just steel against quickness."

"The Misini have plenty of magic, though it's different to ours," Elder Quilqi cautioned. "I'm not at all certain how this fight will go."

Tolor's construct raised up on all eight legs again, the top of its head nearly level with the second row of stands. It crashed back to the ground just as Anuit appeared beneath it. Silluka caught a glimpse of wide eyes and laid-back ears before the Misini was buried in a wave of dust and metal.

The Allwiya's noisemakers went wild.

"Such ease with which they crushed their opponent!" Lugopo called. "A good match to—"

Anuit appeared out of a rift in the air, balancing on top of the construct's head. Her artfully wound scarf was torn and disarrayed.

"Oh ho!" Cosquella called. "Almost got her, they did, but not quite!"

Silluka peered down. Anuit definitely had a speed advantage over Tolor's large and ungainly mechanism, but if it caught her with one of those massive tentacles, she would be finished in one hit.

Anuit rocked as Tolor's beast crawled forward, then gestured and a dagger appeared in each hand. She swung down, embedding each in the top of the head, then held on with one and jabbed more holes in the metal.

OW OW OW OW

The copper plate rose back up, but a few of the seeds and nuts fell out of one side as the giant Allwiya rocked from side to side, trying to shake Anuit loose.

"Their arms have plenty of reach!" Lugopo called. They were more into this fight than Silluka had ever seen them. "Smack the Misini!"

Four arms rose, smacking the area where Anuit was.

"They hear my devious plan!" Lugopo called. Silluka gave them an encouraging smile.

Anuit was faster though, fading into mist and appearing in another place on the creature's head, dodging every smack. Each time she landed, she thrust a dagger into the copper plating.

"How can her knife survive that?" Silluka asked no one in particular. "It must be dull and pitted by now."

Akamu leaned past Ichu. "Misini knives are like Misini claws. Sharp and deadly."

The tentacles moved faster and faster, jumping ahead of where Anuit would move next. The copper screen flopped down.

CALCULATING TRAJECTORY

A hose extended from the side of the mechanical beast's side, blowing steam toward the ground as the tentacles moved even faster, beating a rhythm on its head. The noisemakers in the crowd began to follow the beat, like Tolor's construct was a giant drum.

Another two limbs joined the four, leaving only two still on the ground. They all flailed, striking so fast there was no place for Anuit to land.

At which point Anuit stepped into mist again, and five copies stepped out. Two grabbed the end of a tentacle, somehow melting it to the head of the giant Allwiya before another smashed them into mist. A third was swiped from the surface, arcing out over the arena before disappearing. The last two began climbing down the front of the head, toward the glass eyes. The top of the head was a mass of dents and holes, steam leaking from multiple places. One of the arms twitched uncontrollably and another slowed its rhythm, some piece inside broken.

"She's going to pull it off again, isn't she?" Cosquella said. She had leaned over the seats in front of her and Silluka hooked her stump around her arm to keep her from tipping forward.

The other arms followed Anuit's descent, slapping the front of the head and the copper plate, which fell off to reveal STRUCTURAY INTEGINE COMPROMSIEG, the shapes still being ferried around by several quirra on leashes.

There was definitely a shape in one of the glowing eyes, tentacles waving wildly, but Silluka was watching the seventh and eight tentacles, smoothly and slowly lifting off the ground. The two copies of Anuit were almost to the eyes when they struck, like a hand clapping over an insect. Under one tentacle was only a puff of mist, but Anuit stepped out of nothing, balancing on the tip of the other tentacle. She took a bow.

The Misini in the crowd roared out their appreciation.

The tentacle dropped out from beneath her and Anuit barely caught on to where the top of the glass eye was connected to the body, her scarf flapping in a billow of steam from the construct. She scrabbled as three tentacles arced back, getting distance, then struck fast as whips.

Anuit let go, dropping into nothingness and appearing on the ground, halfway across the arena.

The three tentacles impacted the glass eye with a crash, then a wet squelching sound. Ichor began to drip from the eye socket. The giant Allwiya went still.

Anuit took another bow as the Misini in the crowd hissed and cheered. The Allwiya were silent.

"This sport is becoming more and more deadly," Cosquella said.

* * *

"I do not like these recent deaths in the arena," Elder Quilqi said, later that evening. Lugopo and the other Allwiya had excused themselves, to commiserate with the others in the city at their champion's death. The rest of them, Akamu included, sat around the table in their home in the refugee camp. They filled the main room, which served as kitchen and living area. There were three tiny bedrooms on one side, and a communal outhouse not far away. It was passable as accommodation, though better than any of the hidey-holes Silluka had found in their village on the coast, when she ran away from the farm.

"Does it mean something worse?" Cosquella asked. "You said the fights don't usually end in death, you did."

"They don't." Akamu had both hands on Ichu's shoulders, standing behind his chair. "The judging committee should never have allowed Anuit to continue to fight after the last one. The Misini have been insinuating their way into the highest levels of government in Chimor for decades. This is one result."

"Not just the Misini," Elder Quilqi cautioned. "I told you these arena fights have more meaning than at first appearance. The balance of the gods is shifting, and not to the Huaca's benefit. Cities and deserts, I think this is all rolled into what I've been warning Nina about, with the landmasses collecting together. There's much at play here, and the deaths in the arena are only one indicator."

"You mean this is more than just Anuit's arrogance?" Ichu asked. "Have her gods influenced her directly?"

"Quite possibly. The Clade and the Huaca's gods don't get along well," Akamu said. He squeezed Ichu's shoulders. Ichu had been calmer since the stone warrior returned, but he was still twitchy, as if the changes from the vial were continuing to affect him. She hoped Akamu could help him. This wasn't the time to prod him about it.

"You mentioned the power of our gods was waning," Ichu pressed. "Are they really interested in this city?"

"As one of the largest concentrations of Huaca on this island, they are," Elder Quilqi snapped. "They may not pay attention to individuals, but control of an entire city is a great prize. And I think The Clade is trying to take it from them."

CHAPTER TEN

The Gates of Chimor

Ichu was up early the next morning, anticipating meeting Akamu for practice in the gymnasium. They'd slept together the past few nights, but Akamu said he had business with Nina and the other warrior leaders the night before, and would meet him that morning.

He'd taken Akamu to meet Amoxtli the day after revealing his new abilities, and the two had hit it off, joking about his habits and his trouble with his core. Now he went with Akamu every morning to the gymnasium, drilling how to connect to the new placement of his core, and with Amoxtli in the afternoon, after she had tended to those she helped in the city. Ichu's goal was to learn a full chayu like Silluka, so he could store it in a vial for Akamu, but that was still a ways off. Akamu had told him that—while he was capable of performing the motions—his intent was still weak, and if he connected to the core and performed all of *Jakua's Fight*, for example, the power would burn through him, much like it had done to Silluka when she flew over the canyon, back in the village.

He would become a Mental Adept, but Akamu said he was still too rooted to his body, that he had to be flexible in mental application first. Yet the man had no advice on how to be more flexible mentally. Ichu was planning on trying out different methods today.

He turned on the street leading to the gymnasium, but several Huaca and Misini were coming the opposite way, pushing past him to get elsewhere. He avoided them in their haste, only catching a few words about the front gates.

The gymnasium was empty. This was where both Physical and Mental adepts tested and trained themselves. There were more of these Adepts in Chimor than any other Adepthood. This place *always* had someone in it, unless it was closed. Most practiced early in the morning, especially if they had another job in the city. At this time of day, the place should be so packed Ichu would have a problem finding an open space to practice.

Ichu turned in a circle, looking for anyone. Akamu at least should be here. Had his meeting with Nina and the warriors lasted all night? He hadn't sent a runner with a message.

He went back out on the street and encountered one of the spiky people—the Kawchi, as Elder Quilqi called them—stumping along the street. The creatures were universally stout, with a stubby muzzle, pointed nose, and short legs. On their backs, rows of needles protruded, sharp enough to draw blood. They almost had the shape of turtlemen, but shorter and crossed with a quirra with spines on its back.

"Do you know what's going on?" he asked. "Why is the gymnasium empty?"

"The gates, the gates!" the little Kawchi said in strongly accented language. Ichu couldn't tell what gender they were. They bumbled forward, their legs making a strange shuffling gait. Ichu fell in beside them.

"I heard someone else speaking of the gates. The gates to the city? What's happened?"

"Ooooh. Chimor's gates haven't fallen for hundreds of years, and they aren't now!" The Kawchi pumped a fist in the air and shuffled onward. Ichu was starting to outpace them.

"Fallen to who?" He tried to stick to the shorter person's pace, but it was hard. Their legs were only about half as long as his. He kept having to wait a few steps, then take a few steps.

"Can't say, can't say. Just heard the news myself. I volunteered to bring the information back to my quorum, so here I am, aren't I?"

Ichu stared into the distance, where the gates of the city loomed over the backs of stone buildings. At this rate, the Kawchi wouldn't get there until midday. Maybe this was why he hadn't seen many of them around Chimor.

"Well, I should probably hurry along myself, then," he finally said. "I think a friend of mine is already there." Akamu would be at the forefront if there was a need to defend the city.

"Naturally, naturally. The quorum comes first, after all. Pleasure to speak with you and may your friends come in your times of need."

"And yours as well." Ichu was fairly certain there was a ritual in those words somewhere, but he didn't know enough of the Kawchi people to understand it. He lengthened his stride and soon the spiky person was left in the distance.

Soon, he encountered everyone else. It seemed like everyone in Chimor, in fact, was standing in front of the city gates. Ichu had passed through these for the first time several weeks ago. The gates were wide enough for at least two of their sleds to go through side by side, and maybe all three at once. Now they were shut, for the first time Ichu had seen since being in the city. They were also blocked by a mass of people.

Ichu breathed out, legs in Dexterity stance, as he pulled the air in toward him with his hands. Then another pull, up from the ground, focusing on the new location of his core. It burned very low in his belly. This was the start of *Caterpillar Burrows Through Leaves*, a little-used chayu that let him squeeze into spaces where he normally wouldn't fit. He finished the chayu quickly, the orange aura of Aunt Harvest surrounding him, then he dove into the crowd.

A suitable application of elbows, a few apologies to Misini who hissed at him, and narrowly avoiding stepping on an Allwiya put him close to the front of the crowd. There were stairways to either side of the gate, leading to the gatehouse roof and other overlooks. Stone warriors, their amber armor glowing, guarded each side, and Ichu recognized the one on the left as Kiqema, Akamu's second in command.

"What's going on?" he called to her. He saw the shock of recognition in her face—he hadn't seen her since they were on the sleds in the desert—and she waved him over.

"Akamu is up top with the leaders of the sea, fire, and storm warriors. He mentioned you might come by and thought you'd have information to help their debate. I'm to let you go up."

"What information?" Ichu asked, but Kiqema was already pushing him up the stairs before any of the crowd could surge past along with him.

Ichu raced up the steps two at a time, and breached the top of the guardhouse, the highest landing on the wall of Chimor. It was higher than he had been in the city so far— even higher up than Nina's office.

He was surprised to see the woman herself, talking earnestly with Akamu, another young woman who seemed to vibrate with excitement, and two older Huaca, a man and a woman. The barrel-chested man was as graceful and fluid in his movements as the tiny old woman beside him was quick and jerky, like a flash of lightning every time she moved.

He tried to move closer, but a wall of force stopped him. The five people together radiated power, enough so *Caterpillar Burrows Through Leaves* was stripped from him. None had even looked at him yet, and he could not even approach. From here, Akamu seemed far more serious than he was with Ichu, frowning at something the elderly man was saying. He gestured back and spoke, but Ichu could hear nothing. He looked around for some other way to get their attention, when he realized what he was seeing outside the city.

There was an army of tents outside the gates of Chimor, stretching completely across the path Ichu had taken with the rest of the refugees when they'd arrived. It blocked all passage to and from the city. That must be why the gates were closed. Had this tent city popped up since yesterday? And who was here?

Ichu circled around the wall of power and went to the parapet railing, the warrior leaders still ignoring him, and looked out. From here he could see countless turtlemen—and women—bustling between the tents, setting up cooking fires, talking and laughing with each other, sitting, sleeping, and even sparring together.

The army from the island that had destroyed his village had finally arrived, waiting at the doors of Chimor.

"Not a sight you wanted to see, eh?"

Ichu whirled at the voice. Elder Quilqi had just breached the top of the right stairway, and behind her Silluka and Cosquella followed.

"How did you get up here?" It wasn't a smart question to ask—the elder went where she wanted—but it popped out of his mouth.

"Elder Quilqi told us this morning about the turtlemen arriving," his sister said. "She said she'd been called up here to talk with the warrior leaders."

Ichu glanced back to Akamu and the others, who had broken off their unheard conversation and were glaring at them, though Akamu directed an apologetic look toward him. The five still radiated a force around them, like pushing against a stone wall. He sidled around it to join the elder, his sister, and Cosquella.

"And why are *we* here, eh?" the big woman said. Ichu thought she had the right of it.

"Because you're my champions," Elder Quilqi said. She put a hand on Ichu and Silluka's shoulders—his sister had already linked arms with Cosquella—and walked forward. Before her, the pressure dissipated, though Ichu noticed she kept hold of their shoulders.

"What do barely a Mental Adept and two Physical Adepts have that we could possibly want?" the older woman asked. She snapped and sapphire armor surrounded her, a helm making her look merely old, not aged. "I have a whole contingent of storm warriors at my command."

"And how did they fare against the invading Eztli Mecatl, Tintaya?" Elder Quilqi asked. "I held Loma Tika in my arms as she died. We're in for a long fight here, with stakes as deep as the gods themselves, and I've chosen who I think will help our chances best."

Tintaya's face soured under her helm, but she ducked her chin. "I see, ancient one."

"You sure you know what you're doing, Mother?" Nina asked. She stood head and shoulders taller than the rest of them, even Cosquella. It was as if a tree stood atop the gatehouse.

"I've traveled with all of these people, as I told you," Akamu added, separating himself slightly from the other warriors. "They are competent and capable, even if they are new to Chimor." Ichu could hear the unspoken words— talented for country bumpkins who knew nothing of magic.

The other woman, near Akamu's age, who Ichu guessed was the leader of the fire warriors, suddenly cocked her head, then ran to the parapet and peered over. Ichu felt a rumbling beneath his feet, which could only be the great doors opening. They stopped after only a moment of movement.

"Well, as usual while we were gabbing, the moment passed. There's an Eztli Mecatl from the city out there."

"Who authorized that? This smells like The Clowder's work," Nina grumbled. "They should have asked us, but it's too late now."

"Who went out?" Ichu started for the wall, disengaging from Elder Quilqi's hand as he did so, then nearly buckled from the weight on him. He labored to take even single step, his lungs wheezing. His knees bent slowly toward the ground. Then the elder caught up to him.

"Let's see, shall we?" She looked back over her shoulder. "Tone that down a bit. Best not to crush the lower Adepts. You all must be more worried than a quirra with his tree on fire. Skies and seas, use a little control!"

Immediately, the pressure on Ichu abated, and he sucked in a welcome breath. The elder took her hand back.

"There. Now we can all watch together, like civilized Huaca."

Ichu knew only one Eztli Mecatl in the city. How many were there altogether? Surely more than enough to ensure another one was walking out into that tent city. Surely.

He leaned over the parapet, knowing what he would see. Amoxtli was walking calmly from the gates, all alone. No support and no help. Of course she was. She was a healer, kind, and knowledgeable. She was only doing what she had to. Beneath him, a solid *clang* rang out as the gates closed again. Amoxtli was on her own.

A hush spread among the nearest tents to the wall, and Ichu could pick out individual turtlemen pointing and gesturing to their comrades. A wave-like motion started a few tents in as a particularly large turtleman wearing a metal helmet over the back of his head came forward. The top of the metal was decorated with eagle feathers, and a single perfect pearled seashell sat above his eyes.

He walked, unhurried, out of the tent city and into what must be arrow range of Chimor. On the level below Ichu, a squad of archers was set, bows at the ready, arrows knocked. Yet no one loosed. Chimor held its breath as the two Eztli Mecatl came together. Ichu wondered if any of the crowd down at the gates could see what was happening. Maybe there were peepholes in the gates that could be opened. Farther down the wall were more parapets, cubbies, and walkways, all of which were strung with inhabitants of Chimor. So, the crowd at the gate were just the ones who couldn't get a place?

The turtleman warrior began speaking loudly to Amoxtli in his language, a thing of short, sharp syllables and cracking consonants. It brought back memories of the first warrior Ichu had met, which took the whole village and ultimately Elder Quilqi to defeat.

"Does anyone else understand this?" Tintaya griped. "No? I haven't had time to learn the Eztli language." She made a gesture and Ichu felt as if a cloud rolled over him, bringing sensations of a salty ocean with it. He still heard the turtleman's speech, but it was laden with meaning now. What chayu was that? Something the storm warrior leader had obviously stored, but Ichu racked his mind trying to figure out what animal and sequence it belonged to. There weren't many creatures who could survive the skies above the boiling ocean.

The turtleman made another swiping gesture and Ichu felt the disdain roll from him. He spoke of conquest and growth, that he and his people had traveled far and fast from their home. It was crumpling into mountain ranges, unlivable, and so they had come here to the grand city of which they'd heard so many hints.

Amoxtli held up a hand to stop him. The turtleman leader looked thunderous but stopped speaking.

"You call us heretics and those fallen from grace," she began, in the language of the Huaca. "Yet we came here before it was too late for our home, some leaving even while you drove the underpinnings of our island faster and faster, straining to arrive earlier. You deserve no place here, Xiuhquil, for it is your fault your people have no home."

The warrior shook his head. He spoke again in his language, but Ichu heard of the need of his people, for more minerals and food. Their island was small, and they had outgrown it. There was so much unused space here. Why not come here? They were a strong people and could live in hard places.

"Then why come to this city?" Amoxtli threw a hand out to the desert behind the army. "Live out there with the Allwiya who have failed to appease their gods. Feast on sand, but do not come to this city and demand a place. The true Eztli—those of us who still follow our dead god—have already made friends here and they do not want you or your thieving practices."

Now Xiuhquil held up a massive hand to stop her in return, and his beaky face twisted up in a sneering grin. This time Ichu heard satisfaction and condescension. Did Amoxtli not know they had been *invited* into the city? Gods of the Huaca had personally invited them to compete in the contests of strength that decided the balance of the city. All gods were welcome, and therefore all peoples.

The warrior looked up to the parapet they were on, above the gatehouse, and raised a deep purple vial to his lips. He drank, and his eyes glowed with power, though the purple bled through to the color of old iron.

"Two of your gods, Tiyu Llamkay, Uncle Smith, and Tiye Khuyay, Entle Love, have personally invited us to compete against your best warriors for prestige and entry to this city." Xiuhquil's voice was deep and raspy, used to speaking at length and at volume. There was a gasp from the other onlookers at his accented words. "We demand entry and fair testing, as the other species had. And if our invitation is not honored, we have the means to force our way in."

Ichu glanced to Akamu, whose hands were tightened into fists. The stone warrior whispered something fierce to Nina, but Ichu could only catch the word "traitor." Did he know something about this invitation?

"Why would the Uncles, Aunts, and Entles invite the turtlemen in?" Silluka asked from beside him.

"The minds of gods are not for us to know," Elder Quilqi said, but she was frowning, as if she had suspicions.

"Does he expect the ones up here to answer him, does he?" Cosquella had her hands on her hips, staring at the warrior leaders, in whispered conversation with Nina, who was making negative gestures with both hands.

"You say you have an invitation from gods, but you yourself are godless," Amoxtli's voice rang out, and Ichu looked back over the edge. The old Eztli Mecatl had approached Xiuhquil. "How do you have any say with gods not yours?"

Xiuhquil laughed, a sound like rocks falling. "Better to have no god than a dead god, old woman. Are you the best left of the heretics? Where is Coaxoch?" He leaned forward into Amoxtli, a quick, short gesture, and the old Ezlti Mecatl staggered back. Ichu gripped the railing. What had he done to her?

"Maybe your dead god will fix that!"

Amoxtli continued to stumble back, her hands on her middle, and a babble of noise rose from the others watching. Hands pointed, and Ichu followed their gaze to see Xiuhquil raise a bloody hand.

"What did he do?" Silluka cried. "That poor turtlewoman." Akamu's face was thunderous, though he was silent.

Amoxtli dropped to her knees, a crimson stain pooling in the dust around her.

"Someone help her!" Ichu called. There was no way he could get down there in time. Could he jump off the parapet? If he knew the chayu Silluka had used to fly, maybe. Visions of Amoxtli's neglected house danced through his mind. Her patients she saw every day. He knew a few of them now. Could he take up her rounds? His mind was spiraling at the speed of what just happened.

Xiuhquil dropped something rubbery and soft in front of the dying woman. Something from inside her. Ichu slumped. She was already dead, and the population of Chimor had stood idle. Surely someone could have gotten there in time...

"No," he whispered over the parapet. He'd finally begun learning. He'd found a teacher, and a friend.

Then Anuit stepped from behind Xiuhquil, a spray of mist showing she'd stepped from nothing, as usual. The Misini champion came around his side to stare at the fallen Eztli Mecatl.

"A shame, ya. Not even a challenge for you."

Xiuhquil stood up straight, head swiveling to follow the Misini as she strutted forward. She kept her back to him, reaching out a tentative finger to touch Amoxtli's body with an over-exaggerated shake of her head. But when the turtleman warrior shifted toward her, she produced a knife pointed backward at his midsection.

"Belly wounds are easy to inflict, but I'll follow the trend if I have to, big one." Xiuhquil relaxed back and so did Anuit. She was half his size. "The ones you address on high"—she gestured up to the parapet where Ichu was—"are not the only ones in control of the city, far from it."

Ichu heard a sigh from the older man—the sea warrior. "She's one of The Clowder. Meddling Misini."

Anuit's ear pricked toward them as if she'd heard. "The Clowder is concerned with the fortifications of this city, protecting it from invaders with smarter methods than the brute force of the Huaca." She pulled the knife apart into two duplicates, one in each hand. Xiuhquil tilted his head slightly in acknowledgement. "You may be powerful where you come from, godless one, but here you will find the might of many species arrayed against you. Misini. Huaca. Allwiya. Kawchi. Now, be good while I talk with the other adults. No more killing for now, ya?" She turned away and stepped into mist, appearing at the gates, then on a lower parapet, then the archers' walk, then stepped from nothingness in front of Nina and the warrior leaders.

Immediately the pressure increased on Ichu. His knees bent, forcing him to the ground. Cosquella and Silluka weren't faring much better. Elder Quilqi, unbowed, reached for his shoulder just as Anuit gestured like she was waving a fly away and the pressure vanished. Ichu stumbled to his feet.

"Enough with the theatrics, ya? That's my area. We need to let the Eztli Mecatl in."

"Let them in? We've spent the last month harrying them across the shaking lands," Akamu growled. "We've been trying to keep them *out*."

Ichu was surprised by the anger from the man. Akamu had always been level-headed around him.

"Not all of them, obviously, but The Clowder will take responsibility for them," Anuit replied. "They've requested to be a part of the contests. As the reigning champion, I have say over who I fight next."

"A reigning champion under investigation for killing *two* of her opponents," the fire warrior said.

Anuit waved that comment away too. "Accidents, both. Untimely, and likely due to mixing species in the arena. We all acknowledged this might happen when Chimor answered the gods' requests for contests." She gave a toothy smile. "Besides, who better to fight their champion, then?"

"So now we comply with requests from ones with no gods?" Nina asked. Elder Quilqi grunted and Ichu stole a glance at her, but she frowned at him and shook her head. Ichu thought the high-level Adepts and Anuit might have forgotten they were here.

Anuit raised both hands, displaying the delicate finger pads beneath her claws. "I believe he referenced *your* Uncle Smith and Entle Love, yes? I know none of The Clade would have invited them. These Eztli Mecatl are far from amusing, even the ones already here. But if you want to draw the anger of your gods, then go ahead."

"This is a mistake, Administrator," the young fire warrior protested.

"By all means, refuse the request for sanctuary from a new species, ya." Anuit put her furry hands in the air, one still holding her dagger between two fingers. "Though if I recall, the balance of Chimor depends on all peoples being able to challenge in the area for their gods. What happens if one is denied?"

"They did not ask for sanctuary. They are an attacking force!" Tintaya pointed an armored finger out over the wall.

Anuit shrugged. "Up to you, oh mighty Huaca. I'll simply tell my bosses what you've decreed." She made to walk down the parapet stairs.

Nina sighed and rubbed her forehead. "Fine. Tell them to open the doors, under guard. We can house the ones who are let in with the other refugees. But *no warriors*. Workers and crafters only. If any warriors want to challenge in the arena, they will require special dispensation to appear." She pointed a thick finger at Anuit. "The Clowder had better follow through on their promise. I will personally hold them responsible for the safety of the others in Chimor, with these Eztli Mecatl within our gates."

Anuit gave a mocking bow. "I will tell the other Misini, ya. Remember who has secured the safety of our city in the face of this army, big woman." She stepped into a rift of mist and disappeared.

"I hate that smug feline," Ichu heard Nina grumble as Elder Quilqi gestured him to follow her off the parapet.

"I'll be there soon," he told the elder, heading for Akamu. He needed answers.

New Neighbors

"But this is where *we* live," Silluka told Elder Quilqi. She and Cosquella had rushed down from the gatehouse after Nina pronounced they would be living among the turtlemen. The ones who had tried to kill them, repeatedly. She had to warn Elder Papaki. They'd left Ichu with Akamu, both saying they'd be along shortly.

"Chimor has new refugees on a regular basis, girl. You can't be expected to take up the refugee camp forever," the elder said as they hurried toward the walled area the village had settled in. "Two groups in such a short time is a bit unusual, but I did tell the elders not to expect to stay there."

"The undesirables, they had the better idea." Cosquella's long legs easily kept up with Silluka's pace. "Already taking jobs in the city, learning where they can be useful now they don't have bodycasters lording over them, aren't they?"

"At least some of that backward village had the right idea. Refused to enslave themselves to perfecting movements that don't need perfecting, or at least not that much." Elder Quilqi was frowning though. "Still not sure I agree with bringing the Eztli Mecatl in. Their magic is unusual, and I've seen my share. Uncles, Aunts, and Entles! The gods require intermediaries most of the time, and when that lot pokes their noses in personally, nothing ever goes well."

"Have you seen something like this happen before?" Silluka asked. Once again, she wondered how old the elder was.

"Too many times, girl. The problem with being *interesting* is that you attract the attention of those who think they are *also* interesting."

Was...that a dig at the gods themselves? But Silluka didn't have time to ask. They'd reached the walls of the refugee camp.

The Huaca had taken over most of it in the last few weeks, barring a few buildings that housed Allwiya, and two small families of Misini in one corner. There had been more, and other Huaca living here when they'd arrived, but most of them had moved out into the city by now. Though the refugee area—surrounded by a low wall—was the size of the old village back by the coast, it was only a side nook of Chimor, placed before getting into the city proper. Silluka supposed that was on purpose, to let newcomers accustom themselves to the stew of so many different people and species before immersing fully in it.

Except the elders were never ones to bend to new ideas. They had thought they were the only Huaca before leaving the coast. They were far unprepared to deal with the greater world, stuck in their ways and fossilized. Silluka saw them more and more as Elder Quilqi had always complained about them. They'd taken to the refugee camp as if it was a new village for them to inhabit permanently.

It seemed word had got there before them, or maybe some of the villagers had been at the gates and heard the news firsthand. The refugee camp looked like a kicked ant's nest, people pulling belongings from one mushroom-shaped hut to another, consolidating the Huaca to the smallest area it would fit in. Most of the people who had been defined as "undesirables" had already left, and they had made up over half the village, so there were empty huts mixed between those that still housed citizens.

"Can we protect them?" Silluka asked the elder. "Is there a chayu to keep turtlemen from attacking?" She racked her brain for any of the new chayu segments she'd been learning, but nothing affected a group like this. "What about *Tortoise in his Shell?*" It had kept the volcano from harming the sleds, as they were traveling. "We'd have to keep it up day and night."

"Performed by the ones from your village? The Eztli Mecatl would shred through that in moments." Elder Quilqi shook her head. "If the Uncles, Aunts, and Entles even let chayus like that work against them. The Eztli Mecatl were invited in, after all. Ah, and here they come."

Silluka spun to see a line of turtlemen trudging through the streets. How had they gotten ready so quickly? The inhabitants of Chimor drew back as they passed. The same inhabitants who had completely ignored Silluka's village when it arrived. What did it say about the turtlemen's power that even the non-warriors made passersby pause?

She looked closer to confirm Nina's instructions had been followed. There were no warriors in the line. These were ordinary people. None of the armor and headdresses that festooned the ones that had followed them across the desert and the shaking lands. These turtlemen carried pots and pans, great bundles of beaten fiber, tools, and belongings. The same thick Huaca who had bargained with Elder Papaki when their village arrived went to the first turtlewoman in the line and began to point out spots for them to live, and the associated cost. No different from when they arrived. Chimor would absorb anyone, eventually. That seemed to be how the city survived.

"Do we need to move our things, do we?" Cosquella asked. Silluka eyed where her village had compressed. Their shared house was at the edge of the new boundary, but still within the grouping.

"They won't bother our things," Elder Quilqi said. Was that because her things were also inside? Although the elder traveled very light. Silluka had only ever seen her with a small bag of necessities.

"Better to check, anyway," Cosquella said, and started to their hut. They had to pass the line of turtlemen, and as Silluka followed the tall woman, she heard whispers among turtlemen who looked their way. Most of these were older, though there were a few younglings playing under their parents' feet. She looked back to Elder Quilqi, who was also watching the line with interest.

Cosquella turned sharply at a raised voice in the line and shot back phrases in the speech of the Eztli Mecatl. She'd told Silluka she learned it when the first outcasts came to her farm, when she was very young. She shouted again, her hands shaking by her sides.

Silluka slid her hand around Cosquella's waist, though her girlfriend jumped at the gesture. Silluka had never seen her so worked up.

"What are they saying?"

"They keep saying Chimor will take anyone, to look at me, they do." Her voice was low and dangerous, and she pulled at Silluka's grip, but Silluka held on tightly.

"Why you?" She knew she couldn't keep Cosquella back if she truly wanted to move but planted her feet anyway.

Cosquella asked another question, and the answer came with a rocky laugh from two nearby turtlemen—parents who gestured at their children. Her rough skin trembled under Silluka's touch. "Who are you calling a monstrosity?"

Another answer in Eztli Mecatl and this time Cosquella rocked back as if struck. "They're asking if Chimor always lets in crossbreeds."

"Crossbreeds, eh?" Elder Quilqi tried out a few halting phrases in the same language. When had she picked that up?

The parents' words sounded a little gentler this time, though not much.

"They say they've seen other people like me before. A few Huaca crashed on their island on a boat, years ago. Rare, and most don't live past their first years." Cosquella was shaking like the ground in an earthquake. Silluka pulled her closer.

"Like you how? Do they mean your skin condition?" She didn't like where this was going.

Cosquella asked a question and the turtlemen parents laughed again, correcting her.

"Bones and blood. So much for that 'skin condition' story," Elder Quilqi said.

"What about it? What are they saying?" Silluka was tired of only understanding half the conversation.

"They say my mother...she didn't have a skin condition." Cosquella paused, but it was as if the words were pulled from her. "They say...I'm half Eztli Mecatl."

Silluka blinked, so many things clicking into place in her head at once. Cosquella's *sunqu*, like Ichu's, halfway between Huaca and Eztli Mecatl. Her strange hair and skin, her height. She'd even seen Cosquella's eyes glow red when she was fighting the turtlemen who attacked the sled. She was certain of it now. Maybe that was even why the gods didn't let her access the core.

She held Cosquella close while the larger woman shook in her grasp, suddenly seeming frail. "Come on, let's get to our hut. We can talk about this there."

"Xiuhquil, the warrior leader, he mentioned Coaxoch. She came through our farm, but left when I was young, she did. Maybe she has answers."

Silluka twined her fingers into Cosquella's hand, using her right forearm to brush against her rough skin. It made an almost electric pulse through the sensitive end of her arm. "Come on. Let's get back home."

Cosquella let herself be pulled away from the line of turtlemen awaiting entry to the refugee camp. Silluka ignored the other whispers following them. She would have to learn some of the Eztli Mecatl language, if only to know what they were saying about her girlfriend.

Elder Quilqi followed them, looking thoughtful. But when they got to the hut they shared, Lugopo was waiting, holding onto a peg outside the door.

"I have fortifications ready to spear the invaders with deadly darts!" they announced. They made no move to tap their translation circlet.

"Let's save the carnage until they're moved in, shall we?" Elder Quilqi said. "Maybe throw a spear or two while asking for some honey? We've just had some interesting news."

Lugopo sprang to Silluka's shoulder, hurrying down between their connected arms. "Are you going to spawn? I shall devise a basin to catch the spill. Those who do not survive will make excellent caviar."

"We're not going to spawn anything," Silluka said.

"Unless Eztli Mecatl spawn," Cosquella said in a faint voice. "I don't know anything about it. Maybe *that's* why my mother died."

"Are they increasing their numbers already? No wonder there are so many outside the gates!" Lugopo cried. They scuttled back to the wall of the hut, then up to the roof, where they'd installed a viewing tube. They wrapped three tentacles around it, pointed at the gates of Chimor, just visible over the roofs of several other buildings outside the refugee camp.

"Come inside, squid," Elder Quilqi said. "We have things to discuss, before more Eztli Mecatl and Akamu get here."

Inside, they sat around the one table, all facing the door, as if waiting for turtlemen to crash through at any moment. Sounds of arguments filtered through the refugee camp, and some of them were the rough voices of Eztli Mecatl, speaking in their harsh tongue.

"How can this even be?" Cosquella burst out. "Eztli Mecatl? Me? My father took them into our home, he did. But I didn't think he took them so *far* into our home, he did. And why did they leave then? Because my mother died? Did we offend them?"

"Slow a bit, child," Elder Quilqi said. "Mixed heritages are quite rare, but they have been known to happen. This actually appeases my suspicions about you quite a bit."

"Suspicions?" Silluka said. "What kind?"

"First, I've never seen a skin condition quite like that. But more concerning was her inability to achieve any results with the chayu, even in that suit Lugopo created. Sticks and iron, it would make even a deranged quirra able to connect to the core."

"Success! My invention is truly a devastating creation!" Lugopo raised four tentacles in the air. "Such are the excesses of Whirling Abyss!" Their eyes glanced between Silluka, Cosquella, and Elder Quilqi, and they hastily fiddled with their circlet. "Ah, that is, I am certain this is quite disheartening for you."

Cosquella straightened, taking in a deep breath, then letting it out. "Disheartening? For me, I don't think that's the term. The Eztli Mecatl, they are powerful, and if their blood runs in mine, then I can use that power too, yes? Maybe I *can* learn magic, then." She stared out at nothing for a moment. "But why did my father never tell me this, didn't he?"

Silluka thought back to their last conversation with Cosquella's father, dying from the volcanic ash in his lungs. "I think...he might have tried, at the end."

"Only after nearly eighteen years."

"Maybe...he wanted to protect you," Silluka suggested.

"From whom? We were alone, on that farm, we were. Self-sufficient. We knew of the Huaca to the south of us—your village—but my father hadn't been there since before I was born..." Cosquella faltered. "Maybe *because* I had been born."

Elder Quilqi leaned across the table. "Whatever the reason, I hope you find some peace with it, child. If it reassures you at all, know this must have been a special feat of the gods. Entle Magic and Entle Love must have worked some chayu over you to enable your mother to give birth to you."

"Wait." Now Silluka was confused. "The gods perform chayus too? I thought they created them?"

"Yes and yes." The elder looked peeved at being put off her story. "The gods devise how they shall be worshipped, and they are much more capable of channeling the core than you. Why would they not use chayus?"

"Then...Entle Magic and Entle Love worked with the dead god of the Eztli Mecatl to bring Cosquella into existence?" Silluka hugged her girlfriend closer.

"Perhaps, yes, or they simply changed circumstances so the birth was viable. Whatever happened, girl"—she pointed at Cosquella—"you're quite a special person. I knew

I chose you for a reason. You didn't feel quite like a Huaca to me. Just...off."

"You said you've seen mixed heritages before?" Cosquella held Silluka's hand tight on her arm, as if scared to let her go.

"Rarely." Elder Quilqi sat back. "Misini are more compatible with Huaca. Certainly more than Eztli Mecatl. The Clade is well known enough to the Tiyus, Tiyas, and Tiyes. They've come to agreements beyond your knowledge in the past, when they needed a champion to fulfill both their purposes."

"Then am I a champion of the gods too?" Cosquella asked.

The elder shrugged. "Possibly. Who's to say, with the god of the Eztli Mecatl dead, rather than merely changed in some way? That's news, it is, and no mistake. Or maybe *that's* why you were born, because he *is* dead and Entle Magic and Entle Love wanted something done about it. Things around the gods get funny when they die."

A dead god? What would that mean for them if one of the Uncles, Aunts, or Entles died? Would their chayus simply stop working? Silluka thought back. This was making some memory surface. "Akamu mentioned chayus from Entle Love and Uncle Smith were harder to use. Is that connected to this somehow?"

Elder Quilqi shook her head. "I don't know, and that upsets me. I have a feeling we're going to find out, whether we want to or not. The gods are unknowable, but they're also not subtle much of the time."

Before Silluka could ask what she meant, the elder jabbed a long finger toward Cosquella. "Your problem is that you are going to need to find a teacher. We know you can't summon the ampuka more than a quirra with a broken leg. Perhaps another approach is needed"

"Suit for large lady will need to be adjusted." Lugopo pronounced. "Is not fulfilling full destructive potential!" They tapped the circlet with two tentacles. "Meaning, must incorporate turtleman movements into structure..." They swung off the table and scuttled through the door of the hut.

"Well, that might go spectacularly bad *or* well," the elder said.

Ichu rapped on the open door, Akamu behind him. "Where's Lugopo going like a crab has their tentacle? Have you seen how the turtlemen are taking over this area already?"

"We know," Silluka said. "But more importantly, we discovered something." She looked to Cosquella for permission, and the big woman ducked her head. She was coming to terms with this news faster than Silluka would have.

"Evidently Cosquella gets her build and strength from her mother. Her Eztli Mecatl mother."

There was a stunned silence. Akamu stared at Cosquella, and Silluka felt the pressure in the room intensify. He shared a look with Elder Quilqi, who gave him a knowing smirk and a nod.

"Maybe this can act as a memorial for Amoxtli, in a way," Ichu said. They all stared at him. "The turtleman leader, Xiuhquil, killed Amoxtli at the gates, and with her, any hope of me learning to use Eztli Mecatl magic. She was my friend. That was where I was going every day—to see her. I thought I was lost, after Xiuhquil murdered her in cold blood."

Ichu's hands were clasped at his sides, and Akamu put his arm around Silluka's brother. "Now Cosquella and I can learn together, as a testament to her sacrifice."

CHAPTER TWELVE

Giving Power

Ichu slid into the seat next to the elder, Akamu pacing behind the table. There wasn't much space to move in the hut, and with five of them in here, the room was overcrowded. At least Lugopo had gone outside. When Ichu passed them, their circlet was muttering about adjusting *sunqu* sensing.

"I have news of my own, that may make you rethink any misgivings you have," he told Cosquella. The big woman was frowning more than usual, her hands clutching Silluka's. His sister's stump patted the rough back of Cosquella's hands. No—he looked closer. Not just rough skin, but scales, like a turtleman, altered in color and placement for Huaca skin. Now that he knew, it was obvious Cosquella was halfway between the bulky reptilian Eztli Mecatl and the mammalian Huaca. His eyes caught points along her arms, the craggy skin around her mouth, not quite a beak, and her solid-looking hair. Perhaps that was what came from mixing the hairless turtlemen with hairy Huaca.

"You've tried to use Eztli Mecatl magic, you have?" Cosquella asked, breaking off his examination. "And you think you can teach me?"

"Not tried. I *have* used their magic," Ichu said. "Amoxtli showed me. I met her a couple weeks ago and she was forgiving enough of an unlearned Huaca to invite me in. I wish I had taken you all to meet her." He paused to swallow. She'd walked straight into death. She must have known the turtleman leader would do that to her. She seemed to have a history with him. Why go out alone?

"I have vials in my room already," he said instead. At Elder Quilqi's widened eyes, he hastily explained, some small part of him glad he'd finally managed to surprise her.

"Not like the one I took. I *made* these with Amoxtli. It's the old Eztli Mecatl ways, of giving and supporting, not taking and hoarding like the turtlemen do."

"It's true, ancient one," Akamu added, still pacing. "He's managed to mix the two magics, and the result is a pure core derivation."

Silluka took her hand back so she could gesture. "Giving? Taking? Vials? What are you talking about? Have you been trying to learn another species' magic while Elder Quilqi told us to work on Mental Adepthood?"

"No, hold a moment, girl," Elder Quilqi said. Her old face was screwed up, eyes dancing between him and his sister. "We knew he was altered by taking the first vial, but not how. I see it's caught up to him. This may be the best way forward for him, and for Cosquella." She faced Ichu and that pressure was back, like her gaze was pushing him toward the back wall. It was gentler than what Akamu did, a heavy mitt rather than a brick wall. "For those of us only using Huaca chayus, go slowly, and explain. You seem to have a distinction between the Eztli Mecatl who just arrived and those who have been here some time."

Ichu nodded, trying not to simply gush everything at the others. There was so much he'd learned over the past few weeks. He should have shared it before, when Amoxtli could have lent her expertise. Now he had to. Amoxtli was dead, and Cosquella might benefit from it.

"Amoxtli—who agreed to teach me—was the one who decided on the distinction. She was a healer here. Many of the Eztli Mecatl who arrived after their god died act as doctors, scientists, and engineers. They're a good people. They used each other's strength when their god was alive to build on their island."

He looked between their faces. Even Akamu, who'd been fighting the turtlemen for months, was fixed on him, as if this was all new.

"The ones who left used the power of their god to lend parts of themselves to others. Amoxtli didn't get far enough into it to share the levels of power like we have Adepthood in the Huaca, but they had something similar. The ones who drove them out used different magic, not from their god." He paused. There was a lot of conflict Amoxtli had skipped over, but he'd understood a little from context. "I think it started when their god was still alive, a perversion from giving and lending to taking or even stealing. Maybe that led to the god's death? I don't know. But the turtlemen—what Amoxtli called the ones who stayed behind—started building their power, and I gather Xiuhquil was one of the worst. They used the same power but stole strength from others to make up for what their god used to provide. They made their island speed up so it impacted ours sooner. They destroyed much of the construction the Eztli Mecatl had built."

"But this all started before their god died, did it?" Cosquella asked. "The ones who taught us did not say. I think I heard this Amoxtli's name held in reverence by Coaxoch, my teacher, I did, but I never met her myself. The ones we helped said the others drove them out only after their god died."

Ichu saw Akamu twitch out of the corner of his eye, before the man went back to pacing.

"I think that was the last straw for the Eztli Mecatl," Ichu suggested. "I think they fought against the turtlemen's new ways as much as they could." He found Akamu's eyes, remembering their conversation, how Akamu was so careful not to say Uncle Smith's name. "Their god didn't die a natural death. Maybe he was weakened enough so...what happened, happened."

Elder Quilqi twisted to face Akamu. "I know of what you speak, and best not to elaborate on it here. Let's just say there was a schism in their people around the death."

Silluka and Cosquella were both shooting confused looks at them. "I'll tell you when I can," Ichu promised his sister. "It's dangerous knowledge."

Silluka paled. When the elders in their village said knowledge was dangerous, it usually pertained to one of the Uncles, Aunts, and Entles.

"Fine, so Eztli Mecatl are the ones who came to our farm, they did, and turtlemen are those who followed after." Cosquella crossed her thick arms. "What of all else, eh? Giving power to others and you learning Eztli Mecatl magic?"

Ichu smiled at her. He hadn't had a lot of connection with his sister's girlfriend yet, save they were both struggling with their chayu and connecting to the core. This was a development that might affect both of them, together.

"When Nu'oona told us our *sunqu* had moved, I started thinking. I *knew* what mine was caused by. It was that vial I drank from the turtlemen." He shook his head. One of the stupidest decisions of his life, though it was for his sister's protection—or at least he had thought so at the time. "So, I started to track down Eztli Mecatl in the city, to see if they could help me."

It was also to see if they had access to more vials. The need still ran through him, though he kept it away with a firm will. He still hadn't tried one he'd made, even with Akamu saying it was pure. What if made his need for them even worse? But he'd have to use one again at some point, especially now he knew about Cosquella.

"Amoxtli taught me how the Eztli Mecatl gifts work, and if I'm right, and you can access the same magic I can, then I can teach you." Everyone was looking at him. "It's a strange blend of Huaca and Eztli Mecatl magic."

"Then, I can learn magic, I can?" Cosquella looked like she might tear up. She squeezed Silluka's hand, and Ichu tried not to grin at Silluka's wince. Cosquella had turtleman strength in those arms. "When can we start?"

Akamu leaned into the conversation. He'd been pacing like a caged jakua while Ichu talked, almost as if he wasn't listening, but Ichu had been around the man enough to know that meant he was assembling pieces of information to unlock a greater puzzle.

"You both should start soon, but not just now. We have something else to talk about." He gestured outside the hut, where the shouts of turtlemen moving into the refugee camp mixed with Huaca consolidating their homes like a wall against invaders. "They will be bringing their own magic to Chimor, and to the tournament. Don't forget that's why they're here. Evidently two of our gods have invited them in. Unheard of!"

Elder Quilqi waggled a hand. "Not usual, in any case."

"Ancient one, I know you said we should talk about this, but I feel it's necessary for all here to know. I've used *Tortoise's Hard Shell* too many times in the past few weeks, and I am concerned *someone* may take notice. Is there anything you can do for a few moments?"

Elder Quilqi narrowed her eyes and the pressure grew in the little room again, Ichu pressed down in his seat.

"You mean you wish to talk of Grandmother and Grandfather's children behind their backs?" Ichu blinked. He hadn't heard it put that way before.

"If you please," Akamu gave a small bow. "It's important."

Elder Quilqi turned her eyes up in thought. "Doors and floors. Not a lot of room in here for a chayu, but I may have a morsel saved up from quite a long time ago indeed. I'd been keeping it for a stormy day, though now might be as appropriate as any other time."

She stood, gesturing with both hands, out, then above and below, rolling forward, then a flick to one side. Was that all to store a chayu? Akamu's gestures were usually quick. What did it mean that the elder had locked the chayu behind so many movements?

A wave spread around her, rippling with purple, gray, pink, red, yellow, blue, brown, and orange. All the colors of the gods swirling around each other, though the gray of Uncle Smith and the pink of Entle Love were fainter than the rest. It encompassed all of them, and the sounds from outside fell away, making Ichu work his jaw in the sudden silence. He felt deaf.

"This will work for several minutes. *Dolphin Stuns Her Dinner* is not a chayu I've seen practiced here in many years, and I think we will have a little protection because of it. Still, better to speak fast." Her voice was tinny, as if coming from underwater.

Akamu nodded, and stopped pacing, gesturing with both hands. "You saw the muted colors in the ancient one's chayu. Ichu has come across the same resistance with Uncle Smith and Entle Love's chayus when storing them in vials." Silluka gave him a sharp look at that, but Ichu motioned that he would tell her later. "It is the same with all four elemental warriors, and there have been complaints across the city. That Uncle and Entle are not favoring us like they should, and we don't know why."

"It was true at the coast too," Silluka said. "I remember the elders speaking about it."

"We also know of a connection between Uncle Smith and the Eztli Mecatl." Akamu acted like he wanted his amber armor on, but Ichu thought he was resisting the urge. "I told Ichu of it, in private, but I have it on excellent authority that the god of the Eztli Mecatl did not simply die, but was killed...by our Uncle Smith."

Elder Quilqi fixed him with a glare. "You're absolutely certain? Gods' blood, boy, this is not something to play around with."

"Absolutely certain," Akamu said. "I have a contact with an Eztli Mecatl who prefers to keep herself secluded. She did some testing on one of the vials from the turtlemen and confirmed it."

"And you trust her?" Cosquella said.

"I do. In fact, you even said you know her. She was in the first wave who settled here. Her name is Coaxoch."

Cosquella sat up straight at the word.

"Your old teacher?" Silluka asked her, stump gently brushing her arm.

"Yes, I do know her, me. She is a great woman, she is," Cosquella said. "My father cared for her a great deal and made her my teacher when I was toddling around his farm. But he sent her away before any of the others left, as he was concerned with her safety, he was. I still miss her."

"She arrived here safely, shortly after," Akamu confirmed.

"Could I see her?" Cosquella leaned toward Akamu as if she would go right now, but Akamu shook his head.

"She does not live in Chimor any longer, but in the stable desert. You would have to pass the entire turtleman army to get to her."

"*Dolphin Stuns Her Dinner* will not hold forever," Elder Quilqi warned. "State your worst fears now, before it weakens."

Akamu met her eyes. "Coaxoch claimed Uncle Smith was trying to taint the competition the gods have in Chimor. He is a traitor to the rest of the Uncles, Aunts, and Entles. He is trying to influence the results, and I believe, bring down the might of the Huaca."

"Only time for a few more words," Elder Quilqi muttered. "What else?"

"But he's not acting alone, is he?" Silluka said. "He *and* Entle Love invited the turtlemen inside Chimor to fight. If *he* killed the god of the Eztli Mecatl, what did Entle Love do? And what does that have to do with Cosquella's birth?"

"I do not know," Akamu said. "And that scares me."

"Never good to meddle in the gods' affairs," Elder Quilqi said. "And even more important, where are these two rogue gods, that their power is not being transferred to the Huaca? Hmpf. For now, I believe Ichu and Cosquella should learn what skills they may have in common, and Silluka must test soon for Mental Adept. I want us all in top fighting form for the coming days."

"Fighting?" Ichu clarified. "Not just ability to manipulate the core?"

"I am very specific with my words, boy," the elder grumped. "Now, any other revelations that would bring the gods down on us or can I retain some small part of *Dolphin Stuns Her Dinner*?"

No one else said anything, and Elder Quilqi made a grasping gesture. A wash of color collapsed into her, and the sounds of the outside world flooded back in.

CHAPTER THIRTEEN

Tortoise's Growth

True to Anuit's word, Misini took up places around the refugee center as soon as the turtlemen moved in, and Silluka saw them skulking around the alleys, twirling knives, their eyes flashing in the dark like jakua. A few seemed able to step in and out of mist like Anuit, but Silluka guessed the ability was that of a higher practitioner level, given Anuit's status in the city. None were as dexterous as the champion.

So far, the turtlemen behaved themselves, but it had only been one day. The next morning, Elder Quilqi and Akamu accompanied her to the gymnasium. Lugopo was riding the elder's shoulder, carrying half a dozen gadgets in their tentacles. Ichu was somewhere else with Cosquella, trying to understand how the Eztli Mecatl's power worked. Silluka carried her suit in a bag tied to her back.

As they passed the little wall surrounding the center, two Misini arrowed toward them, knives out.

"I think you can see we're not Eztli Mecatl, yes?" Elder Quilqi sniped. She held out both wrinkled hands, twisting them in the air. "No scales, see?"

"What of the one staying with you, ya?" A male-presenting Misini with a ruff of fur around his neck pointed a knife at the group. The diaphanous silks barely concealed his body, and Silluka jerked her eyes up from his fur-covered belly and legs.

"I personally vouch for her," Akamu said, "as leader of the stone warriors. Is that enough for you? Suffice to say, she is elsewhere today."

The other Misini sneered and brought her knife forward, but Anuit herself stepped from mist and smacked the woman in the back of the head. "Not these. Go find others to entertain you." There was an exchange of hisses from all three, making the hair on Silluka's neck stand on end. The Misini champion faced them again, her slitted pupils wide and fixed on Elder Quilqi.

"You seem to make a nuisance of yourself, eh, old one?"

"Get along, kitty," the elder answered. She seemed relaxed, but a wisp of power sent chills up Silluka's spine. Lugopo crept down the elder's back and hopped over to her, their tentacles shivering.

Anuit didn't back down. "The Huaca are weak. You of all people should know this. We have stories of you, *ancient one*. You pop in and cause trouble. The Clade is strengthening their hold on this city. Soon it will be a vassal of Ninun."

"I've been gone far too long then, if that's the case. Claws and Clowder, if overgrown furballs are taking on the warriors, things are in a sorry state here."

"Why, you..." Anuit's knife was in her hand in an instant, flashing toward the elder's face. Silluka didn't even have time to react.

Elder Quilqi grabbed the knife blade in one hand, pulling the Misini forward with it. Anuit's eyes widened. Silluka grunted at the weight of the air around her, like she had picked up five more heavy backpacks.

"Bad kitty. I think it's time you entertained your hedonistic gods elsewhere." The elder made a complex gesture with the hand not holding the knife and a veil of mist opened behind Anuit. Silluka heard Akamu grunt in surprise. "Fetch."

The elder jerked the knife away and threw it—twisted and bent—into the mist, then poked Anuit in the nose with the unharmed hand that had grasped the blade. The Misini fell back, yowling, and disappeared into the mist, which folded around her and vanished.

The pressure intensified, driving Silluka to her knees. She heard Akamu stagger behind her. Above the elder's head, a large slit-pupiled eye opened in the air, winked once, and disappeared. The pressure on Silluka vanished.

"Humph. Well, that was unfortunate, but in one part at least, Anuit was telling the truth. The Clade is getting nosy." Elder Quilqi dusted her hands off and pulled Silluka to her feet. "You see what I mean about time being short? Good thing I've gotten word your test for Mental Adept will be in three days, girl."

"Three...? But I'm not ready! I haven't stored *Tortoise's Growth* or *Quirra's Day* yet." Silluka grabbed her stump with her left hand, as if she could protect it.

"Let's get to the gymnasium before anything else happens," Akamu suggested.

"Agreed," the elder said.

Silluka thought while they sped through the city, seeing more Misini in the shadows of buildings. Huaca looked over their shoulders as they went about their business. She had spent every waking moment of the last two weeks practicing *Jakua's Fight*, *Tortoise's Growth* and *Quirra's Day*. The second two were harder than *Jakua's Fight*, and it seemed she would never remember them. She'd practiced both with and without the suit, although after what happened when one of Lugopo's gods intervened, she practiced without more often. It seemed *all* the gods were more active in Chimor than on the coast.

"We're going to solidify your testing chayus today," Akamu said when they were finally within the walls of the gymnasium. The only non-Huaca here was Lugopo, and the little Allwiya had been quiet on the walk. "I've heard about the armor the Allwiya made you. It will help you."

"To reign destruction upon the judges!" Lugopo's circlet crowed, though perhaps not as chipper as usual.

"I will be one of the judges," Akamu said.

Lugopo smacked the circlet with a tentacle. "To have a very good test without destroying any judges at all."

"I trust you can keep this creation in good working order while we practice?" Akamu nudged the suit Silluka had lugged to the gymnasium with a sandalled toe.

"It is crafted to the finest order, blessed by Whirling Abyss themself. Since my supplication, I have made more updates so it may turn Silluka into a deadly foe!" Lugopo swung down from Elder Quilqi's shoulder, scuttling along the collection of wood and metal. Their usual mood had returned, now they were talking about their invention. Without someone in it, it looked to Silluka somewhat like a cactus had died and begun rotting.

"Quick quick! Inside!" Lugopo waved three arms toward her. "The suit should no longer scald when the connection to the core is too strong. Only minor burns, even at over one hundred Tortoises!"

Silluka watched Elder Quilqi, who was trying to hide a smile. She seemed to brush off confronting one of the most powerful Misini in the city, and whomever that eye had belonged to. No one had mentioned it on the walk here, and Silluka was fine with that. The less said of the gods, the better.

The old woman was dismissive of the suit, too, but seemed content to let Silluka discover for herself if it was actually useful to her progress. She'd said before it was a crutch more than not, but Silluka could feel the power in it.

"I just need to avoid tying up my *sunqu* again," she said, starting to pull it over her legs.

"Again?" Akamu asked. "You've done that before?"

"Yes." Silluka struggled to get the mesh up around her torso, Lugopo making adjustments as she donned it. "After the fight with the desert Allwiya. I'd started out with two hands, thanks to this"—she waved her stump as she thrust it inside the arm of the suit—"but the right hand was crushed and the chayu I was using wasn't the same intent. Elder Quilqi said I'd tangled my *sunqu*, but she fixed it."

Akamu was frowning, glaring at the elder, who was trying to look innocent and failing. "This is not a simple problem. Not only do you confront Anuit and one of The Clade without a thought, ancient one, I've only seen two other people with tangled *sunqus* and both of them never channeled the core the same." He faced the elder fully. "You untangled it? Not even Nina has been able to achieve that."

"Well, her mother must not have taught her everything she knew, hmm? Failing magic! Let's get back to the task at hand, shall we?" The elder waved a hand at the suit and Silluka's progress. Akamu narrowed his eyes, but helped her the rest of the way, latching the suit up with Lugopo's help.

Silluka smiled to hear someone else get run afoul of the elder's avoidance. She watched the two as the last fasteners and bolts were connected on the suit, Lugopo fussing over everything. It felt...lighter? More mobile? The little Allwiya had changed some things in the last week. She wondered what Whirling Abyss had done to Lugopo when they passed their supplication. They were due visits from their other two gods, but no telling when that would be.

Once the suit was on, Akamu straightened, his hands behind his back, and Silluka was reminded of when he worked with her as their sleds passed through the shaking lands. *This* was the commander of the stone warriors. This was the man who reported to Nina, who might be the most powerful Adept in Chimor, not counting Elder Quilqi. No longer the gentle man who rested his hands on Ichu's shoulders, who had gently kissed him goodbye when neither was certain of when or how they would see each other again.

"We'll skip the morning ritual this time. Show me *Tortoise's Growth*."

"All of it?" Silluka tried not to gape. Even with the suit helping, she'd barely made it through the whole chayu before. The morning ritual was what opened her *sunqu*. Without it, she wouldn't be able to store the chayu.

"Now. You're testing in three days. You will have to impress not only me, but the other judges." He stood, head high, eyes studying her every twitch. She felt as if she'd been caught out in the open. A subtle pressure she could *almost* understand bumped against her. Despite her intentions, her eyes flicked to Elder Quilqi, who gave her a subtle shake of her head.

"You may be the ancient one's champion, but you will gain none of her mercy before the judges. Best not to rely on it."

Mercy? From Elder Quilqi? Silluka's hand tightened. The artificial right hand of the suit creaked in response, the fingers clenching together. She set herself for the chayu, running it through her mind.

"Confidence!" Lugopo climbed to the elder's shoulder. "One will not vanquish enemies in battle without it!" They tapped their circlet. "That is, it will be a great boost to your actions."

"Can I ask a question first?" Silluka tried to ignore Lugopo's pep talk.

"Questions are welcomed, in their own time," Akamu said. It had the feeling of a line he had repeated often. "Best ask before you begin and get it off your mind."

"Can you tell me who the judges are?"

Akamu's eyes widened slightly, but his stance—a solid Basic stance—didn't shift. "I thought you would have guessed by now. You met them all, on top of the gates."

"The leaders of the warriors?"

Akamu gave a short nod. "Indeed. Myself, Tintaya of the storm warriors, Puric of the sea warriors and Coya of the fire warriors. I am at least familiar with your background and situation. The others will only see a backwater girl who is barely a Physical Adept."

Silluka waved the suit's right hand. "And what of this?"

Akamu barely spared it a glance. "We've had many before us who have differences in their bodies. That is not what we're testing for in a Mental Adept. Any further questions before we begin?"

Silluka took the hint. "I'm ready."

"Good. Then show me *Tortoise's Growth*."

This chayu was longer than *Jakua's Fight*, and generally the segments moved slower. More of it was defensive and blocking moves, like *Tortoise Pulls His Limbs In* and *Tortoise's Hard Shell*. The group chayu they'd performed on the sleds to protect them from the volcano was also part of the sequence, though *Tortoise in his Shell* worked differently for only one person. All the group chayus did. Yet there were still surprising shows of strength, like *Tortoise's Heavy Foot*, near the beginning, and *Tortoise Chews Through Sticks*, another chayu she'd never heard of before, which gave enough power in her one hand to crack stone.

Silluka set her feet in Strength stance, using the backs of her wrists and her knees in *Tortoise Pushes Forward* to begin. Much of this chayu was in Strength, Blocking, and even Unmovable stance. If storing *Jakua's Fight* meant she could have taken on Hufi's whole squad, learning *Tortoise's Growth* might keep her from harm should the desert Allwiya attack again. She only needed three of the main chayus for Mental Adept, but Akamu knew many more, able to release a chayu at any time. She was only beginning to grasp the power behind the more advanced Adepts.

Sweat poured down her face as she progressed through the moves. Many required tension in muscles she rarely used to form blocks. But she was pleased to see the form of Tortoise rising around her, his plodding pace following her moves.

It was only near the end when she faltered. Tortoise, encountering obstacles, was turned on his back, but she couldn't remember how to escape his peril.

"Tortoise Rocks on His Back," Akamu barked.

Yes. That was it. Silluka hunched in, transitioning to a forward roll that would trip any attacker. The chayu, released, would let her evade foes with quick side-to-side motions.

She had been moving constantly, if slowly, for nearly an hour and a half when she reached *Tortoise Sleeps*, the end of the entire sequence. She let her arms, burning with fatigue, fall to her sides, her knees shaking. She could feel the chayus trying to find purchase within her *sunqu*, then spreading out to the rest of her body. But she hadn't performed the morning ritual, and she'd performed

Tortoise's Growth sloppily. Most of the energy fled from her.

"You will need to practice most of the next three days," Akamu said. Silluka winced, then took the flask of water Lugopo offered up to her with five tentacles. It was almost as big as they were.

"Any comments?" she asked Elder Quilqi.

The elder held up wrinkled palms. "I have no say in this test. Pretend I'm not here. The leader of the stone warriors is the one who has authority over what you do here."

So she needed to put in more practice, then.

"Are you ready for *Quirra's Day*?" Akamu asked when she'd had enough water. She knew this one even less well than *Tortoise's Growth*, and now she was exhausted. But she was testing in three days.

"You will only get a few minutes' rest between chayus in your test," Akamu added. "There will be no help."

Silluka closed her eyes, trying to remember the sequence. *Quirra's Day* was the longest of the three, as Quirra was a busy and energetic fellow, investigating everything and learning about the world around him. Many of the chayu segments here were practical, like *Quirra Hibernates in the Winter*, to insulate the body from extreme heat or cold, or her favorite, *Quirra Hides His Nuts*, which made the hands extra dexterous. *Flying Quirra* was part of the sequence too, though she wouldn't be flying over any earthquakes this time. It had many other uses, depending on the stance and intent, and she had connected too strongly to the core that first time. She'd thought about that time a lot since then, remembering the pain of the power flooding through her, dimming her vision. She'd done something similar the first time she completed *Jakua's Fight*. Elder Quilqi had said her power was like a beacon. Was everyone else capable of the same feats? Was she special in some way?

"Whenever you're ready." Akamu's wry tone cut through her retrospection, and Silluka's eyes flew open. Elder Quilqi had taken a seat, and Lugopo was beside her, their tentacles crossed over each other like they were crossing their arms, but too many of them.

But rather than scatter her thoughts, the revelation seemed to solidify a certainty deep within her. She *was* special. Elder Quilqi thought so enough to single her out. She'd done what no others in her village had. And she wasn't alone. Her brother had figured out how to mix two different magics, Cosquella was the child of two species, and Lugopo, well...who could doubt Lugopo?

She set in Dexterity stance, which was the base of almost all of *Quirra's Day,* and began the sequence with *Quirra Runs Down a Branch.*

The segments of the full chayu fell into place for her, one after another, and Quirra's form rose around her, his speed and balance shoring up her movements, compensating for her missing hand. With the suit on, there was nothing she couldn't do. This might have been the longest of the three, but it felt the most natural to her.

If Akamu had called out any tips to her while she moved through the sequence, she didn't hear them. She moved with Quirra.

After *Quirra Curls Up,* she blinked and realized the day had shaded into early afternoon. How long had she been moving? They'd come to the gymnasium in early morning, and she'd performed two full chayus. Elder Quilqi was gone, probably on one of her mysterious errands.

Silluka gradually became aware of Akamu's gaze on her, measuring. That pressure was back.

"If you perform all three chayus like that, you will have no problem in your test," he said.

"Such inspired movement! You are certain to obliterate all who stand before you!" Lugopo thwacked their circlet. "That is, pass your test."

She blinked, and for just a moment, the pressure around her receded. Akamu's body was tinged in a mass of colors— all the hues of the Uncles, Aunts, and Entles. Jakua roared along his biceps, Quirra curled around his wrists, Eagle sat on his shoulder, his legs twined with Tree's roots,

Caterpillar and Rat lived in his belly, Coyote paced along his thighs and Crow sat atop his head.

She turned her head and caught Lugopo. They were surrounded by the familiar splotchy white and black glow, but around their body floated intricate mechanisms and strange, undecipherable glyphs.

Before she could look closer at the revelations, the vision was gone and the pressure against her redoubled. Akamu's lips turned up in a grin.

"You saw it, just for a moment, didn't you?"

"What was that?"

"The realm of Pressure Adept. I wondered when it would happen. You're so close. This is why the ancient one wants you to test." Akamu waved a hand sideways. "Well, that and the Eztli Mecatl, but no one knows what to do about them yet."

"Then you really do think I can pass this test?"

Akamu turned serious again. "Practice these three, one after the other, tomorrow and the day after. Once each." He leaned in. "If you really want to impress the judges, do not perform the morning ritual first. Only on the day of the test, prepare yourself when you get up with the morning ritual. Then store these last two chayus for the first time in the test."

Silluka considered. She had been dragged, literally kicking and screaming, to her first test, which she had failed. She was actually looking forward to this one.

"I'll do that. A shame Elder Quilqi didn't stay until the end." What would Silluka have seen around her?

"I think she saw what she wanted," Akamu said.

Silluka watched the rest of the gymnasium. Practitioners generally kept to themselves or worked in small groups with their friends. There was no one close enough to hear them.

"If you're sharing tips..." she started.

Akamu raised an eyebrow.

"Why do you call her 'ancient one'? And not just you. Almost everyone else who knows the elder calls her that."

"It is important to know the weaknesses of all you meet," Lugopo added.

Akamu cocked his head. "For one who champions you, she is scarce with what information she shares."

"You have no idea," Silluka complained.

"Better to share strategic knowledge, so you may entrap those who try to use it against you," Lugopo said, then adjusted their circlet. "Or she may simply be secretive."

"I doubt most who address her as such truly know the reason why," he began. "But instead learn it by watching others."

"But you know," Silluka pressed.

"I know," Akamu confirmed. "It is a sign of respect, and especially with both her and Administrator Nina claiming her motherhood of the administrator, there are plenty of people in Chimor who know she is to be addressed as such."

Silluka noted the tentative words around Nina's parentage. That was a question for another time.

"Then what does it mean?"

"*Ancient one* is an old address, saved as a term of respect only for those few who have ceased aging."

Silluka stared. That...had not been what she was expecting. Yet suddenly all the elder's vague references to where she had been and all that she had seen made more sense.

"And that is unlocked how? By connection to the core? Practice? A chayu?"

Akamu crossed his arms. "*That* part, I do not know. Nina has dropped a few hints that she has some insight into the topic, but I fear even she does not fully understand the method."

"Will work on a technological answer," Lugopo chirped. "Perhaps removing all those hard bones will help." They swarmed up to Silluka's shoulder, three tentacles probing the joint.

"I doubt that's it," Silluka said. She was soaked with sweat, and tired.

"Doubt what's it?" Both she and Akamu whirled at Elder Quilqi's cracked voice.

"Or perhaps it is the amount of core stored in the *sunqu*," Lugopo pondered. "An implanted meter would show what power is required for ageless—"

Silluka flicked the Allwiya's circlet with a finger.

"That is, I shall devise new techniques to study this," Lugopo finished, their eyes focusing on the elder.

Elder Quilqi scanned all three of them, even Akamu looking a little guilty. That sense of pressure bumped up against Silluka again, and this time it felt as if it were measuring. But it was gone before she could feel anything else.

"Then you've performed all three full chayus, have you, girl? Shells and steel, the turtlemen have wasted no time. I've come from the arena registration office and the Eztli Mecatl have already started signing up their champions for the arena fight. I think we should sign you up too, as soon as you test."

Silluka gaped. Between Akamu's pushing and the elders, she felt like a piece of jerky being tugged between two ravenous jakua.

"I can't fight a turtleman," she grumbled.

"You can and you will," Elder Quilqi said. "Because powerful entities are closing in on Chimor faster than you can imagine. These fights have meaning. The more the Huaca lose, the weaker the Uncles, Aunts, and Entles become. The gods are in contention now, and it's going to require all of us to come to their aid."

CHAPTER FOURTEEN

Broken Vials

Ichu worked with Cosquella inside Amoxtli's little house. It was deserted, now its resident had been slaughtered by the turtleman leader. A perfect place to practice arts that were not quite of the Huaca. A tribute. Ichu wouldn't have felt comfortable in the gymnasium now, and he felt this gave a little respect to Amoxtli's legacy. He'd tried to look into her contacts for those she tended to in the morning, but he hadn't found any schedules yet—not that he could have read them—and didn't know enough people in the city to seek them out himself.

"I am hoping Silluka performs well, I do," Cosquella said as they moved the late Eztli Mecatl's table to one side of the room. "I wanted to be with her there, today."

"You'll be there at her test in three days, as will I," Ichu told her. "But we both need to learn what we can do if we ever want to equal her or even support her. I have a feeling she will need it." Elder Quilqi had been pushing Silluka to do more, faster, and he sensed the elder was very nervous about something, even if she didn't share what it was or give any outside indication.

"You say you have learned the Eztli Mecatl magic. But that was working with one of them, it was." Cosquella set a chair down with a thump. "Will it work with the two of us?"

"Only one way to find out." Ichu stepped up to Cosquella. She was taller than he was, her shoulders broader. That intimidating Eztli Mecatl heritage. She smelled sweet, though, like a field of wildflowers. It was obvious why his sister was drawn to that power. He lifted a hand. "May I?"

Cosquella's chin went up. "You said you had to touch each other a lot, did you?"

Ichu lowered his hand. "Only to make a connection. Nothing we can't tell Silluka about."

"Fine." Suddenly Cosquella looked embarrassed. "It's only...I hadn't had another close friend like Silluka before, me."

The simple confession left Ichu feeling suddenly protective. "Cosquella, you and Silluka are perfect together. Your strength and her drive—you're amazing together. The whole idea of the Eztli Mecatl magic is to support each other, to give when needed, and receive when you are vulnerable. There's a beauty in it I found with Amoxtli. It makes me dislike what the turtlemen do all the more." He opened his hand toward her. "I'd like to show it to you."

Something melted in Cosquella. Her shoulders sagged, and she nodded. "I'd like that."

Ichu tentatively reached out, his index finger just touching Cosquella's temple. She didn't quite flinch, but he could tell she had to stop herself. Her skin was not as rough as it looked. It was actually smooth, but textured, like little scales.

"Here is a connection point," he said, "used for giving abilities of the mind, and of speed, from what I know." He took his finger away and Cosquella visibly relaxed.

"This will feel strange." She tensed again and he reached out one finger to touch between her eyes. This time she did flinch back. "This is a node point for both Huaca and Eztli Mecatl. It feels even more uncomfortable the more of the core's power you have within you. Amoxtli didn't mention much about it, but I believe it can transfer some of the strongest mental attributes."

He continued, marking every point he could remember from what he and Amoxtli had practiced. Ears, cheeks, throat, shoulders, biceps, elbows, wrists, fingers, heart, stomach, *sunqu*, pelvis, thighs, knees, feet...there were many possible connections to transfer gifts from one practitioner to another. As they progressed, Cosquella became more comfortable with his fingers on her, even asking questions about the exact placement. Some of the points benefitted from fingers turned vertical or horizontal, or even the hand placed fully flat over the largest areas, like the heart or *sunqu*.

"Now you," he said, and Cosquella blinked at him. She lifted a massive palm, wider than his hand, her nails black and thick, turning it over in the air.

"I only practiced this for a short time," he clarified. "Part of this is simply to be certain I remember as many points as possible. I know there are more, but Amoxtli didn't get to share them all with me. It's possible we'll learn more from other Eztli Mecatl, but for now, we need to encode as many as we can in our memories. It's like memorizing a chayu. Make it so natural to your body that your hands can perform the action without conscious input."

"I see," she said. She pursed her lips, small wrinkles forming around the edges, and Ichu recognized how her mouth was like a softer form of a turtleman's beak, though much more mobile, the color and flexibility more like a Huaca.

She repeated the points he'd demonstrated on her, her fingertips surprisingly dry and not rough, but again, textured, or ribbed, like her fingerprints were exaggerated. He carefully controlled his mouth not to show any sign of a smile. He wondered if Silluka had a chance to appreciate those unique fingers yet. If he said anything here, he was certain Cosquella would never work with him again.

"Good," he said instead. "Remember those places. I'm going to try making a sacrifice to you."

"What will I feel, eh?" she asked.

"You tell me when you feel it," he answered. "I want to make sure this is working before trying anything more complex."

"Fine then."

He followed the same sequence Amoxtli had tried on him that first time, connecting with her heart, stomach, *sunqu*, thighs, knees, and feet. Even before he was done, he could feel the energy leaving him, heard her breathing speed up.

"That's working, it is," Cosquella's voice was excited. The moment he took his hands from her feet—looking much like Amoxtli's, now he was close to them—she was away and pacing. Ichu felt the drain within him, as if he'd practiced chayus all morning.

"Now see if you can give it back." He tried not to sound concerned at how weak he felt. This was the issue with giving to others without the support of the core and the gods. There was only so much to give. One person's energy was much the same as another's, comparatively.

Cosquella stopped pacing and took him in. She must have seen something, because she frowned. "This is your energy, it is." He nodded.

She followed the same sequence on him, and the energy flooded back once she made the connections. He took in a deep breath.

"Good. Now do the morning ritual with me."

"But I've never been able to make that work, me," she said. "The energy, it doesn't stick to me."

"That's fine. I've been practicing now I know where my *sunqu* is." He'd gotten better at connecting to the new position, even if Lugopo still recorded a reduced amount of "Tortoises" when he performed a chayu. "It will help to open you to the gods of the Huaca. You're at least partly under their eye. Maybe it will give you a little more energy to work with."

Cosquella was even worse than Silluka had been when she first started, but he walked her through the morning ritual, performing it well enough himself to capture at least some of the energy in his *sunqu* when they were done.

"I shake like a leaf when I try chayus, I do," Cosquella complained.

"Then you've never felt the effect of a chayu before, have you?" He grinned, hoping what he planned would work.

"Never."

"Let's try an easy one. You know *Jakua's Claws*?"

Cosquella waggled a hand.

"Try it with me anyway." It was a simple chayu, quick to perform and mostly focusing on hand and arm movements. It could be performed in Basic stance rather than Dexterity with no real loss of power. In some respects, Cosquella was the opposite of his sister. She had both arms, and was much more capable physically, but lacked the mental connection to the chayus he and Silluka had. *Jakua's Claws* had been impossible for Silluka, using the methods of their original Huaca, simply because she couldn't make the required finger motions. Cosquella could, if shakily.

They performed the chayu together, and the ampuka spread around him, tinged yellow to show the connection with Uncle Sky. There was no ampuka around Cosquella.

"Quickly, while it's active." Ichu turned to her, careful in how he moved his hands. With *Jakua's Claws* active, he could tear through cloth, flesh, bone, and even stone with just a touch. Depending on the stance, it could be adjusted to rake, grab, tear, or even catch objects.

He hadn't given this chayu to Amoxtli, as they'd focused on longer ones, so he let his previous connection with Cosquella guide him, touching once over her heart, then at her elbows, wrists, and each finger and thumb. As he did, the aura shifted around him, moving through his hands to her.

"It's working!" Cosquella moved back after he finished, the loss of the chayu leaving his hands feeling suddenly weak. "I feel the power behind this, I do." She looked for something in Amoxtli's house she could demonstrate on.

"Outside," he suggested. The stone wall of the edifice the house was carved from was rough and pitted from decades—centuries?—of use.

They went to the back of the house, which pointed directly at the wall of Chimor. Cosquella placed one hand flat on the stone, and gripped, her fingers digging in like it was made of soft mud. She pulled a chunk of stone free, crushing it to dust in one hand. Then she closed both hands together and squeezed, meshing the particles into a lump of glowing rock.

"Aie—it's hot!" She dropped the stone, which was shaped like the inside of her palms, and it sizzled on the ground. She turned over her palms, which weren't even burned.

"A powerful chayu," she said.

Ichi stared. "It's not supposed to be that strong. I can break rock with *Jakua's Claws*, but to press stone chips together like tree resin…" He tapped the popping and glowing rock with the edge of one sandal, but hurriedly pulled his foot back from the heat. "Your hands aren't even burned."

The aura was already fading from Cosquella's hands. "Then why was it stronger, was it? Does it come from us working together?"

Ichu shook his head. "I don't know, but we need to experiment more with this. The Eztli Mecatl magnify their efforts by working together. Maybe this is the same."

They tried several more quick chayus, *Tortoise's Heavy Foot*, *Tree in the Wind*, and *Quirra Washes His Paws*. In each, the effect was amplified when he sacrificed it to Cosquella, though the duration was shorter. Soon the alley behind Amoxtli's house was covered in pits and scratches, and Ichu felt as drained as if he'd won another bodycasting competition.

"Whether it's the chayu passing through first my *sunqu* and then yours, or amplified because of your strength, whatever it is, I think we can say this was a success," Ichu said.

"I agree, I do." Cosquella was standing even straighter, her head nearly brushing Amoxtli's ceiling. "This is the power you feel from the chayu?"

"It is. There's only one last test." Ichu went to the drawer Amoxtli had shown him, filled with the Eztli's Mecatl's vials. If they could store this power, both of them would be closer to matching his sister in strength.

He held one of the small vials in front of himself, gathering his nerve. He had not yet given himself leave to use the vials he and Amoxtli created. His memories of that first time still woke him, some nights, his *sunqu* clenching.

Would they work for Cosquella too? Either way, they would have to actually drink these to test them. The last time he did that, Elder Quilqi and Silluka pulled him from the brink of death. Surely, this would be different? Amoxtli had never said there was a risk to using the vials. She seemed to think it was a natural part of the magic. Akamu had said they were safe. Now that his *sunqu* had moved, could he absorb a vial with no ill effects?

"What is the method for storing the magic in the vial?" Cosquella asked.

Ichu shook off his thoughts. He couldn't show her any of his worry. "Amoxtli said she wasn't certain if I'd be able to do it. It's a higher skill, like Mental or Pressure Adept for the Huaca, at least for the Eztli Mecatl. I don't know how the turtlemen have changed it. It was powered by a god, but now there is no god to oversee it. Yet Amoxtli still made several vials with me."

"A conundrum then. Shall we try it?"

Ichu thought. "Amoxtli was the one to make the vial, after I gifted the chayu to her. But I have to give the chayu to you. Maybe we can try together? The chayus I passed to you were amplified. Maybe working together will help. This magic is based on sacrifice, after all."

"What chayu?" Cosquella paced across the little room's floor.

"Offensive, defensive, or utility?" Ichu asked her. "That's generally how I break down their use in my head."

"What about a defensive one? May be useful in a pinch, it might, and I feel I have the offensive part taken care of." She clenched a fist.

Ichu nodded. "You know *Caterpillar Weaves His Cocoon*?" At Cosquella's frown, he gestured to the open floor. "Just follow me. It's mostly core muscles."

Cosquella followed his direction and movements, though not well. Ichu was able to connect to the ampuka again, feeling the cocoon of protection form around him, orange with Aunt Harvest's power. Once again, Cosquella was left with nothing after.

"Now what?"

Ichu brought the vial to his forehead as he'd seen Amoxtli do. He closed his eyes, trying to feel out the power in him and give it to the vial as he'd given power to Cosquella. But the vial didn't have a *sunqu*, nor points of power. It didn't have a body. He sighed, opened his eyes, and lowered the vial.

"I don't even know where to begin."

"Maybe I can do it, since I'm half of an Eztli Mecatl?" Cosquella suggested. "Transfer it to me."

Ichu shrugged, the vial in one hand, and touched her temple, throat, shoulders, heart, *sunqu*, and knees. That felt like the right combination to transfer the chayu, but the connection was sluggish, as if something was in the way. They could both feel it.

"The vial," Cosquella said.

"Oh, of course," he answered. It had been in his hand while he transferred the power. Maybe there had to be nothing between them...

"No, I mean *look* at the vial, I do!"

Ichu turned over his hand to see an orange glow in the vial—not enough to even partially fill it, but a skim of viscous liquid in the bottom.

"Maybe it transferred through the vial when it went between us?" Ichu's eyes roved the room as he tried to rationalize what had happened. The rest of the ampuka surrounded Cosquella. Had any been lost? Had the chayu multiplied like before?

"Then can we do it again? What if I pass it back to you?"

Ichu gave her the vial, and she began the sequence, touching points on him. Afterward, there was a little more in the vial, yet he felt the effect of *Caterpillar Weaves His Cocoon* more vividly, as if it had been amplified by its passage.

"It's stronger, and there's more in the vial, too," he said.

"How many times can we pass this chayu, can we?" Cosquella wondered. Ichu had never done it more than twice, once to Amoxtli or Cosquella, and once back to him. Could the Eztli Mecatl keep transferring power between two people? Surely *someone* had tried on an entire island of inhabitants over hundreds of years.

"Maybe it will amplify each time," he said.

But when he tried to give the chayu back to Cosquella, his *sunqu* seized and he doubled over, breaking the connection with her and dropping the vial like it was filled with lightning. Cosquella stumbled back from him as if pushed and gripped her belly.

"That answers that question, it does," Cosquella panted when she could breathe again.

"Agreed," Ichu mumbled. It was like he'd taken a dagger to his intestines. He waited, testing his *sunqu*. Had he injured himself again, mixing magics? When would he learn?

But then the feeling faded, and Ichu stood straight. It was as if he'd been punched in the gut without tensing first. The pain was fast transforming to a dull ache, but not debilitating.

"I...don't think that was anything permanent," Ichu hazarded. "When I first...when I first drank from a turtleman vial, the effect was slower building, but worse. This feels more like...a warning."

"I hope it was." Cosquella's face had gone gray and she winced as she moved, testing out the injury. "I would not want my first brush with the core to be my last, I wouldn't."

Ichu looked down to the floor, where the vial lay broken, glowing orange energy leaking out to dissolve into the air.

"Should we try again?"

"One more time," Cosquella said. She looked through the single window in Amoxtli's home. "And then we should get back to the others."

They decided to try *Quirra Hides His Nuts*, simply as a chayu with general utility. They passed the chayu to each other once, passing it through the vial, this time the yellow glow of Uncle Sky surrounding them. There was only a sliver of power in the vial, but it was something. Whether it only gave a fraction of the power, or only lasted a few seconds, there was no way to know until they tried.

"Time to get back," Cosquella said. "I feel bad about leaving Silluka all day, I do, but at least we have an exciting tidbit to tell her."

Ichu hesitated only a moment before smiling back at her. He had contemplated waiting until they'd fully researched what they could do, even keeping it from Silluka, but Cosquella was right. If only for safety when they used the vial, someone else should know.

Besides, he wanted to see the look on Elder Quilqi's face when they showed the glowing energy to her.

On the walk back to the refugee camp, there was a palpable air of tension. The Misini guards were everywhere, and there were already rumors of turtlemen harassing Chimor residents, trying to haggle vendors down to unreasonable prices, and generally proving a nuisance. Ichu wanted to simply blame the people as a whole, but he had seen the line of craftsmen and workers who set up house in the refugee camp. These were not the warriors who had attacked them. This was everyone else, dragged along from the destruction of their island. They simply wanted to live. Were their cultural differences great enough to warrant so much friction?

He almost bumped into Cosquella as they turned into a cross-alley a few streets away from the camp. When he looked around her sizeable shoulder, he also saw the group of three turtlemen youths leaning up against the wall of the alley. No Misini were present here. He knew enough of them now to identify one as dressed in their feminine-presenting garb, and the other two in male. They were passing a half-used vial between them guiltily, as if it were a cast-off they found in the trash. Each would take a small sip, sigh, and pass it to their neighbor.

When they saw Cosquella, all three pushed away from the wall. One growled something in their rough tongue, and Cosquella jerked back as if struck. What she said back in their language did not sound agreeable.

The three spread out across the width of the alley, blocking the way.

"They say there is a new rule in the refugee camp that no crossbreeds are allowed. They're making this up, they are."

"I gathered that part," Ichu said wryly. "Shall we go a different route?" The best fight was one he was not in.

But the lead turtleman drank a third of what was left in the vial and passed it along. The others did the same. Their eyes began to glow that unearthly purple.

"I would like to, I would, but I don't think that's an option," Cosquella said. She fell into a Strength stance, hands clenched.

Then the three were on them. Ichu started *Jakua's Claws*, but had no time to finish it. The motions were still useful to block, but if he'd had the chayu saved he could have used its full power. Beside him, Cosquella swung a meaty fist that connected with one of their assailants' beaky mouths. The turtleman rocked back, but not enough to make a clear path for them.

Ichu ducked a punch that splintered stone behind his head. These turtlemen were determined, and strong, bolstered by whatever had been in that vial.

But they had their own. "Drink it!" he called to Cosquella.

She growled something and fished out the vial from a pocket while her other hand deflected a fist coming for her head.

Ichu went on the offensive, forcing the three turtlemen to deal with him. Unaided by any chayu, their blows fell hard on his arms as he blocked their strikes. Even with only one vial split between them, these turtlemen were strong. He heard a crack as a blow landed heavily on his wrist and pain blossomed. Maybe not a full break, but their blows were hard enough to fracture bone.

Cosquella raised the yellow liquid to her mouth and tilted her head back in one motion. His eyes followed the glow. He could almost taste it himself, but was forced to raise his guard at a fist that would surely pulp all the bones in his arms.

But the hit didn't land. Cosquella, surrounded by the ampuka, picked their opponent's punches out of the air with swift dexterity, redirecting them so their punches landed on each other instead, driving them apart. Her hands moved faster than he could follow. *Quirra Hides His Nuts* was used to increase dexterity. He'd never seen it used offensively before, but then, Cosquella had no training with the chayus.

She squatted, and suddenly the legs went out from under the middle of the trio, putting him flat on his back. Ichu hadn't seen what she did, but dashed through the opening, getting behind the other two, pushing one face-first into the alley wall, wincing at the pain in his wrist. He heard a *crack* from behind him and looked over his shoulder to see the last one reeling back from Cosquella's punch.

There was power here. Amoxtli had said the turtlemen perverted the magic so it was taken, not given. Could he strip the power in that vial away from his opponent? He pushed the turtleman farther into the stone, ignoring what must be curses in his native tongue. Ichu barely kept from getting pushed back, while letting his intuition guide him. He touched the back of the turtleman's bald head, then ran a finger down the raised and plated spine, where ridges under thick cloth felt like a wall of bone or shell. The turtleman's curses turned fearful, and they struggled, but weakly. Ichu dared to imagine he felt strength flowing into him. Was this actually working? He should stop, but the urge to make the connection was increasing. He needed to see what would happen.

He kept one of his opponent's arms pinned flat to the wall, touching the back of the bicep, elbow, and hand. That limb dropped uselessly, and he did the same on the other arm. The turtleman was barely conscious now, and Ichu darted away for a second to pick up the vial Cosquella had dropped to the ground, thankfully not broken in the mud of the alley.

He held it in one hand, keeping the turtleman easily pinned with one hand to his back plates, then flipped him.

The turtleman's eyes rolled. He should stop. But he didn't want to. Ichu touched the turtleman's heart, *sunqu*, knees, and feet, the vial in that hand.

A sense of peace descended on him. Was that all? That's what his intuition suggested for connection points.

He heard the *thunk* of their last assailant hitting the ground and stepped back. The sharp pinch in his wrist disappeared and he rolled his hand in wonder.

The one he had grappled slid down the wall. But something was off. He looked smaller. Was the turtleman...collapsing? What was happening?

"Cosquella?" his voice shook as he pointed. She came up beside him, the aura faded from her arms.

"Is he...disintegrating? What did you do?" There wasn't an accusation in her voice, just concern.

"I tried to take away the power the vial had given him, but..." He watched helplessly as the turtleman slumped and curled, a line of what looked like dust floating away from him.

And toward Ichu. He stepped back, but the dust followed him. It was centered on his hand, the one with his now-healed wrist, and he opened it to see the vial filling with a purple so deep it was almost black. He hastily dropped it, but the line of particles only increased, the vial rolling and hopping along the ground to the remains of the turtleman, which were fast disappearing.

In moments it was done, and a full vial rested where a being had stood mere moments before.

"I didn't mean—" He couldn't finish the statement.

"No, you didn't, did you," Cosquella said. She put a massive hand on his shoulder, and he narrowly avoided flinching. He hadn't meant to *kill* him.

"They attacked us, and we have new magic we don't understand, we do." Cosquella's voice was firm. "We cannot be at fault for what we cannot know. My father, he said that. Maybe as a lesson from his own actions, it was."

Ichu swallowed, looking at the vial. He had killed others before, even other turtlemen, but not like this. His opponent had been helpless, and Ichu could have stopped, but he felt compelled to complete the sequence and make a full connection. Was this the difference between giving and taking? When giving of yourself to someone else, you could decide when to stop.

"We must go, before the others wake up, they do," Cosquella said. "Take the vial with you. We will decide what to do before we arrive home, we will."

Ichu moved as if in a daze, picking up the uncomfortably warm, dark vial. Cosquella pulled him behind her, heading to the refugee center. As they left, his arms felt like lead, as if the fight had drained even more from him than he expected.

CHAPTER FIFTEEN

Mental Adept

Silluka paced across the little house, swinging around Elder Quilqi sitting in a chair each time she made a lap.

"I knew it. You are spawning now? Such increased activity is good to push eggs out," Lugopo observed from the elder's shoulder.

"No, I'm worried," Silluka said, not even acknowledging the Allwiya's strange question. They'd been going on about it ever since they learned about her girlfriend's heritage. "Cosquella is usually here before me. I should be wrung out from everything Akamu put me through today, but I'm doing this." She gestured to her nervous pacing. "I just want to lie down, but I can't stop."

"You've been increasing your *sunqu*'s power, girl. It does wonders for your energy levels."

"The Misini are supposed to be guarding Chimor from the turtlemen, but they're using it as an excuse to harass Huaca too. The turtlemen have set up guards around the camp, and they keep accosting the ones who come in. Are they going to stop her, now they know what she is?"

"Your brother is there with her..." the elder started, before the door banged open, revealing Cosquella guiding Ichu, who clutched a turtleman vial to his chest. It seemed even darker than the others they had seen.

"We took a little detour, we did," Cosquella said. She guided Ichu to a seat and sat him down, even as Silluka went to her.

"You had trouble with turtlemen? Or with Misini?" Silluka hugged Cosquella, reaching up on tiptoes to peck her on one rough cheek.

"Trouble...ha. You could say that." Ichu was staring off, that vial still in his hand.

"Where did you get that?" she turned to Cosquella. "He didn't steal another one from a turtleman, did he?"

"Steal!" Ichu's laugh was not so much that as a bark.

It took some time to get the story from them, and soon after they started, Elder Quilqi sat up, then started frowning, then started pacing herself. Silluka felt no urge to move from Cosquella's side.

"And you took that vial as a trophy when you killed one?" the elder broke in when they described how Ichu had knocked down one of the turtlemen and he didn't get up. Then Cosquella and Ichu almost fell over themselves explaining what *else* they had found that day. They seemed eager to get away from the topic of the fight, in fact. Ichu especially liked to recount how he used to win in sparring matches. But maybe they were both just excited about this new magic. Silluka watched the joy in her girlfriend's face. She almost would have been jealous of Ichu being with her, except she knew how much he doted on Akamu. He would never do something like that to her.

"Bones and dust! You two have been busy." Elder Quilqi crossed her arms, and Lugopo repeated the gesture on her shoulder with four tentacles. "The amount of magical mixing going on is alarming to say the least. But at least I know how to pick my champions." She rounded on Cosquella. "So, you're finally showing up. You say you've drunk one of the vials you made? Any ill effects? Pain in your *sunqu*? Dizziness?" The elder peered at Cosquella and it seemed the air thickened in the room. Cosquella rocked back and Silluka held her arm to steady her. She was getting tired of the more advanced practitioners throwing around whatever that trick was.

"Then are we just tools to you?" she asked the elder, suddenly angry. It felt good to let go of some of the day's frustration. "Game pieces to one who'll live forever while we wither away, *ancient one*?"

"Live forever?" Cosquella asked. "How's that work, does it?"

Elder Quilqi grunted. "I see someone's been spreading tales about me. Akamu, was it? No matter. That's nothing important compared to what's happening here." She turned back to Silluka and the burst of power hit her like a hammer, making her wheeze. She could actually feel her *sunqu* contract, as if in terror. "No, I am not using you as a *tool*, girl. You four are my champions. There are plenty of us dried-up sticks wandering around, if you look in the right places, but *this,*"—she spread her hands to encompass them all—"this is something new I haven't seen in all my years. New mixes, new magics, gods uprooted. I haven't seen that sort of turnover since...well, no matter. What's important here is we have a half-Huaca, half-Eztli Mecatl who's only learned magic from a Huaca once he'd been isolated from his gods."

Ichu opened his mouth to protest some part of that, but the elder held up a hand. "Let me get a look at both of you together. Cosquella has some threads that..." The air got thick again and Silluka felt as if she was standing with a weight on her back. She could feel more of the intent in the pressure now, though. This was analytical, searching. What the elder had done moments before was sheer intimidation. What did it mean that she was starting to understand the weight pressing on her?

"Yes. I thought so. I've glimpsed this in the Eztli Mecatl warriors who were following us. Your *sunqus* have a link now. There's a bond between you."

"I've felt that," Ichu said, his voice excited. "With Cosquella, like we're closer than before." Cosquella was nodding along and Silluka tensed. Was there more here than she thought, after all? "It's like she's another sister now." He reached out a hand for Silluka, who hesitantly took it. "I'm glad I can see her in some small part like you do. She's an incredible woman, strong and unbreakable." He put her hand in Cosquella's, where it almost vanished in the larger woman's grip. Something melted in Silluka and Cosquella enveloped her in a hug.

"I'm glad you've got to experience the chayus finally," she said. "It's such an amazing feeling." They really were alike and had been all their lives. Both of them different from those around them physically. Both treated as other.

Cosquella pushed back from her, making one hand into a giant fist. "I've got more behind these hands now, with the power of the chayus, I do. Just need a little help storing them up."

"Touching, but we all need to pay attention to what's around us," the elder said. "The turtlemen will take notice of their members dying. The other two must have moved the body of the third when they revived."

Ichu and Cosquella exchanged glances, and Silluka could see them recounting the encounter in their minds.

"Possible, it is, but I cannot say for certain," Cosquella said.

"The other two were knocked unconscious, but they must have woken up after we left, then found their comrade missing...this." Ichu held up the vial, still clutched in his hand. The elder glared down at it as if it had personally wronged her.

"Don't drink that," she said shortly. "The ones you made with the Eztli Mecatl woman are clean, but not this. Not until I have a chance to study it." She turned her head to Lugopo. "Do you have a tool able to discern its pureness?"

Lugopo swung down from her shoulder, landing on Ichu's thigh and reaching for the vial with three tentacles. "Can adjust my chayu sensor to detect the power of this vial."

Ichu let go—unwillingly, Silluka thought—and Lugopo scrambled away, the little blue and green Allwiya scuttling out and to their house, then returning with yet another creation seemingly made from metal wire and wood chips. So, it hadn't been lost after all. Lugopo must have stored it with their other inventions. They held up the vial and pressed the device to it. A kaleidoscope of color bled out against the wall: mainly slate gray, but with flashes of yellow, pink, and red throughout.

"New update, inspired by Whirling Abyss," they said. "This will show how gods contaminate objects!" They tapped the circlet. "That is, what gods have tinkered with mortal minds." Another tap. "How they play with our lives." They shrugged with another two tentacles and went on. "Seems like your Uncle Smith, Uncle Sky, Entle Love, and Aunt Healing all had input."

"Meddling minds! With the Eztli Mecatl god dead, it seems Tiyu Llamkay still has a large effect on them, even now."

"Well, he did have a large...influence on the turtlemen, from what we know," Silluka said carefully. There was no chayu here to keep the god's ears from hearing them. She wondered what deeper layers there were to Elder Quilqi's words.

"Uncle Sky's presence must come from *Quirra Hides His Nuts*," Cosquella volunteered. "That was the chayu I used, it was."

"And every time harm and connection come into play, Love and Healing are there," the elder said. "The gods do more than we give them credit for, often."

"It is interesting, this *combination*, though, isn't it?" Silluka asked. They kept hearing about Uncle Smith and Entle Love together.

"That it is. And something we can discuss later." The elder's words were warning enough for all of them. "As for the vial, I would not use it, for fear of *undue* effects." She waggled a finger between Cosquella and Ichu. "Neither of you. Shaking Islands, now there's two I have to warn."

"But you're certain the vials we create are safe?" Ichu pressed.

Elder Quilqi pursed her lips. "Against my better judgement, I think so. But I feel as if there is some mechanism I'm missing. This mixing of magics is a novelty. Perhaps it's simply my *old* mind trying to make sense of it." She shot a sidelong look at Silluka.

"You're not going to let that go, are you?"

"Absolutely not."

* * *

The elder had told them to stay close to their house that night, though Silluka would need to go back to the gymnasium in the next two days to prepare for her test for Mental Adept.

She paced the three steps across her bedroom. The anxious energy had left her while learning of what her brother and Cosquella had found, but now it was back. They had been fortunate to find one of the family dwellings in the refugee camp where she, Ichu, Cosquella, and the elder could all have a separate room. Now, she was regretting being alone.

As if in summons, there was a timid knock at her door. Silluka knew that knock. For being such a big woman, Cosquella was surprisingly shy at times.

"I heard you pacing, I did," she said when Silluka opened the door.

Silluka let go of the door and pulled her in, her hand barely reaching around Cosquella's palm. She pulled the other woman close, then let go to reach around her and pull the door to. Cosquella gave her a pointed look.

"Don't want to disturb anyone else," she said. She hooked her stump around Cosquella's elbow, reaching for the bed with her hand and pulling Cosquella to sit beside her. Her knee vibrated up and down with her nervous energy.

There was a comfortable moment of silence between them. There hadn't been many since they entered Chimor, and just as few while they were running from the turtlemen across the desert. She'd really only known the big woman a few weeks, but it felt longer than that, their attraction for each other tempered by their trials along the way. They'd both lost their parents, they were both on the fringes of their societies, they both looked different.

"Are you and Ichu well, after this afternoon?" Her brother had been more agitated than she had seen him in some time. They'd both had to defend themselves in the desert. It felt different within the confines of the Chimor.

"We will be well, I think." Cosquella looked down. "They wanted to do us harm. That was certain. They didn't expect us to have so much power. And it turned back on them. None of us knew what would happen. Your brother blames himself, he does, but I think he'll see the right of it, once we practice making the vials."

"How did it feel?" Silluka asked. There was no need to quantify. Cosquella had been struggling for weeks to feel any hint of the ampuka, to store part of the core in her *sunqu*. Nothing had worked until now.

Cosquella melted into her, leaning her head on Silluka's left shoulder. Silluka felt the solidity of her, the power.

"It was wonderful, it was. Your brother performed the chayu, but I did it with him. The Eztli Mecatl gift is completely opposite how the turtlemen act. He sacrificed to give me what he had created, he did, and it amplified between us. I'd never felt such energy within me."

Silluka smiled, pushing back into Cosquella. She'd thought the other woman's skin was rough when they first met, but the more she came to know her, the more she found it simply...textured. Like running fingers over a collection of polished pebbles.

But she was still antsy.

"What if we go up to the parapet over the gate?" she suggested.

"The elder said—"

"I know, but it's almost dark. We can slip past anyone else out there."

"If you think we'll be safe..."

"We will be." She was almost a Mental Adept. Surely she could protect her girlfriend.

They snuck through the refugee center, leaving out the back way to slip across the streets toward the gate. Whether the turtlemen had set guards elsewhere, or the Misini had cleared a path, or they simply were lucky, Silluka didn't know.

She pulled Cosquella, her hand in the larger woman's, up the stairs and on to the gate rooftop. The turtleman's army was spread out below them, hundreds of twinkling lights from campfires and torches. All the new refugees in the city and there were still this many out here.

"It is everyone from their island?" she asked.

"I wonder if anything is left on their island. It crashed hard into our coast, it did," Cosquella said.

"What do you think of them, now you...know?" Cosquella had been raised fully Huaca. Did she have any loyalty to the Eztli Mecatl?

"The ones who taught us, they were good people, they were, but these?" Cosquella shook her head. "I'm certain some of them are, but we've tangled with their warriors, and now even their tradespeople bully us."

Silluka stepped up to the parapet, one foot on the crenellation.

"When I performed *Flying Quirra*, I flew across a canyon deeper than this drop. It's like the thrill of the magic in you, isn't it?" Silluka reached out with her hand to run fingers down Cosquella's arm.

"And now you're testing for Mental Adept, you are." Cosquella stepped closer to her. "Things are moving fast."

Silluka stepped back down and relaxed into Cosquella's side. "There are still two days. I just want to be, for now."

"I can help with that, I can." Cosquella put her other hand on top of Silluka's, and a thrill ran through her. She shifted sideways until their thighs pressed against each others', both looking out over the army.

"Then let's be. Together." Silluka raised her hand to Cosquella's face, running fingers over her cheek. Like pebbles in a stream.

She leaned in for a kiss.

* * *

Two days later, Silluka entered the large room at the back of the gymnasium. It was closed off from the rest of the building, but open to the sky, light shining down from a clear day. Akamu was waiting for her, his amber armor active and reflecting every stray ray of light. The other three judges were with him, each in their own armor: sapphire for the storm warriors, bright orange for the fire warriors, and a deep purple teal for the sea warriors.

She had armor of a sort as well. She'd spoken several times with Elder Quilqi and Lugopo about wearing the suit. Lugopo was all for it, naturally, and their argument consisted of a lot of reasons why the suit would give them unlimited power, intimidate the judges, and potentially challenge the gods themselves. Elder Quilqi stated again that the suit was a crutch, but admitted it would be a "helpful gadget, for a time."

Silluka eventually decided to wear the suit. She had stored *Jakua's Fight* while wearing it, and while she had not stored the other two, at Akamu's suggestion, she felt it would be better to have all three either stored with the suit or without, rather than a mix. The elder was convinced it would make a difference whether sections of the chayu could be released with or without the suit, but Silluka was uncertain. When she had fought the Allwiya's insect-like vehicle in the desert, she had accidently tangled her *sunqu* because she didn't know her intent had been different with and without a right forearm and hand.

But if she was aware of that difference, could she hold the difference of her intent in her mind while performing the chayu so that it wouldn't make a difference?

She would see today.

"Are you ready?" Akamu leaned down as she entered, guiding her to the other three judges.

"I think so. It's a bit nerve-wracking to be in front of all of you." She'd only started to realize how far ahead of her the leaders of the warrior sects were, and how far their leader, Nina, was above them. And Elder Quilqi was more advanced than any of them? Silluka didn't even know what the adepthoods were, for certain, past the Pressure Adept, the stage after Mental Adept.

"It is, usually, especially when you're all alone in here with us." Akamu gave her a wink as he guided her to the middle of a circular ring under the sun. It was inlaid in the stone floor, much like the one in the elders' building back in the village by the coast. "But someone made a fuss about not being allowed in, and, well, things spiraled from there."

He left her with that mysterious tidbit and took his place with the other three warrior leaders at the head of the room, each staring at her impassively. Coya, the leader of the fire warriors, paced back and forth like a caged Jakua, while Puric, the elderly leader of the sea warriors, lounged against the back wall. Tintaya of the storm warriors and Akamu both stood with hands clasped behind their backs, heads straight up.

"Which chayus will you demonstrate for us today?" came a deep voice behind her. She turned as Nina strode into the room. Silluka's breathing sped up as the pressure increased, forcing her shoulders down.

"*Jakua's Fight, Tortoise's Growth,* and *Quirra's Day,* Administrator." Silluka was happy her voice hadn't squeaked. Was she now being judged by the administrator as well?

"And that...contraption you're wearing. Will it interfere with your motions?" Administrator Nina took a station between Akamu and Tintaya, taller than either of them by head and shoulders.

"No, Administrator." Silluka swallowed. Was she not allowed to wear this?

"It has the smell of the Allwiya gadgetry," Coya complained, still pacing. "This is a test of the Huaca, not of another species."

"Yet there is nothing to say it is not allowed," Akamu argued.

"Circles and suns, Nina! At least don't smother the girl before she has a chance to show you what she has."

Silluka spun to the voice, to see Elder Quilqi leading Ichu and Cosquella, Lugopo riding her girlfriend's shoulder.

"Speaking of unprecedented," Tintaya began.

The pressure in the room decreased, reluctantly, Silluka thought, giving one last press down on her head and neck before it retreated.

"My *mother* and I have come to an arrangement," Administrator Nina pronounced. "In exchange for her and her fellow spectators, I've agreed to lend my voice to the final judging."

Even Puric frowned at that, levering himself up from the wall.

"This is traditionally our purview, Administrator," he said blandly. "You are the judge of any we cannot, but a Mental Adept is a simple test for us to observe."

"Yet this is how it shall be," the administrator said, and all four of the warriors ducked their heads at the force in her voice. Maybe she pressed into them with her will like she had to Silluka.

She snuck a glance at her friends and family. Lugopo gave her an enthusiastic wave with four tentacles, but thankfully made no comments. Spouting about how she would bring destruction to the warriors would not help in this context.

Silluka stretched, feeling the confines of the suit as it guided and corrected her movements. Every action perfect, just as the people of her village practiced all their lives, but with the intent of a soon-to-be Mental Adept behind it. She felt Nina's eyes on her, as an almost physical force, but dared not look back.

"Shall I still call the test?" Akamu asked, and Nina bowed her head. As if that was a signal, Coya stopped pacing, and Puric stood straight, two warrior leaders to each side of Nina's bulk in the middle. All five Adepts stared at Silluka, and once again, the feeling of a weight on her increased until it was as if she carried rocks strapped to her back and front. She wasn't off-balance, thanks to the suit, but she felt slow and heavy.

"Silluka. You come here, having demonstrated the intent needed to connect to the core, to fill your *sunqu*, and to use that power in your chayus. Are you ready to formally test for Mental Adept?" Akamu stared straight at her.

Her mouth was dry. She hadn't been prepared for any of this. All Akamu and Elder Quilqi had said was that there was a test, with judges. Were there certain words she was supposed to say?

"I am," she replied, staring back at the judges.

"You can perform the three chayus, as stated, reliably?"

"I can." Silluka lifted her chin. She'd only known them for days, but she'd known their parts all her life. She could feel how the different sections fitted together. Was this the intent that came with being a Mental Adept? To know instinctively how to move?

"And have you stored all three chayus already in your *sunqu*?"

Akamu's mouth lifted in a slight smile the other judges couldn't see, and she remembered his words when they practiced.

"I have only stored *Jakua's Fight* in my *sunqu*."

Coya grunted at that, which Silluka considered a win.

"Then you are prepared to also perform the morning ritual before these three full chayu and store the other two as part of this test?"

"I will."

"Know that if you fail to store a full chayu, fail to complete a chayu or any segment of a chayu, or leave the circle in the middle of the floor, you will fail your test and will only be able to schedule a future test when all four— five—of us deem you are ready."

"I understand." Silluka kept her shoulders relaxed only with an effort.

Akamu looked down the row of Adepts, and each one gave a quick nod. That seemed to be the formalities out of the way, as Puric slumped back and Coya began to pace behind the others.

"Begin the morning ritual when you are ready," Akamu told her.

Silluka took in a deep breath, then released it. On her next breath, she spread her arms—both with hands and fingers thanks to the suit—in *The Wing Grows*, the first move of the morning ritual. It was as much a warmup as it was a way to open to the core.

Once she finished, several minutes later, the ampuka glowed about her, bright with all the colors of the gods. Even the gray of Uncle Smith and the pink of Entle Love were present in dim colors.

She concentrated and pulled the ampuka into her *sunqu*. She'd gotten better at this over the past weeks since learning about it on the sleds. Now, she could press all but a sliver of the ampuka deep inside, leaving only a small shine around her. The suit helped the process, refining her movements. It was even more fluid than before, the joints moving with tight precision. Lugopo had refined it further since being blessed by their god.

The energy of the core burned within her, but Silluka relaxed, her chest out, stomach tensed. She was ready to run miles or take on an entire army.

Or perform three full chayus in a row over the next half a day or more.

"Eight Tortoises of power!" Silluka turned at the exclamation. Lugopo held their refitted device to measure ambient power. "Shall this handcrafted device also be destroyed by your power?" They tapped the circlet. "I am hoping so!"

Silluka turned to the judges, ready to defend the Allwiya, but Tintaya was looking expectantly over her head.

"What is a 'Tortoise' in this context? You have devised a way to measure chayu power?"

If she had a chance to warn her, Silluka would have cautioned against asking Lugopo such an open-ended question. Instead, she ran through *Jakua's Fight* in her head, readying the component parts, getting her intent in line with what she would do.

"Yes, one Tortoise is base energy for a competent Physical Adept to perform *Tortoise Shoulders His Load*."

Lugopo scuttled down from Cosquella's shoulder and swarmed across the floor outside the ring. They held their device aloft with two tentacles, signing with another three. "Scale must be adjusted for further adept levels. More tribulation is needed." Tap. "More data. This test will be a perfect place to gather it."

"I still think they shouldn't talk," Nina grumbled.

Akamu cleared his throat. "Perhaps we can continue and see Lugopo's results at the end?"

Tintaya waved a hand and Akamu turned back to Silluka. "You may begin *Jakua's Fight* when ready."

And this was it. Once begun, she would lock herself into the movements for the next hour.

Silluka went into Dexterity stance, beginning with *Jakua's Claws.*

As she performed the chayu, the shape of Jakua grew around her, pouncing, swiping, lashing his tail, climbing and springing on his enemy, hiding to save strength and heal. The different aspects of the chayu poured into her, each one ready for a different purpose, but unused for now, ready to be drawn out later, when she learned how.

As she passed through the last moves of *Jakua Rests,* she became aware of the suit's glow around her. This time it was not hot enough to burn her, though it was uncomfortably warm. Silluka kept the wince from her face, standing tall as she rested.

Sweat dripped from her brow, but this was only the first of three chayus. The other two were longer. She recalled Akamu and his warriors taking days to recapture their powers when they were escorting the village on their sleds. Their movements seemed easy to her then. Would she be able to conserve more energy in her *sunqu* with more practice?

"Twenty-five Tortoises of energy this time! Such power shall rock the foundations of Chimor!" Lugopo raised three tentacles dramatically, their device held aloft. They were met with silence and tapped their circlet. "That is, there was a twelve percent increase. Quite illuminating."

Silluka could feel the chayus settling over where they had been stored before. There was not as much of a rush of energy this time, likely because she had already stored it. She controlled her breathing and focused her intent on *Tortoise's Growth*, the next full chayu. Her *sunqu* had been partially depleted to power this first chayu, but she had enough power to store the next two chayus. She hoped she did.

Akamu looked to the other judges, where they had moved around the edges of the circle through the first part of the test, observing her movements and technique for error. Behind her, Elder Quilqi and Ichu had taken seats to watch, while Cosquella stood, shifting nervously, and Lugopo prowled the back of the testing area on five tentacles, raising their device for readings.

"Approved." Puric was the first of the judges to speak.

"Fine technical detail," Tintaya said. She had spoken quietly with Lugopo as Silluka performed the first chayu.

"I'd argue some of the intent was weak in places, but passable," Coya said.

"I also approve," Akamu said, and looked to Nina.

The big woman came forward, pacing around Silluka, touching the suit at certain points.

"This creation, it acts as a further refinement of your skills. I would say it is an outside influence in your test, yet it does accommodate for your lack of a forearm. Be cognizant of how you direct your intent through it. This is the reason it becomes so hot. It is channeling the power of the core on its own, alongside your actions."

She stared at Silluka for a few moments more, and Silluka was ready to be told to leave and never come back, Elder Quilqi or no. Silluka was a country bumpkin from the edges of the Huaca. What could she possibly do more than those raised all their lives in Chimor?

"I approve," Nina said finally, and Silluka slumped in relief. "Let's see what you and this suit are capable of."

Silluka set herself and began *Tortoise's Growth* from Strength stance.

This chayu was half again as long as *Jakua's Fight*, and Silluka began to feel the drain halfway through. The suit was feeding off her movement, and her *sunqu*. It was draining what she had stored in the morning ritual faster than she would like. She would have some capacity left after this, but not much, and she still had another full chayu—the longest of the three.

The metal parts of the suit had gone red with heat and smoke rose from the wooden portions by the time she got to *Tortoise Sleeps*. The shape of Tortoise was all around her, his lumbering hulk describing shapes of power around her. She had not stored this chayu before, but she could already feel the segments drawing into her flesh.

She pulled her arms in front of her, rounding her shoulders over for the last move, barely able to resist the heat in the suit.

Around her, the shapes swirled inward, the magic lining up to store within her. The metal was a blaze against her skin, the smell of woodsmoke heavy in her nose. She felt a scream bubbling up within her. Her *sunqu* was almost empty. There was no way she had enough for *Quirra's Day* after this.

As her vision dimmed, she saw Tintaya take a step toward her, ready to catch her.

Then the suit connected with the full chayu. It went from blazingly hot to bitterly cold in an instant, the metal creaking alarmingly as it pressed into her skin, squeezing her. The shapes of Tortoise around her pulled inward violently, rushing to fill her body. Energy rushed into her *sunqu*, filling it more than it could possibly hold, spilling out around her in a blinding flash of colorless light. Silluka raised her hands, to shield her eyes, but her arms were glowing too. The inside of her eyes were glowing. All she could see were rings of light and shadows.

Then *Tortoise's Growth* was inside her and she fell forward to her knees, her teeth knocking together from the cold of the metal.

She looked up at the shocked faces of the judges, save for Nina, who looked thoughtful. Silluka pushed to her feet, her knees complaining at their abuse. She twisted to see her friends, but Elder Quilqi was in front of them, holding to Ichu's shoulder and Cosquella's hand. Lugopo looked like they were melting over her shoulder. Their device trailed from one tentacle.

"Approved," Nina's voice rang out. "Let's see your last chayu."

Silluka looked to the front, but the other warrior leaders said nothing, not even Akamu. She looked back at Elder Quilqi, who had crossed her arms. The elder gave her one small nod.

Filled with energy, and very confused, Silluka began *Quirra's Day*.

This was the chayu she knew least of the three, and it was the longest, though she felt the most connection with it. She and the suit moved as one, the extra energy from storing *Tortoise's Growth* sustaining her. In Dexterity stance, she began *Quirra Runs Down a Branch*.

Silluka let the suit guide her movements as she progressed through the chayu. Each part came naturally after the last. This was her favorite of the three full chayus she'd learned, even if it was the most complex. Especially with the suit, each segment of the chayu felt like a natural extension of her body.

Her attention didn't precisely wander during the chayu, but her mind became a separate entity from her body. She took stock of the others moving around the room while her body shaped the moves, Quirra's antics growing around her in ephemeral shadows shaded in the auras of the gods.

Her mind focused on how her body moved, even though it felt like the form of the chayu was controlling her, rather than the other way around. Lugopo's adjustments to the suit made its motions smoother than ever, and she discovered each movement made a connection to her core as her body locked into the exact place it should. Now she observed it, she sensed the suit was taking a bit of her energy every time, along with a bit from the core, gradually heating up.

By the time she neared the end, the suit was painfully hot, like a hundred wasps stinging her skin. She gritted her teeth against it, but there was no way to stop. The last few moves of *Quirra Curls Up* stretched before her, and she noted Elder Quilqi taking a defensive position again in front of her brother and Cosquella. Coya had ceased her interminable pacing and all four judges stood in a line, faces set, Nina slightly in front of them.

She was ready for the chayu this time when it set into her bones. The burning heat turned again to freezing cold, but Silluka wrestled against it, keeping the excess from escaping, wrestling it with her mind, restraining it from fleeing and storing as much as she could within her.

Her body was in agony, but her mind floated free as the shapes of Quirra's many escapades flooded into her. Her vision tunneled. Had she made too strong a connection to the core again? Was she going to pass out?

But no, even as her eyes rolled back, she saw into another place.

There were dozens, no, *hundreds,* of people moving around, in all sizes and shapes, each glowing despite the blinding light of what looked like a sun beneath them. As her (mental?) eyes adjusted, she saw there was an entire city in her vision, made of the same glowing substance as the sun beneath it. People passed in and out of dwellings like a city. Then realization slammed into her. This was the *core* she was looking at. Those were *gods,* in their physical forms. Just as she began to search for Uncle Sky, or Aunt Harvest, or any of her gods for confirmation, her mind snapped back, and she was in the testing room again. She blinked away the core's light, then realized what she saw was *herself,* glowing with almost as much light as in the vision. Even Nina had a hand up to shield her eyes.

"I believe I can say that was a success," Akamu finally managed as the light around Silluka dimmed. "Are there any who disagree?"

Coya opened her mouth, but Tintaya and Puric both shook their heads as Nina thundered, "Approved. Silluka, you are a Mental Adept."

Silluka turned to see Cosquella beaming at her. Lugopo held up a smoking mass in three tentacles. "Over eighty Tortoises of energy! The last reading, at least, when you destroyed another of my creations. This took much more effort to make!" They tapped their circlet. "That is two you have burned out. Good job!"

CHAPTER SIXTEEN

Registration

Ichu left the little house early in the morning. He had been stuck in the refugee camp for the last two days save for Silluka's test, but he had heard other Huaca whispering of another cross-species challenge coming soon in the arena. This was his chance to show off the new magic he'd been studying with Cosquella. He'd never be able to test for Mental Adept in the conventional way now his *sunqu* had shifted, but winning in a fight against one of the champions of Chimor? That would attract the warrior leaders' notice, and maybe even Nina's.

Silluka's test had been eye opening. He'd almost been pushed to his knees when she finished her second chayu, only saved by Elder Quilqi shielding him as she'd done up on the parapet. That wasn't normal for a Mental Adept test. He could tell that without Elder Quilqi muttering to Nina afterward where they couldn't hear. Silluka was amazing. Unusual. Had she always been such a prodigy, when no one had bothered to teach her, back in the village? What she could do was far beyond what the elders could ever teach them.

Akamu had spoken to him after, but even he was distracted at Silluka's performance. Ichu had to do something extraordinary to get their attention. He didn't work like a Huaca anymore. He was part Huaca, part Eztli Mecatl, and Cosquella was the same, though in a different manner. Perhaps they could test together, after he won a fight? Was that allowed? Would they even make up one Mental Adept?

He turned down a side street, skirting the outline of a turtleman guarding the entrance to the refugee center. They'd staked out their territory, leaving the Huaca there with few choices. The Misini had made a show the first few days, but when there was no overt killing, they had retreated into the shadows. That didn't help the shift in power between the groups. Once again, those who had been "undesirable" in the past had the best strategy: incorporate into the larger Chimor before it was too late.

Ichu had hidden the vial created from his turtleman assailant in the same chest with the others. He'd thought about carrying it around with him, but the pull of it was too strong—even more than the others. He could not drink that vial, knowing how it was made, what the sacrifice was. Both Elder Quilqi and Akamu said the other vials he made were safe. But though the power of them pulled at him, he couldn't bring himself to drink those yet either. He tried to put the terrified face of the turtleman out of his mind.

There had been other quiet clashes between Huaca and turtlemen besides the one he and Cosquella were involved in. Except for his fight, the Huaca always lost, save when Misini finally appeared to head off the fight. The Clade was definitely making a bid for power in Chimor. Akamu said the capricious gods of the Misini had been trying to gain the upper hand for decades, and now the Huaca gods were weak enough to challenge. Their first step was to take control of the safety of the city.

Ichu hurried toward the center of Chimor. He knew where the registration center was, next to the arena in which they'd watched both fights, but he hadn't been inside it before.

He was almost there when a hulking turtleman stepped in front of him, blocking his path. Ichu rocked back on his heels, his stance lowered into Dexterity, his hands clear of his tunic.

"You. Weak Huaca. Give victory to me."

So, some of them had learned his language.

Ichu held up his hands. This turtleman—turtlewoman?— didn't have any of the armor of the ones encamped outside the city, but she was bigger than him, with a thick wooden stick hanging from her belt. She wore a vest and pants that looked as if it were made of Jakua hide, the fur still on.

Plaits of grasses were arranged along her bare head, forming a sort of open hat.

"I have no quarrel with you. I'm simply wanting to get into this building."

The turtlewoman leaned forward. "No registration. Only with approval."

Now Ichu braced himself, running through *Tortoise's Heavy Foot* in his head if he needed to perform it quickly to boost his strength. His chayu were weak, but since finding the new placement of his *sunqu*, there was at least some effect.

"I don't believe you need to approve me to enter."

The turtlewoman nodded. "Everyone must give victory to me." She pulled a vial from inside her vest, a thick reddish liquid inside. Ichu's eyes went to it as it simultaneously turned his stomach, knowing where it came from. He wished now he'd stashed a few of his own inside his tunic. If this wasn't a good chance to drink one, when was?

"And if I don't give victory to you? If you give victory to me?"

The turtlewoman smiled at that. "We test. Who gives to the other?" She opened the vial and drank it. Ichu began *Tortoise's Heavy Foot*. It was a shorter chayu but still took more time than drinking a vial or releasing a stored version. Could he take on this opponent by himself? This was not one of the warriors who had chased them from the village. No warriors had been allowed in the city.

The turtlewoman let him complete the chayu. She'd likely seen other Huaca do the same thing.

But then she was on him, the moment he finished. Her eyes glowed red, her muscles taut, seeming larger than before. The effect of the vial?

He didn't have time to think. He pivoted on his back foot to the left, the turtlewoman's fist passing a finger width from his head, then drove a knuckle into her forearm, *Tortoise's Heavy Foot* amplifying his strike.

The turtlewoman grunted and shook out her arm, grabbing his tunic with her other hand. She lifted him bodily off the ground and pulled back her fist for a strike.

Ichu blocked it with both hands, thankful the chayu gave him extra strength. His hands still stung from the impact.

Then he was back on the ground, falling backward into a roll. He came to his feet, only to find a Misini sparring with the turtlewoman, weaving and ducking around her strikes like a wraith.

"Stay. Still." The turtlewoman grunted, but the Misini—it was Anuit, again—vanished and appeared behind the turtlewoman, a dagger pricking her neck. Was she watching Elder Quilqi's group? Why did she always turn up?

"We've warned you, Eztli Mecatl. No picking on the children, ya? No bloodshed."

Ichu drew himself up, but Anuit spoke over him as soon as his opened his mouth. "You are nothing, Huaca. Barely a Physical Adept. Not worthy of this place, or Anuit. Begone and stop tempting fights."

"I will register for the arena," Ichu said. "Neither of you will stop me—"

There was a sharp point of pain in his neck, and he stopped, back straight. Anuit—another Anuit—stepped from behind him, holding an identical dagger. "You think you can challenge Anuit, big Huaca? Your old woman, maybe she is an interesting challenge, but you? Bah." She leaned close, whiskers tickling his ear. "Do as you will. Get yourself killed. My gods will be amused, and I will gain prestige with them."

Then the point of pain was gone, and the other Anuit dragged the turtlewoman, grunting and straining against seemingly overwhelming strength from the catlike person, out of the way of the registration office.

As she was pulled away, her muscles bunching, eyes still glowing crimson from the vial, the turtlewoman laughed like rocks grinding together. Anuit pulled her around a corner, but the laughter followed Ichu, his eyes stuck to the corner as if they would come back any second.

A sudden weakness flowed through him, like the turtlewoman was taking some of his strength with her. Was she? The turtlemen worked better together. He had felt something similar when he and Cosquella defeated the three outside the refugee center. He frowned at nothing, because there was nothing to do about it. He had to learn of the differences in his magic, and this was the fastest way without a teacher. He had to use the vials he made in true combat. It was the only way to know.

Was he doing the right thing? Yes. He had to prove to himself he was still capable. He was the bodycasting champion of his entire village. Surely so many sparring victories meant he could face off against one of the contenders of Chimor. There had to still be contests between Huaca. He'd sign up for one of those first, test his mettle. They would be much less deadly than the champion matches Anuit had fought in.

He'd thought about joining the brawling club Cosquella told him about. She enjoyed the physical nature of it, but Ichu wanted the benefit of the connection to the gods. That club was for non-adepts—purely non-magical fights. Those training in adepthoods faced off in the arena, or tested, or both, to show their ability.

He went inside the registration office.

The building was one of the ever-present stone monoliths of Chimor, butting up against the arena, which stretched through the center section of the city. The inside of the building was hollowed out, the ground floor open on all four sides. The middle contained a group of desks, run by different species, though there were no other candidates here this early in the morning. He went up to the desk with a Huaca behind it, who was chatting with the spiky Kawchi next to him. He only turned away to glance at Ichu.

"No Huaca fights available. Only cross-species."

He turned back, but Ichu stepped up to the table, forcing him to pay attention.

"No fights between the same species? Why not?"

The man shrugged, obviously eager to be rid of him. "Orders from the city administration. And you know where they get their orders."

Ichu cocked his head. "From where?"

The man looked at him like he was a baby. "The gods, man. Where have you been living?" For some reason, now he was paying more attention.

The Kawchi next to him piped up in a squeaky voice, "Rumors, rumors! All around. They say The Clade called this one in. The Clade!" The Kawchi looked around uncertainly, as if one of the gods would step from a wall. Or maybe just one of the Misini.

Ichu looked to the other tables, one run by a bored-looking Misini. A larger Allwiya, almost as tall as his knee, perched on a second, and the last had a floating Yakurikra hovering behind it, tentacles waving lazily.

The Yakurikra seemed ill-equipped for combat, based on the healer who had treated him. Maybe they tied their opponents up in their tendrils?

He approached the Allwiya table. At least he knew their methods. But the Allwiya gestured abruptly with three tentacles, then started off into a long explanation—presumably—of which Ichu could only grasp a few words. There were a lot of negative gestures, and the table had no lists on it with the Allwiya's arcane scrawl.

"No fights available?" he hazarded.

The Allwiya made an affirmative gesture. He knew that one.

He went to the Yakurikra table.

"There is nothing for you here, I am afraid," came the languorous voice from the middle of the orb of their body. "As my friend Kuluni says, the only challenges open are the Misini, or..." they trailed off.

"Or what?"

One tendril pointed to the back wall, where a sheet of paper with scribbles on it was held by an iron nail driven into the stone. Cracks trailed away from the impact.

Ichu had a guess as to what that form was for. Hesitantly, he headed for the Misini table.

"Level?" The Misini almost snarled. This one was male-presenting, outfitted in diaphanous silks and other sleek fabrics that swirled around them, giving peeks of his gray and white fur beneath.

"Do you mean my Adepthood?" he asked.

"What else, big Huaca? You want to fight? You need to be Mental Adept not to die in the first few seconds. Want to give the crowd a show. Preferably Pressure or Elemental Adept, ya? So what is your level?"

Ichu considered lying for only an instant. Despite the Misini's seemingly universal aloofness, he'd seen how deadly Anuit was. But she was a champion. He hadn't seen any others. Perhaps there were easier opponents.

"I'm almost a Mental Adept," he hedged. "I think I can take on—"

"No." The Misini scooped up the list on his desk, covered in looping scrawls. He jerked his chin toward the list on the back wall, fangs glinting from the sides of his mouth. "Fight's two days from now."

Ichu turned to the list nailed to the stone wall. And it had been nailed there. The list was not pushed over the nail. Instead, the nail had been pushed through the list, into the stone.

There was only one opponent name on the list, or at least he assumed it was a name. There were three places with that same sequence of pictures, but two had writing matched beside them. The first had been crossed off, but the second was a series of loops and crosses, similar to the writing on the Misini's list.

Ichu couldn't even read Huaca script, much less the pictographs on this list. But as a guess, this was for turtlemen challengers.

There was a piece of burnt wood hanging next to the list, and Ichu reached for it. He couldn't test yet, and no other fights were available, not with magic at least. One chance to prove himself. To prove the vials he made worked. It was this or nothing. Or waiting. Waiting until Elder Quilqi determined he was ready, despite his magic being completely new, according to her. Waiting for some sign he was ready to fight again. Could he even know what that sign was?

Or he could find out by the direct route.

He picked up the charcoal and carefully drew out the two chayu signs that made up his name—two of the few he knew—in the last open slot on the list.

He walked out of the registration office.

* * *

"You are wanting death then?" Lugopo's translation circlet chirped. "Can assist with death if needed."

"I want you to *protect* me from getting injured. Like you did with Silluka. Can you make me something? A gadget, a way of using my magic better? I don't need a suit like her, but anything else would help. This fight is in two days."

Lugopo crossed two tentacles in front of themself, then another two on top of them. They sat on the chest in Ichu's room where he stored his vials. Another three tentacles signed at him. "You were the one to dismiss my inventions as toys and trinkets when they can destroy nations!" They raised two tentacles to the sky, then tapped the circlet. "That is, may cause discomfort to others."

"Fine. I apologize for my comments earlier," Ichu said, glancing at the open doorway. Silluka was on the parapet again with Cosquella, watching the turtleman army. Elder Quilqi was on another of her mysterious errands that took her all over the city. He'd asked her where she was going, only to be met with one of her non-answers.

"Apology accepted." Lugopo uncrossed their arms, then seemingly unable to stop themself, gestured with all six. "So many whispers from the unknowable gods! Obliviation, waiting to be bestowed!"

"Then what do your gods whisper around me?"

Lugopo looked upward, as if listening, and a cold shiver ran down Ichu's back. *Were* the Allwiya's mad gods whispering about him?

"A difference in magic. A new way of interacting with the gods." They rubbed two tentacles together. "Many possibilities. These vials you create. What is their efficiency level?"

"Their...what?" Ichu was lost.

"How much magic can you store?" Lugopo signed. Their signing was quick and choppy.

"We didn't even fill one vial, between Cosquella and I." Ichu went into more detail than he had to the others about transferring the magic back and forth and how it amplified.

Lugopo scurried back and forth along the chest, stopping to sign here and there. "Yes. There must be many efficiency improvements possible. But to pull the energy from one? Or the other? Or the core?" A white and splotchy black aura began to glow about them. They spun back to Ichu. "How close to destruction will you risk yourself?"

"Destruction? I want to win the fight, not burn to a crisp."

Lugopo tapped their circlet, still signing. "Burnout from core is likely"—another tap—"possible. This is needed in two days?"

"The fight is in two days," Ichu corrected. "I'll need to work with Cosquella to store as many vials as I can."

Lugopo produced a stick of chalk and a small slate tablet from somewhere. The little Allwiya was only as big as his fist, but seemed able to produce more objects from under their tentacles than physically possible.

"One day to be inspired by the gods, create a device no one has seen, capable of boosting magic of a new variety of ways, before you use it in a battle certain to destroy you!"

Ichu opened his mouth to object, or apologize again, but Lugopo tapped their circlet.

"Brilliant! I shall begin immediately." They leapt to Ichu's shoulder, producing a small length of string, which they quickly wound round his neck, bicep, elbow, wrist, and each finger.

Lugopo leapt back to the chest and waved two tentacles at him, signing with another two. "Go away. Come back tomorrow morning."

Ichu thought about objecting that this was his room, then thought better of it. He went to find Cosquella.

He had to wait until she came back with his sister. Silluka had taken less time in the past few days to train, not that he could fault her for that. But that meant she spent more time with her girlfriend. While commendable, that also meant Ichu couldn't practice his newfound magic, which also required Cosquella.

Elder Quilqi came back first, and Ichu tried to look busy, but the elder pinned him with a glare. "Squeaking floorboards! You look like you're waiting for a quirra to get caught in a trap. What are you up to?"

"Just waiting for the others." Ichu tried for nonchalance, but he had never been good at that. "Hoping to practice some more with Cosquella."

"You can still connect to the core by yourself, correct? You only need her for those mysterious vials. I'd like a better look at one of those."

"What for?" he asked, despite himself. If he actually got some information out of the maddening old woman, it would be worth the effort. "Can you tell me more about how they're made?"

"Hmm. Get me one, then, wherever you have them stored." Elder Quilqi gestured with her chin toward his room, and Ichu tried not to flinch. It was the most obvious place he would put them. She wasn't spying on him.

He ducked back into his room, about to apologize for interrupting Lugopo, but the little Allwiya was hanging upside down on his wall, suspended by a set of nails they must have installed in the last two minutes, though Ichu hadn't heard anything. A bright white-black glow was around them, and their circlet was chirping and pinging like a little lost bird. Their tentacles—all but the two that held them suspended—waved languidly in the arm, creating arcs Ichu could almost connect to images. The movement drew him in, until he shook his head, going to the chest. How long had he stood there?

He slipped out the purple vial containing *Eagle Watches from on High* and went back to the elder, looking only once over his shoulder at Lugopo. Maybe he would sleep out here tonight, if the little Allwiya was still in his fugue.

"Took you long enough." The elder accepted the purple vial from him, the feeling of weight in the room suddenly deeper, as if he had an entire basket of bricks on his back. She brought it to one eye, starting into it, or maybe through it. What could she see with her old eyes? How long had she lived? Silluka had accused her of being immortal, but the elder hadn't denied the accusation.

"This is part of *Eagle's Sight*, though I'm not certain which one. Either *Eagle Watches from on High* or *Wind from Eagle's Wings*. Whichever, it was performed well. I would expect nothing less. But this is not one you made with Cosquella, is it? There is a powerful Eztli Mecatl influence in it—more than the girl has right now."

"This one was made by myself and Amoxtli, before..." The pang of sadness at the old Eztli Mecatl's end was more than he expected, for only knowing her a week. "Cosquella and I only made two, but one broke and the other she used."

"Well, it's clear of whatever nonsense the warriors put in theirs." Elder Quilqi's mouth pinched like she'd eaten a bitter melon. "They feel contaminated, like a dumping ground used for a graveyard."

Ichu swallowed. He'd hidden the third vial he and Cosquella had made. The one that had sucked in the essence of the turtleman attacker. The knowledge sat on him heavier than the oppressive weight of the room. He didn't know what to do with it, nor what it would impart if he drank it. The need burned in him, tempered with his distaste of the results.

"You're certain this is safe for me to use?" A nod from the elder would be another affirmation he could stop pushing down that urge when it came up. He was so tired of being afraid of this new magic.

"You feel it, then? The need to drink more of the vials?" Elder Quilqi looked into his eyes, and the pressure deepened. Ichu's knees shook with the effort of holding him up, but he got the feeling this was nothing for the elder, merely a slip of her power let loose.

"Yes...yes Elder," he stammered.

"But you haven't. You're strong, I can say that much." She stood up and Ichu sagged as if his bones had been removed. "Yes, it's safe. It's good you are able to resist that pull if needed, but I'd encourage you to drink this, now I've checked it. Get used to the effects. It's liable to be a bit different from what you're used to."

He'd been holding back for so long, ever since he drank that first vial. The explicit permission was too much to bear, and he snatched the vial from the elder's outstretched hand and uncorked it. The smell washed over him as he raised it to his lips. It was like running across the grassland of the coast, seeing the shore far beneath, the salt smell mixed with fertile soil.

He drank the vial.

Instantly, the chayu blasted through him. He hadn't known there was a buildup before, as all the moves fell into place, but now it was easy to recognize in comparison. Eagle's wings soared out from his sides, in the purple of Entle Magic. Connections trailed out from him, as Eagle's sight revealed hidden information to him.

Silluka had sat at this table with Cosquella earlier this afternoon, talking. They had also snuck out of the house a few nights before Silluka's test. Lugopo's trail was heavy here, back and forth across the house. Little items and contraptions were hidden everywhere. How had he not noticed them before? If a turtleman tried to force their way in, they would be in for a nasty surprise. He could even tell the contraptions were fine-tuned *for* turtlemen. They wouldn't go off unless the exact right conditions were met.

Then he took in Elder Quilqi. The woman was practically glowing, little lines of connection trailing from her to all over Chimor. He guessed the strong lines trailing away were likely for Silluka and Cosquella, but there were more than two. One large glowing line went off toward where the warrior leaders held their offices. Maybe to Nina? Others trailed far down, or high in the air, but the strongest cable of light, as big around as the elder, plunged straight down into the earth. To the core?

As he watched, lights winked out, hidden, until he could see the elder's smirking face.

"Hits differently all at once, yes? Gods' chayus, it's almost like you're working on a reasonable level."

Eagle Watches from on High was almost gone, the vial empty and the chayu used up in moments. It had never acted so powerfully. Had the results been focused when he worked with Amoxtli, as when he transferred the chayu to Cosquella?

"You have connections everywhere," he breathed.

"I'm old. I've gotten around. Nothing so unusual. What *is* unusual is that you were able to see, just for a moment, into the realm of the Pressure Adept. Was that an artifact of Amoxtli's skill? Or the way the Eztli Mecatl magic transmutes that of the Huaca? Hard to say."

Ichu didn't know where to start. His mind buzzed around the information, aware the elder hadn't answered his original question, but too tantalized by the implications.

"Pressure Adept? Is that what you see in others?" The weight in the room had dropped away, he realized, as he drank the vial. Now the elder was hiding her power again.

She scoffed. "Hardly. It's a start for what you will need very soon, though. You'd best get to refining with Cosquella and use whatever nefarious contraption the squid dreams up for you. You'll need practice with the girl if you want to have any chance at that arena fight with Xiuhquil in two days."

Ichu's tongue tied itself up once again, trying to ask too many questions at once. "Xiuhquil?" he finally managed. That had been the turtleman leader who killed Amoxtli.

"Yes! Who do you think signed up for the fights in the arena? You can't read their script yet, I see—just signed your name to whatever was around."

"But no turtleman warriors are allowed in the city without permission! When was he allowed in?"

"He hasn't been, officially, and a name on a sheet isn't enough to tear the city apart over a possibility. I'd assume the workers will smuggle him in somehow if he's not given permission. I haven't quite determined that bit, but he's being quiet for such a large specimen of Eztli Mecatl." Elder Quilqi crossed her wrinkled arms and stared at him, as if she couldn't believe his stupidity. He was inclined to agree.

"I'd love to stay here gabbing at you, but I assume you want to start training with the big girl, yes?" the elder hooked a thumb over her shoulder.

As if on cue, the door opened to admit Silluka and Cosquella, giggling together about something. Cosquella had his sister's hand in hers, but Silluka used her stump to tap the larger woman on the chest as she walked backward into the room. She didn't like to touch others with her stump.

"Well, we'll try again harder next time, won't we?" Silluka said, then realized who else was here. Her smile faded. "Something happen? You look like you tried to eat a cactus, Ichu."

"I'll need to borrow Cosquella from you," he said. "I need to understand how this new magic works, if that's alright." He looked between both women, asking for permission.

"Well, we were planning to go up to the walls again tonight," Cosquella said. "We've been watching the army. It's like they're waiting for something out there, it is."

"Waiting for their first challenger, I'd wager," Elder Quilqi said. "Xiuhquil was set to show the strength of the Eztli Mecatl against one of the fire warriors tomorrow, but she got a bad case of reasonableness and backed out."

"Xiuhquil, who killed Amoxtli?" Cosquella asked, her stony face growing even more severe.

"The same. And the city would have held against any actions of the army, except that arrogant feline Anuit stepped in to claim the right, a day later." Elder Quilqi gestured toward Ichu with one hand. "And then so did this idiot."

Silluka turned on him, her eyes flashing. "You did *what*?"

He'd been planning to tell her, if the elder hadn't gotten to it before him. He shouldn't have signed up for the arena fights in the first place, but he had to prove himself. It would force him to understand his magic.

"I didn't know it was with Xiuhquil," he said. "They aren't allowing Huaca to spar with Huaca any longer, and I have no other way to show my ability. Another rule change The Clade is pushing."

"But why did you sign up for the arena at all? The elder already told me I was going to have to fight."

The scenario shifted suddenly in his brain. Silluka had always been brave, but with no resources to back that up. Now she had the ability to match her courage. Was she upset he was getting to fight *before* her?

"You don't think I can handle myself," he said. "Ever since you decided to take flight like some goddess"—he waved one hand in the air—"you think you can do everything. Remember who provided for you when our parents died, and even before that. I'm the best bodycaster in the village. I can take care of myself."

"Can you?" Silluka caught her stump with her hand. "Against one turtleman, who's definitely going to be more powerful than the ones we fought on the sleds? Akamu had to save us there. He can't do that in the arena."

That was low, but Ichu kept his anger inside. He'd dealt with his sister her whole life, when she complained about the extra lessons their parents paid the elders to teach her, to bring her into citizenship despite her handicap. She rejected all that and tried to live as a thief on the streets of the Huaca, despite having a home, small as it was, to come back to.

"I've protected you my whole life, Silluka, and I'm not going to stop now, even if you're starting to realize your own strength."

"By throwing your life away?" Silluka gestured at him with both arms. He could almost feel her nonexistent fingers on her right hand wagging at him.

"Anuit is sparring him first, she is." Cosquella's input was quiet, but her voice was loud enough to carry, despite that.

Silluka slumped. "Anuit. Of course that...Misini took the challenge first. She's killed everyone she's faced. Is it too much to hope she kills Xiuhquil too?"

"Perhaps that is her plan, it is," Cosquella said. "Let the turtleman champion in, then kill him. It would be a good way to turn the army outside away, it would."

Ichu kept his mouth shut, letting the argument ebb away. Silluka was concerned for him, that was natural. Gods, *he* was concerned for himself. If he knew the Eztli Mecatl leader was the one he'd challenged, he never would have done it. It was definitely time to learn to read.

CHAPTER SEVENTEEN

Questions and Answers

Silluka turned to Elder Quilqi, who'd been watching them fight like a long-suffering mother, trying to stay out of it. "Shall I sign up after Ichu then? If Anuit doesn't kill him, maybe all three of us can take Xiuhquil down for good and kick the turtlemen out of Chimor."

She expected the elder to laugh at her, but she put a considering hand to her chin. Silluka caught Ichu biting his lip like he did when he was trying to be the big brother. When would he realize she could take care of herself? What level of Adepthood would finally show him?

"Perhaps," Elder Quilqi said slowly. "I can't know what the gods have planned. There is a lot going on with these Eztli Mecatl, more than is visible to most. The Misini are nearly as bad. Feuding Gods! What is happening in this city? All this power collected here will certainly attract too much attention. The last time I was here..." She seemed to acknowledge Silluka and the others hanging on her words and waved them away. "No matter. We need to focus on the present. These arena fights are not just an exciting afternoon for the crowds. They have real power here. Anuit's two wins have set the gods off already, strengthening The Clade and weakening both the Uncles, Aunts, and Entles, and the Allwiya's gibbering horrors."

"Is their power related to Chimor? We've had barely any weather since we've been here," Silluka asked. There had been no hurricanes or tornadoes. They weren't near enough to the coast for tidal waves, but earthquakes and volcanoes didn't seem to happen here. No one had to call on the gods to protect them. "You've told us these arena fights are important, but *why* are they important?"

Elder Quilqi looked between them, then called out, "Lugopo, how much more time do you need on your latest gizmo?"

Lugopo skittered out of Ichu's room, for some reason, already signing. "Crawling Dark of Squirming and Manylegs of Reaching have given such inspiration! Certainly they will ask for my supplication after this triumph!"

"Then you've started."

Lugopo held up a bead or nut in one tentacle. Immediately the room seemed to dim, as if Silluka's eyes were locked on the little object. Her fingers tingled and began to shake. Lugopo hid the thing away again and the room snapped back to normal.

"Started, but not quite ready! Still need to place safety mechanisms. Ichu stated he did not wish to destroy himself." Lugopo did the equivalent of an Allwiya shrug. "Will take longer that way."

"What was that?" Silluka gasped for air. Cosquella was clutching at her chest and Ichu looked hollowed out, leaning heavily against a chair. Elder Quilqi, of course, was unmoved.

"Mixing of magics leads to new combinations! New ways to destroy the world!" They tapped the circlet. "Er, *explore* the world! Whirling Abyss' blessing gives new insight—too much to do!" They scampered back into Ichu's room and the door banged shut, though Lugopo wasn't big enough to generate that much force.

"Looks like we have a few hours at least," the elder said, and gestured to the chairs around the table. "Sit down. Time for a story."

Silluka exchanged a look with Ichu, their fight forgotten, at least for her. The elder never offered information freely. She sat, and the other two followed quickly. Cosquella, sitting on her left, found her hand under the table and gave a reassuring squeeze.

"Chimor is very old," the elder began. "Not the oldest or the most powerful of the permanent cities, by far, but it has transformed into an important center for this island, especially over the past few decades. It is important enough for the gods to fight over it, because Chimor used to be an island, thousands of years ago."

"The city itself was an island?" Silluka asked. She imagined the city by itself, braving the boiling ocean. She'd known it was old, but to be measured in even hundreds of years was unknown to the coast where her whole family had lived for generations. The storms and earthquakes eroded the coast. The land raised or sank. Other islands collided as they approached, giving rise to volcanoes and tidal waves taller than Chimor's walls. Even trees and bushes grew on the order of weeks and months, ready to shelter the changing land. How could anything survive that long?

"You children have barely seen what lies in the world ocean—what you call the boiling ocean." Had the elder been off the island completely? "Some of those older, more powerful cities trawl the waves still, vying for dominance. That is where many of those powerful individuals I'm concerned about live. Chimor simply chose another option, to call more islands to itself for protection."

"Then the Huaca started out on Chimor, did they?" Cosquella asked.

The elder waggled her head. "The Huaca there built a wall all the way around the island." She gestured in a circle around her head, implying the walls of the city were those same ones. "It helped to fend off the worst of the attacks and the weather."

Silluka's mind whirled at the thought that the entire city used to be an island. It was simultaneously large, and very small compared to the land around it.

"And you're saying this is why there is no weather here past a little wind or rain?" Ichu asked. "I've seen the width of the walls and the stonework. It was built to withstand winds like we got at the coast. I'd bet Chimor's buildings could even contend with earthquakes."

Elder Quilqi pointed a finger at him. "Correct, and they did. The builders knew how to construct buildings to last.

Why do you think they are all solid stone, hollowed out?" Her finger crossed to Cosquella. "Your point is salient too, girl. You asked if all the Huaca lived there. The answer is no. When Chimor sailed the seas, the gods were different. Some had not been raised, and others had not been killed. Grandmother Life and Grandfather Death were still in this world then, still waxing in power. The way you practice chayus now is not the only way to call upon the gods, even the gods of the Huaca."

Silluka wanted to know more, much more, but all this had come from her asking about the upcoming fight. Elder Quilqi never volunteered anything not pertinent to what they were doing. "So what does this have to do with The Clade pulling strings and the arena fights?"

"Indeed. Ocean and land, there's too much to even hint at what's happening! You children are so young. But I'll try to be concise." The elder put both hands together, fingers touching. "Chimor used to be an island, belonging to gods—some gods—of the Huaca. The decision to pull other islands to it, made by mortal or immortal minds, gave it protection and solidity that helped it outlast many of its competitors. Some of them now make up the shaking domain you crossed on the way here."

"And the stable desert around Chimor?" Ichu asked.

"The first ring of small islands, fused so closely to Chimor they buoy it, above the planet's core." Elder Quilqi made her hands into a ring on the table. "Chimor's plan might also be its downfall, though. Each new island had its own gods and people. The Misini were the first encountered that were not Huaca themselves. Until that point, the magic here had been at least stable."

"It's not stable now, is it?" Cosquella leaned forward, caught up.

"You yourself are a good example of how it is not. And it's accelerating faster. The main arena was created to pit Huaca against Huaca, to determine whose god was stronger and who would be admitted to join with the Uncles, Aunts, and Entles. Each island had their chance. Some survived and joined the city. Others died."

"But the Misini made a conflicting pantheon of gods," Silluka said. The realization came as she said it.

"Correct again. Now the arena served two purposes: to choose the most powerful of the Huaca gods, and to show which were stronger, the Huaca or the Misini. In all the centuries, The Clade has never beaten the Uncles, Aunts, and Entles. The fights were separated by species for a reason, until The Clade were able to override the ruling."

"And the Kawchi, Allwiya, and Yakurikra aren't powerful enough to challenge either group," Ichu said, standing to pace. "That's why Akamu was so upset about..." He trailed off, looking around like a god would jump from behind a door. "About what the secondborn did to the turtlemen."

"And now the Uncle and his *lovely* sibling have invited the Eztli Mecatl to the tournament," Silluka continued his thought. "Why? When? Why does their army simply sit outside the walls. Why not attack?"

"Because the cats have destabilized the power inside Chimor, they have," Cosquella said.

Silluka stared at her girlfriend. Was this why Xiuhquil was so eager to fight? To win? Was it a way to conquer Chimor without even killing anyone?

"Then if Xiuhquil beats Anuit, what happens?" Silluka stood up now, Cosquella releasing her hand. "Anuit has already beaten the Huaca and the Allwiya. Is only one fight needed, or does a species need to win multiple fights to gain dominance?"

"The gods dance to their own music," the elder said, spreading wrinkled palms out in front of her. "Who can say if only one fight is a deciding factor, or if there must be many over weeks or years. Time is different to the gods."

"Or to an immortal?" Silluka pushed.

"Precisely." The elder didn't take her bait.

"And why do you care what happens to Chimor?" she asked. "You said this wasn't your birth city either."

"Yet it is an important one, and I have the feeling foul play is afoot, which I do not enjoy." Elder Quilqi's tone gained a core of iron. "Someone is trying to change the rules by which this island operates, and my champions are not powerful enough yet to block that tactic head on."

Ichu was scowling at that, and Silluka narrowed her eyes. The elder had some plan with them that seemed to reach even past Chimor. "What aren't you telling us about this fight?"

"Lots, girl. Fur and scales! I said I was trying to be concise. There's far too much you don't know—can't know, at your level—but I need others to help me get to the bottom of this. Chimor is a first step, but an important one. The world is hurtling toward a reckoning."

"Then I should fight after Ichu, just to be certain," Silluka decided. Ichu took a step toward her, but she put out a hand. "No more talk about how you can protect me. I'm a Mental Adept. You're still a Physical Adept, however good at the chayus you are. Do you know how many chayu segments I have stored within me? Seventy-three."

"Which you cannot yet release," the elder pointed out.

Silluka clenched her jaw. "Should I sign up or not?"

"Peace, girl." Silluka felt that annoying weight on her shoulders under Elder Quilqi's glare. She would figure out what that was and how to stop it. "Yes. After careful consideration, I think you *should* sign up after your brother. I need to keep my champions alive."

"Are two allowed to fight at once?" Cosquella asked. "I can help Silluka out, I can."

The elder rubbed her chin. "Possibly. There have been allowances for multiple lower Adepts against a higher Adept, and the Eztli Mecatl power levels are not as well understood as the other species." She pushed up from the table abruptly. "I'll go have a word with the registration office. See if we can come to an understanding about how Chimor should protect its own. I'll be back later."

She marched out of the house before Silluka could think of anything else to say. She locked eyes with Cosquella, then her brother.

"So, we're all going to fight Xiuhquil?"

"I only wanted to practice with Cosquella," Ichu grumbled. "If I'm going to fight, I need to store some longer chayus. Or at least ones that will pack a punch against a turtleman."

"There are a few in *Jakua's Fight* that might help," Silluka volunteered. "I don't think you know all of them. I haven't seen you use them, at least." She looked to Cosquella. She was a little jealous of the two of them working together, if she was honest. Although Akamu had been the one to help her store the chayus. She hadn't seen him with Ichu as much lately. Was it his role as the leader of the stone warriors that took him away?

"That would be helpful." Ichu broke into her thoughts. "I can show you how Cosquella and I transfer the chayus."

Cosquella took her hand again and Silluka smiled at the pebble-like texture of her skin. "I can actually feel the ampuka, I can!"

"Xiuhquil won't stand a chance." Silluka grinned.

Over the next few hours, Silluka showed Ichu *The Bush Conceals Jakua* and *Jakua Leaps Up a Tree*, both good against taller, stronger opponents. She also showed a few chayus from *Tortoise's Growth* and one from *Quirra's Day*. Ichu learned them all quickly, only needing to repeat them once each before the moves started to fall into place for him. Silluka tried not to feel jealous of him, but it was hard. He'd been doing this his whole life.

When they'd selected the chayus that might be most helpful in a fight against a powerful turtleman, Ichu and Cosquella showed Silluka how they committed a chayu to the vial. They performed the morning ritual together, opening their *sunqus* to the core. Then Ichu performed *Tortoise's Heavy Foot*, an obvious choice to have at hand. The rich brown of Tiyu Tiksimuyu, Uncle Earth, surrounded him as he drew close to Cosquella. Her eyes flicked to Silluka, as if asking permission to be this close to her brother. Silluka nodded, just slightly, entranced. She imagined her hands touching Cosquella's temples, shoulders, heart and *sunqu*, thighs, knees, calves, and feet. The turtlemen's magic was very intimate.

Ichu held a vial in one hand as he made the connection. While the ampuka bloomed around Cosquella, some went to the little vial, filling a fraction of it up with glowing liquid.

"Amazing!" She stamped a foot, rocking the house. "I can feel Tortoise's power." Then she looked at the vial. "But there's so little of it in there. Not like when..." she abruptly stopped at Ichu's stricken look.

"What did you do?" Silluka knew when her brother was trying to hide something. He was a terrible liar. She felt there was a piece missing when they told of their fight with the three turtlemen, so happy to switch to how they had created vials between them. She looked from one to the other. "My brother *and* girlfriend? Are you both going to hide the truth from me?"

"I am sorry, Silluka, I am." Cosquella knotted her hands together, worrying at her large fingers. "We decided not to share that—"

"Share what?" She rounded on Ichu. "What did you do?" He was always trying to protect her without her agreement.

He spread his hands, stepping away from Cosquella. "Silluka, I...it was a mistake, one I don't want to repeat."

"And you told Cosquella to keep it from us? Like you tried to do the first time, on the sleds?"

Cosquella placed a hand on her stump. "No. It was me, it was, to tell him to keep this away from the others. No good can come of it and he won't do it again, he said."

"Do...what again?" Now Silluka was worried.

Ichu sighed and slumped. "The magic of the Eztli Mecatl—the original people Cosquella's family learned from—works by giving strength and ability to others. The turtlemen's—those who use their magic now their god is dead—works by *taking* from others."

Silluka squinted, looking between them. "I think I see the difference, but what does this have to do with anything?"

"What I learned from Amoxtli was giving magic. It's beneficial to everyone. But something happened in the alley, fighting the turtlemen. I found out I can do both kinds of magic."

"Giving, and taking?"

Ichu nodded. "I might as well get it." He went in his room, and Silluka peeked after him, seeing Lugopo sitting on the chest, signing with some arms while others used arcane tools on the strange nut that sucked the energy from a room. Ichu stepped around them and opened a drawer in the chest, withdrawing a blue and a yellow vial, then another deep purple black, like a bruise. Even from this distance, it felt wrong.

He brought all three closer and Silluka almost recoiled from the purple vial. It was a similar feeling to the others she'd seen the turtlemen carry.

"You can sense it, can't you? Two of these were made when I gave a chayu to Amoxtli. But I didn't take the other one *from* turtlemen who attacked us. I accidently *made* it from him."

"Made...what from the turtleman? Took what?" Silluka asked.

"Everything." Cosquella's voice was bleak. "It wasn't pretty, it wasn't."

"I was trying to take the strength from him after he drank his own vial," Ichu explained. "I connected with him, but it took too much. We left the other two alive, but there was nothing left of him, not even bones." Ichu shivered, holding the vial up to the light. It seemed to drink it in. "His essence filled up the empty vial Cosquella used. Why can I make this, but not even fill a vial up halfway when I make one with Cosquella?"

"Taking is easier than giving?" Silluka ventured. She tried to hide her disgust at the story. The turtlemen's magic was evil, destructive, compared to the Eztli Mecatl. She could see how much the memory weighed on her brother. "I know that sounds trite, but maybe, in the absence of a god, it was all they could do, with no real connection to the core." She wondered how their magic worked, after all, with no god to facilitate it. "Maybe using a person up completely generates as much power as the little bit we take from the core."

Ichu looked at the vial again, seeming nauseated. "It does make a kind of horrible sense. So if we try to give more of ourselves, then maybe we'll fill our vials more?"

"I would not want to try that, I wouldn't," Cosquella said. She was still surrounded by the rich glow of *Tortoise's Heavy Foot*, though it was starting to fade. "And we can only transfer it twice between us."

"Let's see what we can do with what's left," Ichu suggested, and this time Cosquella made the connection to him, the vial in her hand. Silluka watched, thinking of the woman's strong hands on her instead.

When they finished, the vial still only had a small amount inside it, and plenty of empty space. She watched the viscus liquid slosh slowly. "You said you can only do that twice?"

"Transferring it between us makes it stronger, it does," Cosquella explained. "But only to a point. After that it hurts the *sunqu*."

"So, you can't add any more of that chayu." An idea was welling up in her. "But can you add a different one?"

Ichu stared at her. "That's brilliant. I don't know."

He began *Jakua's Claws* and when the ampuka was bright about him, took the vial back and connected with Cosquella at the heart, *sunqu*, and arm connections. The vial filled just partially with the yellow of Uncle Sky.

"Back to me, quickly," Ichu gestured, and thrust the vial at Cosquella. She made the connection back to him and the vial filled a little more. The two colors in it stayed separate, as if they were oil and water.

"I think we just found a tactic against Xiuhquil," Silluka said. "How many chayus can you hold at once?"

"Generally, only three can be effective at a time. The first starts to wear off by the time I've finished the chayu for the third." Ichu raised the vial, now maybe a third full. "But with this, I don't know. Perhaps five or six."

"Try it," Silluka urged. She would have herself, but she didn't think the magic would work for her and didn't want to risk a change in her magic like what happened to Ichu.

Ichu held it out to Cosquella, but she waved it away. "I tried the last one, I did. You try this."

Ichu licked his lips. Silluka could see the eagerness in him, though he hid it well. He stared at the vial for a long moment, then popped the cork and drained it.

The ampuka passed from the vial to Ichu, surrounding him instantly, and he gasped.

"Yes, it works! I can feel both." He looked around, as if for something he could destroy in the small house, then went outside. Silluka and Cosquella followed him.

Ichu plunged his hand into the ground, passing all the way up to the elbow with seemingly no effort. He pulled and a giant chunk of dusty ground ripped from the ground. It was a good test. *Tortoise's Heavy Foot* was able to give the strength needed, but it was for blunt impacts. *Jakua's Claws* could grasp, slice, and claw, but it didn't have the strength behind it. Both together were a powerful combination.

"We need to combine more of these," Ichu said. He dropped the plug of earth back into the ground and stamped around the edges. Each footprint smashed the ground together until there were no seams. Tentative heads poked from other Huaca houses at the noise, but Silluka waved them away. They had enough odd goings-on at their house that most of the curious onlookers vanished.

Back inside, they set on a sequence of chayus, meant to work with each other. Along with *Tortoise's Heavy Foot* and *Jakua's Claws*, they chose *Quirra Hides His Nuts, Tortoise's Keen Eyes, Branches Withstand a Gale,* and *Raven Spreads Her Wings. Tortoise's Keen Eyes* was the only new one Silluka taught the others, having learned it as part of *Tortoise's Growth*. It was similar to *Eagle Watches from on High*, but kept the attention on the immediate surroundings, rather than linking to how signs connected to the rest of the world. It would be a good observation chayu to determine if an opponent had any hidden tricks.

Learning, perfecting, and storing the chayus took most of the rest of the afternoon until Elder Quilqi returned.

"Cosquella will be fighting with Ichu," she announced. "And Silluka is by herself afterward. I tried to have all three of you fight Xiuhquil, but the powers that be dismissed his danger after Anuit tangled with him. Can't say I blame them that much." She pointed at Silluka. "That means you're officially signed up, as is your large friend. Congratulations on getting a match in the Chimor arena."

"Then we need to keep practicing," Ichu said, the worry in his voice creeping out.

Elder Quilqi watched all of them. Not with that strange heavy pressure but simply observing. "It's late, and you look like you've been at it since I left. Take a break for tonight, and don't wear yourselves out. Use tomorrow to work out the kinks, but your match is the day after. You're not going to fix anything fundamentally wrong in that time. Work on your strategy instead of tiring yourselves."

"You sound like my old teacher," Ichu grumbled.

"I've had my share of sparring matches," Elder Quilqi replied tartly, "of great portent and of little. The same strategy applies to both."

Silluka gratefully took the excuse to peel Cosquella away for an evening walk, leaving from the Huaca side of the refugee center, where there were fewer turtleman patrols. With Lugopo still communing with their weird gods in Ichu's bedroom, the house felt too small for a little privacy.

Silluka took her girlfriend firmly by the arm, wrapping her stump around her pebbly skin. Her feet were already taking her to the parapet above the gate. The turtlemen were on her mind, and she replayed the connection Ichu and Cosquella made, fingertips touching key points on the other's body.

"How are you doing, with all these new revelations?" she asked as they climbed the stairs.

"You mean with me being half Eztli Mecatl, you do." Cosquella squeezed her arm. "It's not so bad. I knew I was different, I did, and this at least gives me a good reason why I'm so bad at the chayus."

They breached the top and stood on the parapet in the early evening, the sun quickly disappearing behind the rocky outcrops that marked the edge of the desert and the start of Chimor. Fires twinkled in the turtlemen's camp, and many of them wandered around—attending to business, talking, eating, sparring, and laughing. There were enough here to make a strong attempt at laying siege to the city, but they simply stayed put. Their warriors had chased Silluka and her village across the desert. Why simply stop now? Unless Xiuhquil could guarantee their victory with an afternoon of fights.

Cosquella ran a finger across her cheek and Silluka jerked back to the present. "I don't think you came up here to stare at turtlemen, me."

Silluka laughed. "I didn't. I just got to thinking. But I suppose we'll find out more at the match." She raised her hand to Cosquella's cheek in return, then brushed across her temple, ears, jaw, and neck. All points she'd seen Ichu use.

"What does that feel like, to give your magic to someone else?"

Cosquella considered. "It's giving up a valuable part of yourself, but with the promise it will be used well in the future, it will be. It's pride in the power you can contribute to a common cause."

Silluka trailed her hand down to Cosquella's heart, then down her belly. Her *sunqu* was lower than on Silluka, down almost to where her legs met her body. "Can you feel it gather here?"

"Hmm. I do. A warm feeling all over, it is." Cosquella leaned forward. "Perhaps I can share the feeling with you."

Silluka kissed her, and indeed, she started to feel a fire in her belly.

CHAPTER EIGHTEEN

The Gods' Arena

Ichu worried at a nail head, hammered into the stone behind the gates leading to the arena. Shouts and cries of the crowd rang down into the covered hallway where he waited. A couple small rooms led off to the sides for people to relax between fights, but he was too keyed up to use one.

For the last two days, he and Cosquella had stuffed every helpful chayu they could think of into vials. Amoxtli's house had a whole drawerful of them, which prompted Ichu to wonder how the turtlemen produced them, or if they were a product of Eztli Mecatl ingenuity and a limited resource. It made him even more regretful about the one they dropped and broke. Added to that, Lugopo still hadn't delivered the creation Ichu had asked for. Every time he looked in on the little Allwiya, they waved him away with "Working!"

Now half the vials were in pouches at his sides, while Cosquella had the other half. He'd even, against his instincts, placed the dark purple vial at the end of the line of vials. If he had nothing else left, then maybe he would use it, despite the consequences. If his life was forfeit, then what did any ill effects matter?

He was wearing heavier clothes than he usually wore, leather coated with oils and resins to thicken them to resist cuts and punctures. He hoped they would be enough.

All this thinking wasn't getting him into the right frame of mind to fight Xiuhquil. He peered through an opening in the gates, seeing the dusty arena laid out, as a particularly loud call rang out from his side of the stands. The fighting floor looked bigger from down here than from up in the seats, which were packed. Word had gotten out about the turtlemen's champion. And where was Cosquella? She was supposed to show up with Silluka, who was queued to fight after him, and him after Anuit.

"Don't worry your pretty head, big Huaca," a voice hissed near him. Ichu turned to the Misini, who was herself pacing up and down the corridor. "I'll wear the strong, scary Eztli Mecatl down for you." She paused and put a long, clawed finger to her lip. "Or maybe he'll trip over his own feet and break his neck. You can never tell."

"I thought you usually went for the eye?" growled Ichu. He didn't want to anger Anuit—he'd been on the wrong end of her dagger once already—but Cosquella's absence was weighing on him. Had her registration been disallowed after all?

Anuit's pacing paused for a moment. "All a coincidence. Both accidents. They put me against opponents too far below my level, ya."

"Then have you actually fought an Eztli Mecatl before?" Ichu taunted. "Not just danced around one, threatening them? I have." Was she actually nervous? Maybe some higher authority had called Anuit on her actions. In this case, Ichu wouldn't mind too much if she killed Xiuhquil, except Elder Quilqi's warning about The Clade having too much power rang in his ears. Either Xiuhquil or Anuit winning would weaken the power of the Huaca gods.

The shouts of the crowd rose to a high pitch and Anuit's jakua ears swiveled as the announcer boomed a welcome.

"I'll have to leave this lovely conversation, big Huaca." She glided forward to the gate. "My time to put down this invasion against Chimor is here. It will be a nice star on The Clade's bid for the city. Your Huaca gods are past their prime."

"...we welcome Anuit of the Misini!" the announcer's voice boomed, and the gate ponderously swung upward. Anuit turned away from him and lifted her chin, diaphanous fabric swirling around her body, and leaving little to the imagination. Ichu would have looked away, except her fur hid most everything as well as clothes. She seemed comfortable with her near nakedness as she pranced out the gate, raising a hand to the section of seats filled with Misini.

Ichu followed close as the door swung back closed, watching through a peephole beside the gate. It was like a front-row seat to the action—save it was actually harder to see what was happening at ground level. He kept looking behind him, waiting for Cosquella and Silluka, but they weren't here yet. Maybe Anuit would kill the turtleman after all, and he wouldn't have to fight. Good for him, but bad for Chimor.

"And our challenger today is none other than the advance general of our newest Chimor residents, many of whom camp outside our gates even now." The announcer's voice held an edge of derision in it. "Granted a special writ of passage from The Clowder and the Huaca Warriors, here is Xiuhquil of the Eztli Mecatl!"

This announcement was met with boos from all over the stands, as well as hisses, raps of metal on metal from the Allwiya, and a curious clicking. Ichu scanned the seats until he saw an entire section of Kawchi rattling their spines.

The gate at the other end of the arena rose, and Ichu leaned into the peephole, trying to take everything in.

Xiuhquil strode out, wearing his metal helmet, decorated with eagle feathers and a seashell. He wore more armor now, similar to the first turtleman Ichu had faced, back at his farm by the coast. Fibrous sheaths wrapped his arms and legs, and metal plates clanged down his back, completing the image of a jagged shell. A metal breastplate held that same image of a beast's head Ichu had seen on the first invader, with a long jaw and overhanging teeth. His feet were bare, five clawed and scaly toes digging into the ground on each foot.

The warrior raised his hands to the boos, as if soaking them in, and punched one fist into the other open hand with a smack like rocks colliding. He took a vial of red liquid from his pouch and swallowed it back. Glowing red light fell from his eyes, staining his gray cheeks crimson. Even from behind the gate, Ichu was intimidated. He knew the strength behind those fists.

"Begin!" the announcer cried, and Anuit sketched a bow, before disappearing into nothing. Xiuhquil's massive head swiveled, but then fixed on a point of nothing, and he surged forward, faster than his bulk would suggest he could move, metal plates ringing off each other.

Anuit stepped from a spray of mist, directly in his path, holding a knife in each hand, then danced aside as Xiuhquil's momentum took him past her. Ichu heard the *ping* of metal on metal as the knife harmlessly bounced off the metal plates on Xiuhquil's back. An "awwww" rose up from the spectators.

Had he...seen her while she moved? What was required to pierce the Misini's illusions? How did she compare to an adept of the Huaca? She seemed to hold equal sway when talking to Akamu and the other warrior leaders on the parapet above the front gate, and she complained that both her opponents were lesser than her. She might have been the most advanced Misini in Chimor, from what Ichu could guess.

Anuit danced back as Xiuhquil swung punch after punch, nearly catching her whiskers. From here, Ichu could see the concentration on Anuit's face. From years of watching and participating in sparring matches, he could tell she was recalibrating how to combat this opponent. Xiuhquil was more than she bargained for.

The moment Xiuhquil regrouped to firm up his stance, she leapt into the air, coming down as four copies. They spread out around Xiuhquil, but the turtleman sent a kick out to the one on his far right, a foot as big around as Anuit's torso catching that copy square in the chest. The other three copies vanished as Anuit—the real one—flew back with a yowl, tumbling head over heels. Shouts and displeased yells greeted the attack from the stands.

He *had* seen through her illusions. Xiuhquil was almost twice as tall and probably three times the mass of Anuit. Her main weapon was moving unseen and striking from an oblique angle. When fighting the Allwiya, the only thing that saved her was the slowness of the mechanical contraption and its blind spots.

Now that illusion was gone. Xiuhquil advanced on Anuit, still picking herself up, and grabbed her by the ankle, throwing her an even farther distance. She disappeared while in the air, but his beaky face followed her original airborne trajectory, running after.

There was a *whumph* of displaced dirt and Anuit appeared, already scrabbling on all fours to get away from the turtleman's relentless attack. But he was quick—as quick as the warrior Ichu had first fought, or quicker. It had taken an entire village, and Elder Quilqi, to defeat that one. Had the elder killed the previous warrior leader—Xiuhquil's predecessor? None of the others they'd fought had been this powerful. People in the stands were muttering, and he heard hissing from the Misini. It sounded more worried than angry.

Anuit disappeared again, and this time Xiuhquil stopped, head swinging around to cover the entire arena floor, the red from his eyes highlighting his scaly face and beak. Ichu was struck by how much of Anuit's tactics relied on invisibility. But she had also moved faster than possible between points, when she stepped up the front gates to the parapet. Did she have a way to cross short distances in a single step?

Xiuhquil's red eyes seemed to brighten as he stopped his search and ran across the arena, terrifying in his quickness. Metal rattled and banged as his armor plates moved with him. He began punching the air, ducking and moving as if in a fight. The sounds from the spectators were growing, sounding anxious. How many knew what this fight meant for the city? How important *was* it?

"We're here!" Silluka's breathless cry came from behind him, and Ichu frantically gestured with a hand for them to come watch. "The attendants wouldn't let us both in until Elder Quilqi went to talk to them."

"It's going to be very close," Ichu said. He turned away from the peephole only long enough to note Cosquella wearing heavy leather armor, like hunters and jakua handlers used. The heavy axes she'd used to kill the giant Allwiya hung at her sides. A bruise still dotted one cheek from a brawling club outing several days ago. He'd asked if he could attend, just to keep his sparring reflexes up, but she told him it was for non-adepts only.

Silluka was wearing only heavy cloth, wrapped around her. Over that, the metal slivers in her suit caught stray bits of light from torches in the waiting chambers. It sparkled around her, almost like Akamu's armor. Though if the fight got to her, that meant Anuit hadn't stopped Xiuhquil, and neither had he and Cosquella together.

"Where's Lugopo?" he asked. He would need every advantage he could get.

"They said they're still working, and wouldn't come," Silluka said. "I tried—"

There was a cry from the stands and Ichu jerked back to the peephole. He saw the end of Xiuhquil's last punch, the turtleman straightening afterward.

The illusion fell away from Anuit as if pieces of fabric were unraveling around her. She clutched her chest, staggering backward. Her dagger was on the ground, dropped sometime during the exchange. She looked like she was gasping for breath.

Xiuhquil leaned in again, throwing a final jab to the face. Anuit's head snapped back, and she crumpled to the ground in a pool of fabric. The turtleman straightened again, his massive arms raised to the sides, as if basking in the boos and noises from the audience. He seemed to swell, as if taking in their hate.

Or was he? Could a turtleman take power from anyone? Or just other turtlemen?

Attendants were already running onto the field to drag Anuit off. Ichu and Cosquella were next. He ran a hand down the vials strapped to his side and made sure Cosquella's were secure.

"We're going to fight him," he stated.

Silluka reached up to grab Cosquella, hand around the back of her neck, stump pressing into her chest. "You stay alive out there." She pulled her girlfriend down into a firm kiss.

Ichu looked away. Akamu had been pulled into business with the other warrior leaders for the past two days, though Ichu had sent a runner to tell him of the fight. Was he watching now? Was Elder Quilqi with him?

"That's not all we have for you today, my good people!" the announcer boomed. "Our Eztli Mecatl champion has let us know he's ready for his next fight already—no resting needed between!" There was a pause, and Ichu looked up through the peephole. He could just make out the stand on the side of the area where the announcer stood. He was talking with another Huaca and a Misini, gesticulating wildly. Then he threw up his hands and turned back to the crowd.

"We have something even more special for you, in fact. Our new challenger, fresh off dethroning our reigning champion, has told us he wants to take on *all* of his other challengers today at the same time!"

There was a roar from the crowd, and Xiuhquil threw his arms wide. There were a few cheers mixed in with the boos and clicking now. He beat his chest with a *thump* Ichu could hear all the way in the staging area, and the cheers grew louder.

"What does that mean?" Silluka still had a hand around Cosquella's neck. "*All* of us? I'm not ready. You're hardly ready. Lugopo isn't here."

"You have to get ready then, *now*," Ichu growled. "That warrior just took down Anuit without even breathing hard. I don't know how it happened—maybe the elder had something to do with it—but all three of us together *maybe* gives us about the only chance we have to win."

The announcer was calling his name, adding grandiose titles like they always did. He pointed a finger at the women.

"You haven't been in fights like I have. Three on one is just as confusing to us as to our opponent. Cosquella, protect Silluka." His sister started to speak but he rode over her, raising his voice. "Because I have more experience fighting than you. *We* can drink vials." The announcer was calling out Cosquella now, and the gate was creaking open ominously. "You have to perform chayus. It will take longer, but you're more powerful than us." The gate was halfway open, and he stared into Cosquella's eyes. "*Drink* your vials. If you think you need one, use it. Don't hold anything back. Don't try to save anything. Use all your power, and I'll use mine."

The gate was open. Xiuhquil stood waiting in the arena.

"Begin!" boomed the announcer's voice.

CHAPTER NINETEEN

One on Three

Silluka stumbled out of the gate behind Ichu and Cosquella, her mind whirling with strategies. She'd meant to perform a chayu while she was waiting, or at least the morning ritual. She had nothing now, and the other two had vials to drink. Could she...? No, not worth it to even think about trying one of their vials. They would need them, anyway.

When was the last time she did the morning ritual? Earlier today, when she was practicing. Was she still open to the core after this time? She stopped, going into Dexterity stance while the other two went ahead. The suit perfected her form. She began *Jakua's Claws*, simply because it was short and she knew it. This was the base form, meant solely to cause damage. But she was a Mental Adept now. Just as her missing hand didn't hamper the form of the chayu, she knew her intent was strong enough to drive the power of the chayu with the core.

She pulled from her *sunqu*, letting the feeling of *Jakua's Fight* rise up in her. It seemed like the suit was pulling from her too, the metal already heating up. She dug down to where *Jakua's Claws* was stored within her, running up and down her arms, even extending past where her right arm ended. She put the power of her mind behind the chayu.

The glow of the ampuka began around her immediately, rising in intensity over the course of the short chayu. She ended the last movement with a flourish and her *sunqu* contracted, releasing part of its stores. Rather than the shadows that had moved about her while performing the full chayu, it seemed as if this one segment sucked up energy from within her. Spectral arms grew out from her physical ones, great paws even larger than the ones on the village's trained jakuas. The massive paws and scythe-like claws extended past both of her arms, even the one with the hand. Greenish light bathed the sand around her, and she heard gasps from the stands behind her. But she couldn't devote any time to whether what she had done was out of the ordinary.

Ichu and Cosquella were ahead of her, flanking Xiuhquil. They hadn't even begun to fight. Had they drunk vials while she was busy? No, Cosquella raised one to her lips as Xiuhquil watched, head canted. His eyes were still glowing red from the last fight, but he didn't know about their magic, which meant they had some element of surprise.

Silluka ran forward even as Cosquella's eyes glowed with multicolor light, blues and oranges and purples. Her girlfriend lashed out with a long-legged kick, and the wind from it buffeted the turtleman, though it didn't connect. He put a hand up to protect his eyes from the grit even as Ichu struck from his other side, a one-two punch into where kidneys would be on a Huaca.

Xiuhquil spun into a backhand and Ichu went flying.

Silluka couldn't spare a thought for her brother—he'd been through worse—and slashed out with both of Jakua's hands, her left then her right. Even without her right hand, the paw on that side curled the way her hand would have, following her command. The claws raked down her opponent's raised arms, and she could *feel* the feedback as sharp points scrabbled against pebbly skin—much like Cosquella's. But her attack didn't even scratch Xiuhquil.

He laughed, a gravelly, rocky sound, and said something to her, but she couldn't understand him. He reached for her, his arms longer even than Jakua's aura around hers, but Cosquella flung herself at him, her full weight bowling him backward. She was nearly as tall as he was, and heavier than she looked. Xiuhquil toppled back, looking surprised.

Silluka smiled. She knew which vial Cosquella had drunk. One of the parts was *Tortoise Grows Larger*, which increased the user's weight. *Wind from Eagle's Wings* was what she'd used to spray dirt at the turtleman.

Ichu picked himself up as Xiuhquil threw Cosquella back. Silluka caught her before she fell with Jakua's great paws.

"He's too strong, he is," Cosquella panted. "Your fancy new arms didn't even touch him. How did you do that?"

"I'm not sure, but we can take him down," Silluka answered, and went into Strength stance, sacrificing speed for power with her next strike.

Xiuhquil simply stood there, his massive arms raised to the sides. He still hadn't taken a vial, but a shadow seemed to gather around him, pulled from points around the arena.

Silluka spun, following the shadowy lines. Cosquella and Ichu didn't seem to see them. She caught sight of hooded faces in the crowd, red eyes glowing beneath cowls.

"He's drawing from other turtlemen!" she cried, just as Ichu came from behind, one fist swinging in a circle to catch the back of Xiuhquil's head.

The turtleman didn't move and Ichu's fist bounced off, staggering him. As he stumbled, Silluka caught the gleam of vials along his side. He hadn't drunk any yet.

"Drink!" she shouted and caught Ichu's nod. She leapt forward again, slashing, but Xiuhquil only held up one hand, easily fending her off. She forced more reserves from her *sunqu*, strengthening the blows, but they did nothing, though she could feel the power in her limbs. She could have cracked stone.

"I can't touch him," she panted to Cosquella. "And he hasn't even gone on the offensive." He was playing with them.

Ichu drew out the vial in his second holster. This one contained *Quirra Hides His Nuts*, for intricate movement, *Tortoise's Horny Beak*, to harden the skin, *Tree Sap Flows*, to make the blood course faster, and *Hummingbird's Wings*, to speed up movement. It had been Ichu's idea to pair all four chayus. The second after he swallowed the mix of purple, pink, yellow, and orange liquid, he seemed to blink forward, faster than the eye could follow.

Xiuhquil shook his head as a rain of punches drove into him, beating him back by sheer number. Ichu seemed to have multiple sets of arms, blurring in and out.

Cosquella ran to help him, clapping her hands to drive a wedge of air at the turtleman's eyes. While he squinted, she followed with an elbow to his other side. Silluka stepped up beside her, swinging with both arms. Surely with the three of them...

Xiuhquil buckled under the assault, guarding his face and body with arms ridged with fiber and bony growths. The shouts of the crowd filtered into Silluka's ears. They were doing it. They were winning!

Then Xiuhquil roared, bodily picking up Ichu and throwing him, then smashing into Cosquella. Silluka found herself flying backward, though she couldn't even say what he'd done.

She landed on her back and all the breath went out of her. She barely kept from knocking her head on the ground by Jakua's paws cushioning her landing. Dazed, she looked to where the turtleman warrior stood, twenty paces away. Had he thrown her that far? Cosquella and Ichu were on the ground too.

Finally, Xiuhquil attacked. He stomped to Cosquella and stamped on her. On her back, on the ground, she barely caught his foot with both hands. Her biceps bulged with the effort to keep him from squashing her, her teeth clenched, her eyes glowing.

Silluka pushed to her feet, but Ichu was faster, running across the distance in a second to impact the turtleman's plated back with a ring of metal on flesh. Ichu grunted audibly, but Xiuhquil staggered enough for Cosquella to throw him off with a gust of wind and the mass of *Tortoise Grows Larger*.

Silluka was doing nothing to help them. If she had faced the turtleman alone, he would have beaten her senseless in moments.

Even with all three of them, they were barely scratching him. There was a slight discoloration on one of his gray cheeks, but aside from that, no indication he was even in a fight. He wasn't breathing hard. How much was he drawing from the other turtlemen in the stands? The fight was one on three, but how many were propping up that one, lending him strength and resilience?

"Great project completed! Now you will all die approximately twenty percent less!"

Silluka swiveled away from the fight at Lugopo's voice. The little Allwiya was hanging over the wall of the arena, two angry Misini behind them complaining about Allwiya crawling over their seats. Lugopo held up a pendant that seemed to pull at her *sunqu*.

"Get this to Ichu to prevent possible maiming!" They tapped their circlet with one tentacle. "Certain maiming!"

Silluka looked back quickly. Xiuhquil had her brother by the throat.

She ran to the wall, and Lugopo dropped the pendant into her hands. There was a clockwork seed at the center of it that ticked ominously and her hand grew numb holding it.

"Fight and reign destruction upon your enemies!" Lugopo told her.

She ran to Ichu, holding the deadly thing out in front of her.

* * *

"Take this!"

Ichu felt something pressed into his spasming hand as the turtleman raised him off the ground by his neck. The vial he'd drunk was already starting to fade, and he'd made little to no impression on Xiuhquil. How strong was the warrior? Even the turtlemen they'd fought on the sleds in the desert weren't this strong. His fists had made *some* impact on his first opponent.

His vision was going black, and he raised his hand to his throat, clawing at the rough hands holding him.

They relaxed suddenly and he fell back, coughing. As his mind cleared, he saw Xiuhquil sneering down at him. No, at what he held.

The pendant. That Silluka put in his hand.

Cosquella tried to grapple the warrior from the back, but his metal armor and width prevented her from getting a good grip. He shook her away and pointed down, asking a question in his language. He seemed completely at ease.

Ichu had fought people like that before, who were so confident they thought no one could touch them. Xiuhquil was the first who he thought might pull it off.

The chayus in the vial he'd drunk were fading away fast. He reached for another, crabbing away from the turtleman before he could make another move. The warrior simply watched him. But when Ichu brought a new vial up, the multicolored light inside was draining away, before his eyes. His other hand burned with cold, and he brought that up to see the pendant radiating ice blue, growing greater by the second. He pulled out a second vial and third, but they were already empty. He even pulled the last dark purple vial, made from the turtleman in the alley. It was empty. What had Lugopo done?

Xiuhquil laughed and Ichu's head snapped up in time to see the fist coming for his face. Silluka and Cosquella were on their backs again nearby.

He instinctively blocked with his right hand, the one holding the pendant, wincing in anticipation of bones cracking in his arm.

But the punch was merely a punch. Strong, but Ichu blocked it easily. He and Xiuhquil stared at each other in shock, before the turtleman stepped back to raise his arms again.

This time, Ichu saw the buzz of energy Silluka warned them about, flowing into his opponent like drifting shadows from the stands. There were turtlemen there, several slumping in their seats. They'd been powering Xiuhquil, except now a thick stream of the shadow passed to the pendant. Was it sucking power away from them?

He stepped closer, holding the pendant aloft, and the buzzing lines of energy diverted fully from Xiuhquil to the pendant, making it glow even brighter.

"Lugopo, you did it!" Ichu cried. He didn't want to know what mad whispers their gods passed to them to make this happen.

He grabbed Xiuhquil's arms, forcing them down even though the turtleman struggled against him. He was strong, but Ichu was now stronger. Xiuhquil seemed to be deflating, his muscles shrinking. He was even getting shorter.

Xiuhquil wrenched his hands from Ichu's grasp with a circular motion, breaking the ring of Ichu's fingers to thumbs around his wrists. He backpedaled and turned, shouting words into the sky.

But these Ichu could understand, though they were gravely and accented.

"Tiku Llamkay!"

Why was he calling for Uncle Smith?

A light broke in the sky, brighter than the sun, making Ichu's eyes water. It rose over the arena, gasps coming from the crowd.

Then an aspect of the light shifted, and it suddenly wasn't just light, but a head, of a giant Huaca, taller than the walls of Chimor. He looked as if he were made of burnished gray metal, save his eyes glowed bright as the sun. Ichu raised a hand to shield his vision, as did half of the spectators. A deadly silence had fallen, even though he saw people with their mouths open, yelling and pointing.

Ichu fell to his knees as an intense weight smashed into him. He could barely raise his head enough to make out people falling down in the stands. Xiuhquil was prone, face in the dust of the arena, though from his own accord or from the pressure, Ichu couldn't say.

Ichu gasped and opened his hand to let the pendant roll away from him. It was brilliant blue white now, growing brighter and sparking, little strikes of lightning zapping out from it in all directions. It was like a little sun itself.

Then it fizzled, cracked, and split in two, the light escaping.

On instinct, Ichu put out a hand, ignoring the burning from the lightning strikes, and *connected* with the energy.

The weight on him eased, and he pushed to his feet, able to see everyone else kneeling or prone. Silluka struggled to push herself up. Cosquella was flat on her back. Up in the stands, he saw six figures, one of which was Akamu. All were standing, barely.

The thinnest, oldest one, hopped down and marched toward the edge of the arena closest to where Uncle Smith still gazed out over the crowd. He knew that march. Elder Quilqi.

"You have called me, and I have answered, my adopted son," the voice of Uncle Smith boomed out over the assembly.

The last piece of the puzzle clicked in Ichu's mind. He finally realized what he should have all along. The turtlemen's god wasn't dead. He'd been replaced. Tiyu Llamkay had killed him and taken his place. It was why Ichu could use both magics, and why Cosquella could. At least one of the gods of the Huaca was a traitor to their cause, siding with their enemies. Was Entle Love the same?

He stepped forward, as if he pulled a wagon of stone behind him. The energy from Lugopo's charm filled him.

"You have seen the power of the Eztli Mecatl. I have made them a home here. Welcome them as your new allies and conquerors." The voice addressed the people of Chimor.

Ichu took another step, and another. Even the energy from the broken pendant he'd absorbed was draining fast, used to bolster him against the power of a god. His eyes stayed on Xiuhquil, but he could see the turtleman's mouth moving in prayer. There was a line of power, just visible to Ichu's eyes, connecting him to the god towering above them.

Another step. The people in the stands were screaming, some tearing at their skin, hair, or appendages.

Elder Quilqi reached the edge of the arena, looking up in the face there. She raised her finger to point at him, but nothing was audible.

"The time of the Huaca is growing dim. It is an era of change, no matter what you say." Was he speaking to the elder? It was hard to see where the giant face was looking. Instead, Ichu took another step. Only one more and he would be close enough.

The pressure grew stronger around him as he raised his foot as high as he could above Xiuhquil's head. The turtleman's eyes grew wide as Ichu's shadow descended on him.

Ichu let all the oppression of the god flow into him as he brought his foot, far heavier than it should be, down on the turtleman's skull.

The pop, like a melon being smashed, was the only thing audible in the arena, and Uncle Smith's head ponderously turned away from Elder Quilqi and to him, the weight on his shoulders increasing exponentially. He fell to his knees in the gore, watching the line of power between Xiuhquil's body and the god dissipate.

The turtlemen in the audience had been feeding Xiuhquil, and Uncle Smith, in turn had taken that power from the warrior. It was only a guess, but it was Ichu's only chance.

"Such heresy cannot be allowed. I will—"

The last of the line of power blew away in the breeze and Uncle Smith's face disappeared.

CHAPTER TWENTY

Gathering Power

The hand on Silluka's arm brought her back to consciousness. She looked up into Elder Quilqi's worried face.

"Thank the stars you're alright, girl." It was the most concerned Silluka had heard her. Nearby, Akamu was attending to Ichu, and Coya, the fire warrior leader, was pulling Cosquella to her feet. Xiuhquil was...a mess at Ichu's feet. So they had won the fight. It didn't feel like it.

"What happened?" She thought she had seen Uncle Smith appear and talk to them, but that was...silly, wasn't it?

"Gods meddling in affairs they shouldn't, that's what," the elder said. "Burnished bronze! How could I have been so stupid?"

The others came up to them, Nina and the other warriors having come down from their boxes. There was an older Misini with them, his graying whiskers and muzzle at odds with his diaphanous clothing. Above, people were streaming out of the arena, pushing to get out of the exits.

"The Eztli Mecatl outside the gate have begun organizing, ya," he said. "The Clowder is fortifying the walls, but Anuit is out of commission, and without her they are lessened."

"Thank you, Gegama," Nina rumbled. "Please let us know anything we can do to help. We'll need to gather all the city leaders to decide what to do. This level of...betrayal is unheard of." The big woman's eyes were wide. Silluka saw signs of nervousness in everyone. Some were hiding it better than others.

"Then, that wasn't a dream?" she asked Elder Quilqi. "I thought I was knocked out."

Akamu's face was stony. "If you mean that Tiyu Llamkay turned against his people and has been masquerading as the god of the Eztli Mecatl, then no, that wasn't a dream."

Silluka's stomach dropped. It seemed they could speak of the Uncle openly now. That great metal head and torso in the sky. She looked again, but it was really gone, only the sun shining down from a cloudless blue. She still wasn't used to the sky here not being gray all the time, like on the coast.

"It wasn't really him," Elder Quilqi told her, or told everyone, as even Gegama turned to her. "Uncle Smith wouldn't have disappeared like an errant cloud if a god had actually been looming above you all." She swept her gaze across them. "Great apparitions! Have none of you ever seen a god project themself?" There were subtle head shakes, even from Nina. The elder pointed down. "The gods are in the core, a bonus and a detriment to being among their number. Great power, but they have to stay close to that power."

"Was he...was he their god this whole time?" Cosquella's voice was shaky, and Silluka crossed to her, taking her large hand in hers.

"Since before you were born, girl. I told you hybrids were unusual," Elder Quilqi said. Suddenly, there was a lot of interest in Cosquella, who shrank back. Silluka stood in front of her, though her head was only up to her girlfriend's shoulder.

"She had nothing to do with this. The Eztli Mecatl hate her just as much as they do us."

"But what is their plan?" Nina broke the silence, and Cosquella squeezed her hand in thanks. "They coerced a challenge in the arena, courtesy of their traitor god"—she waved a hand in the air—"but then they lost. What now?"

"They have another option," Ichu said. Akamu had his hand on her brother's shoulder, nodding along. They had been speaking in low tones together. "This first way was the easy one, where Uncle Smith could assume more control of

Chimor, start his own species faction with the Eztli Mecatl. But they lost that challenge."

"Yet they still have an army outside our gates," Akamu finished.

"Chimor has never fallen to an invading force," Coya scoffed. She'd taken to pacing again, behind Nina and the other warrior leaders.

"You've fought them just as we have," Akamu told her. "They're a powerful people, and the more we take down, the stronger they'll get."

"Wasn't Xiuhquil their strongest fighter?" Cosquella asked.

Elder Quilqi shook her head. "I wouldn't count on that, girl. He was a leader, yes, but not necessarily their best fighter. He was built up from feeding on his people. I think we should move this meeting closer to the gates and make certain they're fortified."

All of a sudden, the pressure was back on Silluka, bowing her down. Nina had turned toward the entrance of Chimor. "We need to move quickly. The Eztli Mecatl are massing. There is a lot of core energy swirling outside the city, moving around like I've never seen. There's a lot in the refugee center as well."

Silluka realized everyone was bent over, including Coya, and Akamu. Gegama stood upright, though his many fabrics looked flattened against his fur. Elder Quilqi stepped near Nina and the weight lessened on Silluka. "Looks like you still need some practice on not squishing your allies, girl. Control yourself."

Nina grunted and swept a scathing look across the elder. "Maybe if my first teacher hadn't flitted off, I'd have some more practice, Mother." She snapped her fingers and obsidian armor grew about her, climbing slowly up her arms.

Akamu frowned and made a fist. His armor, amber colored, swirled around his feet and crawled up his legs, even slower than hers. The other warrior leaders followed.

"What's happening?" Akamu asked. "Are they attacking our magic? Our armor has always been instantaneous."

"Not so." Elder Quilqi leaned in, inspecting a line of iridescent teal crawling up Puric's thigh. "It's dependent on the local aura of energy from the core. The more energy supplied by the gods, the faster it goes. You lot have just never been where the gods can't reach."

"And you have, ancient one?" Coya asked, but her tone was more threatening than pleading.

"Cracking crystals, girl! I've been a lot of places. Do you want me to recount all my adventures, or do you want to find out why the Uncles, Aunts, and Entles aren't supplying you magic like they should?"

Just then a Kawchi rode up on a long-legged lizard, which flicked its tongue at the group. The spiky person leaned over clumsily to Gegama, almost falling from their mount. The gray around their muzzle implied their age. "Gather, gather! All administrators must get to the gates to direct their forces. The Eztli Mecatl are moving! My quorum has gathered our friends to surround the ones in the refugee camp, but we are being overrun. We need your theatrics, Gegama, and your power, Nina! Come, come!"

They straightened with an effort, nearly falling off again, and the lizard skittered nervously to stay underneath them. Silluka caught a glimpse of six other mounted Kawchi not far off, in the shadow of the area gate. Each rode a similar lizard.

Nina tapped her black helmet, which was only now forming, stars showing in its depths. "Warriors, round up your squads and meet me at the gates." She spared a glare for Elder Quilqi. "Any answers you have would be appreciated, Mother."

"I will see your warriors there," Gegama said, and stepped into mist.

Silluka was soon left with the elder, Ichu and Cosquella. Lugopo skittered up from where they had climbed down the wall of the arena. They went to the broken pendant, cradling it with two tentacles and signing with two more.

"Such bright potential and broken too soon!" They stared up at Ichu. "Your viciousness will be remembered!" They tapped the circlet with another tentacle. "That is, this will take days to fix. Such an inspiration from Crawling Dark of Squirming to let it absorb the god's power! Surely, I shall be called for supplication soon!"

"That's what it did?" Cosquella asked.

"Nearly one hundred Tortoises before breaking!" Lugopo raised the broken pendant pieces high. "I shall make a new scale! One hundred Tortoises equal one Pendant of energy!" They rubbed their head with a tentacle. "What is the scale for a god?"

"We may find out soon enough," Elder Quilqi warned. "How is that confounded contraption the squid made for you? Against my better judgement, I think it served you well today."

Silluka clenched the suit's right hand into a fist. "There wasn't much time to use it in the fight, but I think it helped pull energy stored in my *sunqu*."

"Yes, it let you express core energy to make *Jakua's Claws* physical manifestations. That's not easy to do, girl. That suit has potential after all."

Silluka had thought it was her new skill as a Mental Adept. Had she used a more complex adepthood again?

"Do I need mine too, do I?"

The elder watched Cosquella for a long moment. "Has it helped you?"

Cosquella shrugged. "I don't feel much from the chayus. Never have."

"Based on revelations about your parentage, I think it may not be as useful as we thought."

"My creations are always useful!" Lugopo raised up three tentacles in objection.

"Certainly they are, squid," the elder said. "Yet if there's nothing to channel, even your suit can't boost it."

"Vile slander!" Lugopo tapped the circlet. "I mean, a valid argument. I must adjust it for new, exciting magic!"

"Don't we need to get to the gate?" Ichu was practically dancing from foot to foot, more excited than Silluka had seen him. He always focused where there was an enemy to fight.

"A few moments will let them herd most of the Eztli Mecatl," the elder said. "A stupid idea to open the gates in the first place, but I suppose it couldn't be helped." She jerked her head toward the arena exit. "Let's get to the city entrance, but be cautious. Even with that thing on you, I think you may be at a loss for power for once."

* * *

Soon, they moved as a group toward the gates of Chimor. The streets were deserted, everyone either helping or hiding in their homes.

While Lugopo adjusted Silluka's suit, Ichu and Cosquella performed several chayus in a row, transferring them back and forth to refill Ichu's emptied vials, bled dry by Lugopo's pendant. Cosquella's were still intact, and they divided them up between them as well. Well-armed, they found groups of Kawchi herding turtlemen and women into their homes in the refuge center and surrounding the buildings. They were helped by strange groups of creatures. The seven who had been riding lizards had dismounted and even more giant lizards paced around a group of houses, lunging at anyone who emerged. Another smaller group of Kawchi was surrounded by a flock of crows, diving at any turtleman who so much as peeked from a window.

"Their magic," the elder said in response to Silluka's questioning look. "The Kawchi's quorums can invite beasts to help them, depending on their size and competence. Good crowd control. Administrator Long Quill is quite skilled to invite those desert dragons in. We'd best hurry on." Elder Quilqi's eyes had been on the gatehouse the entire time they walked from the arena. She seemed unhurried, but Silluka kept finding herself lagging behind the elder's long legs.

"One moment!" Lugopo scurried away to their house, returning slowly, dragging a net with Cosquella's suit in it. "May still make your enemies cower in fear!" They tapped the circlet. "Or may be a pile of junk until I fix it."

Cosquella sighed, and lugged the net over one shoulder, Lugopo riding it.

The city gates had been closed since the turtlemen first showed up. They'd been opened only to let the small group of turtlemen non-warriors in and closed again thereafter. Silluka suspected Xiuhquil had been smuggled in at the same time and only emerged when he'd been granted his writ of passage.

Their group climbed the stairs again, finding the parapet over the gates crowded with Nina and the warrior leaders, their group, and Gegama. On the lower levels, the warrior squads were slowly being encased in their respective armor, as they began the group chayu *Tortoise in his Shell*.

"Can those not be stored too?" Silluka asked Akamu as she came up beside him. "*Tortoise in his Shell* is part of *Tortoise's Growth*."

"It is, but the group aspect doesn't work if it's released as a stored chayu," Akamu said. "There's something resisting us. Watch the shield created by Coya's fire warriors." He pointed over the edge of the parapet at a group of turtlemen hammering at a fiery shield just outside the gates. She had to lean far out, and Lugopo, now hanging on to her shoulder, wrapped two tentacles around the slats of her suit. The shield was already cracked and would fall in moments. More turtlemen were hanging back in the mass of tents.

"They probably sacrificed power to the ones attacking," Ichu said, chin pointing toward the main army. "Otherwise, their power would be too spread out."

Silluka stumbled as Tortoise's Shell broke and Lugopo catapulted from her shoulder. She grasped for tentacles and the little Allwiya barely managed to weave through the end of the suit's hand.

She might have tumbled over the wall herself if Cosquella hadn't caught her shoulder, pulling her back into an embrace.

"None of that, you," the big woman said.

Akamu was at the side of the parapet, yelling for his warriors to finish their group chayu. The turtlemen were hammering at the gates.

"Mother, can't you do anything? I don't know what's happening, but we're helpless here."

Silluka turned to see Nina towering over Elder Quilqi, holding up one arm. Her midnight armor was thin, and nearly see-through. The elder's lips were set in a thin line.

"Sailing islands! Do you want to bring every immortal in spitting distance down on us?" Silluka crept closer. Were those the powerful entities the elder kept warning them about?

"We won't have a city left if they break through." Nina pointed back toward the army. "You brought them here with your new 'champions.' Now help defend us from them."

"I did no such thing." Elder Quilqi crossed her arms. "They were coming here anyway. No other place to go for a thousand leagues."

"They could have gone to Ninun." Tintaya stepped into the argument from the other side, but Elder Quilqi scoffed.

"The Misini would have hidden their city from any invaders before they got close. Unless they went right past it and to one of the floating cities off the coast, there's no other stronghold around."

"Then help us defend it, ancient one," Puric said. The old warrior's helm hadn't fully formed, leaving one eye and a patch of his head unarmored.

The elder's gaze landed on Silluka, and she reeled back before Elder Quilqi blinked, and the intent in her gaze went away.

"Humpf. We'll do this the hard way. You keep these unwelcome guests at bay, and my champions will take on any Eztli Mecatl warriors who break in. I'll do what I can, but it will take a few minutes."

"Agreed," Nina said.

"What are we doing, us?" Cosquella asked.

"Get your squid-cursed suit on and go down to the gates," the elder told them as Ichu stepped up beside her. "Your *unique* blend may work when other chayus don't. I dare say some of those warriors are going to break through before I'm done. We're going to have a rough time if the gods *aren't* paying us any attention."

Then Elder Quilqi began *dancing*. It was the only word Silluka could think of. She ducked and wove, moving from stance to stance, arms making intricate gestures. It was not a chayu Silluka recognized, but shared aspects. It tugged at her memory. The elder had moved in a similar manner a long time ago, when she had kept Loma Tika, the storm warrior, descending in a fireball, from decimating their village.

"Go!" the elder shouted.

CHAPTER TWENTY-ONE

Round up

Ichu left Akamu working with his warriors to erect another barrier. The banging on the gates of Chimor was increasing, and Ichu had no idea how they were going to keep the turtlemen from getting in. What was the elder doing, and what did she mean about the gods not paying attention?

He vaulted down the steps, the others close behind, and quickly found the Kawchi occupied in keeping the turtlemen holed up in the refugee center. He saw Elder Papaki poke his head out from a hut, then duck back inside. He hadn't even thought of the elder in days. He hoped those he knew in the village were well, but he didn't have the luxury to think about them now.

He went to Administrator Long Quill, whose group of lizards were busy snapping at turtlemen. "What are you planning to do with them?"

"Contain, contain!" Long Quill pointed back into the city. "The arena's the only place large enough to hold all these prisoners of war. We'll push them there, but someone is needed to guard the gates."

"Is that who they are now?" Cosquella asked. "Prisoners?" Lugopo was helping her into her suit. Ichu wasn't sure what benefit it would give, but anything was a help.

"Their comrades are actively attacking the city," he said. He watched the mass of turtlemen, most without armor. He remembered the power of the three thugs he and Cosquella confronted in an alley. This species was strong and wasn't afraid to take what they wanted. He was sure not all of them were that way. Amoxtli hadn't been. But Amoxtli had been Eztli Mecatl, had worshipped their now dead god. These turtlemen followed Uncle Smith and his turncoat plans. Had the entire species known what was happening? Had each individual made a choice to worship their dead god, or go with a traitor? If so, there were many more who chose Uncle Smith.

"We let them in to find jobs here and integrate. Surely they're not all bad." Silluka was watching the crowd too, her thoughts likely echoing his.

"I don't think they are. Maybe some of them will even tell us who smuggled in Xiuhquil, but we can't find out while the rest of them are trying to break into the city." Ichu rubbed at his chin with one hand.

"Fine, we figure out the questions to ask later, we do. What vials can we use?" Cosquella took out her remaining stock, now fastened to the outside of her suit. Their once-vibrant colors seemed dull and lifeless.

They returned to the gates to find Gegama and several other Misini there. "We will delay them as much as we can, but the big uglies know where the gates are. Our illusions can only do so much, ya."

"Then we'll force them back." Ichu pounded a fist into the other palm. He took out a vial they'd made quickly at the arena, as the gates creaked ominously. There were already cracks running up the left door.

"We've patched the cracks on the outside with an impression of an unblemished door and the certainty the ungainly attackers are making no impression," Gegama said, "but they're only attacking harder..."

The door split, and Ichu gulped down the vial. He braced for the explosion of chayus, *Jakua's Claws*, and *Tortoise's Heavy Foot*, along with *Quirra Hides His Nuts*. Those were the easiest and quickest chayu to transfer and store in the vial. His balance felt sturdier, but when we swiped an experimental hand across the stone wall by the gate, only a few flecks of rock chipped off.

"The vials aren't doing what they're supposed to," he warned.

Cosquella wiped her lips, then stamped a foot into the ground. Rather than making a dent, her boot rang with a wet *slop.* "I can fight them without magic. I've done it before, if this suit doesn't slow me down, it does."

"Mine isn't working either. My suit is resisting me." Silluka was to one side, halfway through *Jakua Crouches and Lashes His Tail*, but the ampuka barely glowed about her. Her movements were clumsier than usual.

"My traps are unimpeded!" Lugopo's circlet chirped from above him, and Ichu looked up. The Allwiya hung from an assemblage of metal spikes hanging above the door. Where had they gotten the material so quickly? It looked poised to fall on whomever came through the door first, and Ichu took a few steps back just as the left gate rattled again. Maybe it would take out a few turtlemen.

"It's not working," Silluka said, and dropped out of her chayu. "It's like I can't connect to the core any longer."

"It must be something to do with Uncle Smith, now he's revealed himself," Ichu hazarded. The door cracked again, the hard wood bowing in. He could see a hint of a turtleman behind it, metal plates attached to one fist.

"*Rattling Leaves*," Cosquella said.

"What?" Ichu looked back to her.

"Akamu said that was a children's exercise to force a connection to the core, he did. Try it out with our suits." She was wiggling her fingers, but their rhythm was shaky as best.

"The movements would need to be exact." Ichu got into Basic stance, trying not to wince as another crack appeared in the door. If this didn't work, their only option was to run.

"Both together," Silluka said, as Cosquella abandoned her attempt and stood in front of them, drawing her hatchets from her belt.

Ichu and his sister began *Rattling Leaves*, first and third fingers, then the second and forth, then each finger dipping in turn, then repeating the rhythm. Slowly, an anemic ampuka began around their fingers. Silluka closed her eyes, and hers disappeared.

"What did you do?" Ichu stared at her.

"I pulled it into my *sunqu*. If I get enough, maybe I can use it to fuel a chayu."

"We're not going to have enough time for that—"

That was when the doors cracked open.

"Run!" Ichu shouted. Lugopo dropped to his shoulder as they took off. Behind them, a *boom* shook the ground as a metal construction of spikes fell, pinning the first wave of turtlemen to the ground.

"Spiky death from above!" Lugopo's circlet cheered.

Silluka continued to move her fingers—both her real ones and the ones on the suit's right hand—as they ran. Every time the ampuka began to glow, she would stop for a moment, and the glow disappeared. Ichu had never been able to make the ampuka work like that. His sister was full of surprises.

The roar of the turtlemen followed them through the city. There were too many to fight, but the inhabitants were pouring out of their houses with whatever weapons they had at hand. Ichu finally slowed with the others, as their path was blocked.

"We'll take down as many as we can, we will." Cosquella brandished her hatchets. Stray midday light reflected off the metal in her suit. They faced the incoming tide of turtlemen.

These were not the craftsmen and artisans who had entered the city before. These were warriors, fed on the skills of the others around them. They'd only get stronger, the more they took down. And they were fighting against regular people. Ichu looked around. Even if some of the Huaca were Mental or even Pressure Adepts, the chayus weren't working. Their gods had left them. Ichu relaxed his shoulders, flexing his hands. He'd take down as many as he could.

That was when the light bloomed in the sky above them, and gasps came from around them. The turtlemen faltered as Ichu shielded his eyes and looked up. There was a figure above them, performing a chayu in the air. An old and spindly figure.

Elder Quilqi.

Around her, a veil of shimmering mesh descended, filtering over the buildings like someone airing out a cloth sheet. It fell all around the city. One edge descended not too far from them, just as the line of turtlemen began their approach again. They ducked under the veil as it closed the distance, but some of them were not quick enough.

It cut through them like a line of razors, leaving only a handful of attackers on their side.

"These I can handle!" Cosquella cried, and Ichu followed her, wishing for a weapon.

With the people of Chimor helping, the few turtlemen who got through were taken down quickly. None were as strong as the first one Ichu had encountered at his village.

After, he went to the gauzy ripple in the air, dividing him from the rest of the turtleman army. They stared back, poking the barrier with weapons. It fizzled where they hit, but did not give. Ichu touched it on his side and found it hard, like resin.

They were locked in the city, and Akamu and the rest of the warriors were on the other side with the turtlemen. The veil extended higher than the walls, in an irregular circle.

"Now what?" he asked the air.

"Shimmering skies, I can't hold this forever!" a voice answered him. He looked up. Elder Quilqi's voice had been as close as if it was in his ear. "I see that energy you're saving, girl. Good idea. Try this."

What looked like a glowing thread descended from the elder, aiming directly toward Silluka. She reached up as it came to her, and when she touched it, her whole body lit up with the ampuka, and she gasped.

"Remember when I said not to try *Flying Quirra* again until you were ready? Ignore that."

Ichu looked at Silluka. She stared back, wide eyed.

"Does she need to fly, does she?" Cosquella yelled up at the sky.

"No need to shout, girl, but yes, she does. You all do. Find Maisah the Flamesmith and get back here as quick as you can. Chimor's going to need more help than I can give it myself." There was a pause. "Now, girl! Start it *now*!"

Silluka dropped her arms to her sides, her shoulders relaxing and her eyes closing. Then she raised her left leg to her right calf. Her arms moved in small twitches, like a nervous quirra, and she put her left leg down and raised her right foot to her left leg. Then she raised both feet off the ground.

She held out a hand to Ichu on one side and Cosquella on the other. Lugopo's tentacles tightened their grip on his shoulder as his sister lifted all three of them up effortlessly, flying up above Chimor. They passed Elder Quilqi, who only pointed one finger, out past the city, to land they'd never seen before. Silluka ducked her head, and they flew forward, past the barrier, over the city, and away from Chimor.

Argument

Tiye Kwirpuyay, commonly called Entle Magic, put their hands on their hips. They stood on one side of a round table, made solid from the core's energy. There were eight spaces around the table, but only six were filled. This room of the palace was one of the biggest, centrally located. A good place to call their siblings together.

"Barbaric. Llamkay goes missing for just a few decades, pops his head out to champion another people, and my siblings tremble like leaves on a windy day."

"We cannot let this insult stand, Kwirpuyay," Tiyu Pacha raged, lightning crashing around his head. The old bore would argue against anything that stood in his way.

"But what do we do if he tries to kill one of *us*?" Tiya Qucha was a small woman, despite having reign over such a large area as the sea. "You'll protect me, won't you, Tiksimuyu?"

"Naturally, dear." Uncle Earth was a dowdy man, a latecomer, and Kwirpuyay had never seen how he'd joined the pantheon in the first place. They seemed to let in all kinds these days.

"We have to fight back." Tiya Qhalikay clenched her hands. She would be the first to war, despite her moniker of "Aunt Healing."

"Even if it leaves our Huaca defenseless?" Tiye Kwirpuyay argued. "They're already fighting Llamkay's new toy soldiers."

A cheetah-like woman burst into their counsel, laughing and swerving drunkenly, followed by more of her kind. She barreled straight into Tiya Aymuray, the youngest of their number, and the goddess yipped and pulled her hands back from what had been thrust into them. For a fertility goddess, Aunt Harvest was a bit squeamish.

"Don't like what you feel?" Cheetah purred over the Huaca gods, to a chorus of grumbling. Her hands gestured to her bare breasts—all six of them, where Aymuray had pulled away. Several of the other Huaca gods and goddesses' eyes traced down. The Clade had no dignity. Hedonistic and opportunistic.

"What are you doing here, cat?" Kwirpuyay asked. "This is a war council."

"Are we not at war as well?" Cheetah giggled, a *ye ye ye* sound from her feline muzzle. "I'd suggest you reign in your errant sibling, Huaca. Never tell when you lot will lose the upper hand, ya?"

"Filthy cat," Tiyu Pacha grumbled, but Cheetah only snorted another laugh. Another furry hand snaked around the god's neck and Cheetah purred into the embrace, leaning back to nuzzle noses with the powerfully built Panther behind her. His sleek, dark muscles shone in the light of the Core below them, but his eyes tracked Tiye Kwirpuyay. Their eyes traced down his impressive thighs and what hung there, despite themself. Lynx was behind both of them, the shorter god hanging on to Panther's tail and snuffling hungrily. Kwirpuyay tossed their head at the display.

"I'm going to get more information," they said, stalking away from the arguing gods. This council had been a mistake to call, especially lacking a fourth of their number. "Try not to let too many of our adepts die?"

But no one was watching the land above. The shock of Llamkay's betrayal had turned all eyes back to the core, ignoring the sigils of communication from the Huaca in Chimor and across the greater continent they were tied to, stuck with these upstart newcomer gods. Kwirpuyay remembered when Chimor had been a powerhouse of magic, a true bastion of the Huaca.

And where was their younger brother after all? He'd made that flagrant display from somewhere, finally letting them see him again. That was when the arguing had started. Started in earnest. There was always arguing going on here.

The core was like a giant and interminable house party, with new guests coming in and splitting off all the time. Well, time being relative. This palace used to be empty save for their siblings. And their parents, but Grandmother Life and Grandfather Death had moved on. No other god had replicated what they had done. All of them wanted to, Smith most of all. Their parents' exit from this world had to be tied into Llamkay's power play.

Tiye Kwirpuyay stalked through palace hallways leading from the council room, sections twisting and branching off as the world plates above them joined and separated. They winced as the walls suddenly turned gooey, their feet sticking to the floor. The city of the gods was kept solid by will alone.

Waving tentacles pushed through the softened wall nearest them, writhing up Kwirpuyay's wrists like blind snakes. They tried to shake them off, but several others signed at them.

<Shall we feast on the Huaca's destruction finally?> a resonant voice shivered through the wall.

Kwirpuyay pulled, and a pile of flailing arms vomited into the hallway, completely blocking their way.

"Never, you old monster." Tiye Kwirpuyay brushed the rest of the grasping tentacles from them, but Manylegs of Reaching wasn't done.

<We have aided your conquest for many years against the furred pests,> they signed. <Remember our might, now your numbers dwindle.>

Kwirpuyay gestured, and another doorway opened to their left. They exited to a plateau, facing out over the fiery surface of the core. There were other islands all around theirs, getting closer like moths to a flame. They were even more worrying now, with Llamkay a traitor.

"Keep aiding us and I promise we will make it worth your time," they called back to the mass of arms.

<And our siblings, and our innumerable children.>

"Yes, yes, all of them." Kwirpuyay sucked in a fresh pool of energy from the open core, tucking it into their *sunqu*, then turned back to the sprawling palace, made of many mashed-together buildings. They pulled open doorway after doorway, creating ones where they didn't exist.

The palace was surprisingly full, for the limited number of gods that lived here. Of course there were also their servants, sages, subjugated slaves, and other immortals. They checked in a room of Huaca crafters, forging weapons to give to aspiring mortals. Another doorway led to a contingent of Misini, disappearing and appearing like quirras, delivering messages of their gods. Once they even surprised two of those spiky Kawchi rutting like rabbits. Tiye Kwirpuyay hastily closed the door. They had found nothing of interest and covered the entire palace.

They concentrated, listening to everything around them for any other clues. The arguing among their siblings in the central chamber was only growing louder as they ignored their supplicants above. Kwirpuyay tuned them out, searching. They couldn't hear him.

Where was Tiyu Llamkay hiding, and what had happened to Tiye Khuyay?

THE END OF BOOK 2 OF THE SHIFTING LANDS

ACKNOWLEDGEMENTS

Once again, I'm writing a book 2. This is always one of the most interesting parts of the series process to me. I've written three "book 2s," including this one, and each time I've found so much fun worldbuilding stuff to play with!

If you've read my other works, you know I love fleshing out the worlds I write, and I'm really pumping that up with this one!

One of the hallmarks of progression fantasy that drew me to start this series in the first place is the characters moving through the world quicker as they "power up" and seeing cool new sights along the way. Even with my obsessive level of outlining and worldbuilding behind the scenes, I find myself using up all those elements and more in each of the Shifting Lands stories. My brain is already full of concepts for book 3, and I'm looking forward to sharing them with you!

Oh, and if you caught a particular title right at the end of the book that seems familiar from a short story in the *Fiery Deeps* anthology, you're on the right track. I did say this world was big!

My books depend on more and more people as I keep writing. It's a challenge to both run a small press and write my own books at the same time, but I love doing it. Thanks, and many hugs and kisses first go to my wife, Heather, for supporting me in life, business, and all my strange hobbies and obsessions for over 20 years of marriage.

Thanks also to the READ group for description and cover critiquing, crowdfunding help, and the amazing art and merchandise they make!

Serene Chia continues to draw some of the most eye-catching covers I've seen. I'm already planning for the third one.

Lastly, thank you to everyone who backed the Space Wizard Science Fantasy Year 4 campaign! We keep breaking through records, and I look forward to each one. Supporting a small, queer, indie business enables me to keep putting out quality books that I hope can rival those from big traditional presses.

ABOUT THE AUTHOR

William C. Tracy writes and publishes queer science fiction and fantasy through his indie press Space Wizard Science Fantasy (spacewizardsciencefantasy.com).

His largest work is the Dissolutionverse: a space opera with music-based magic, including ten books and an RPG. He also has a standalone epic fantasy with seasonal fruit-based magic, a nonfiction book about body mechanics and correct posture, and a hard sci-fi trilogy with generational colony ships and a planet covered by a sentient fungal entity.

William is an NC native and a lifelong fan of science fiction and fantasy. He has a master's degree in mechanical engineering, and has both designed and operated heavy construction machinery. He has also trained in Wado-Ryu karate since 2003 and runs his own dojo in Raleigh, NC. He is an avid video and board gamer, a beekeeper, a reader, and of course, a writer.

You can get a free Dissolutionverse novelette by signing up for William's mailing list at spacewizardsciencefantasy.com

Follow him on Bluesky at wctracy.bsky.social, and Instagram and Threads @spacewizardpress for writing updates, cat and bee pictures, and thoughts on martial arts.

Please take a moment to review this book at your favorite retailer's website, Goodreads, or simply tell your friends!

www.ingramcontent.com/pod-product-compliance
Lightning Source LLC
Chambersburg PA
CBHW031155010826
48971CB00012B/601